Thomas Gray, Richard West

Gray and his friends

Letters and relics in great part hitherto unpublished

Thomas Gray, Richard West

Gray and his friends
Letters and relics in great part hitherto unpublished

ISBN/EAN: 9783337282387

Printed in Europe, USA, Canada, Australia, Japan

Cover: Foto ©Andreas Hilbeck / pixelio.de

More available books at **www.hansebooks.com**

GRAY AND HIS FRIENDS

LETTERS AND RELICS

IN GREAT PART HITHERTO UNPUBLISHED.

EDITED BY

DUNCAN C. TOVEY, M.A

TRINITY COLLEGE.

CAMBRIDGE:

AT THE UNIVERSITY PRESS.

1890

TO

THE MEMBERS PAST AND PRESENT

OF

THE ASCHAM SOCIETY OF ETON COLLEGE

THESE PAGES

ARE AFFECTIONATELY DEDICATED

BY THEIR FORMER COLLEAGUE

THE EDITOR.

PREFATORY NOTICE.

THE Relics collected in this volume are derived from various sources. Some time ago Mr John Morris most generously placed at my disposal the valuable collection of Gray Papers, described in the Appendix to Mr Gosse's edition of Gray (Vol. IV. p. 339). I desire to express my gratitude for the great courtesy through which I have been able to give here in full the Journals in France and Italy, and the notes of travel in Scotland, from that collection.

I must also record my great obligation to the kindness of Mr Chaloner W. Chute, of the Vyne, Hampshire, who allows me to print some letters written by Gray to John Chute which have not yet been published, except in the 'History of the Vyne.'

The collection made by Mitford (now in the British Museum) was I believe intended to supplement his long labours over Gray. It is contained in four volumes (bound in two) of MSS. (32,561; 32,562 Add. MSS.); part of these

materials he used in his latest editions of the
poet's Works and Correspondence; much of them
he never gave to the world. Yet it is to these
I imagine that he refers, when he says (Preface
to the Correspondence of Gray and Mason), "I
have still some materials by me which I think will
not be unacceptable to the public, partly relating
to Gray and partly to those connected with him
and his history, that may serve to illustrate what
is already published, and complete in some points
our acquaintance with the circumstances of his
life." I am here trying to do what Mitford
could have done so well; and where I follow him
I am altogether indebted to his care and pains.
Fortunately his handwriting, though minute, is
generally clear; he evidently transcribed Ashton's
letters in greater haste than those of Gray and
Walpole, and here in some places his writing is
less easily decipherable. Yet it may be inferred
that he is generally faithful even to the punctua-
tion, for this was his principle in copying; and
I believe that access to the originals, had that
been possible for me, would not have improved
the present volume to any appreciable extent,
wherever I have had Mitford to depend upon.

Of the letters now published from this source,
those which will I think be found most interest-

ing to the general reader are described by Mitford
as follows

" Manuscript
Letters
of
Gray, West and Walpole
copied by me
from the Originals
lent
by Lady Frankl^d Lewis†
to me
February 1853
J. M.

N.B. The Mrs Lewis, to whom the letters
directed to Mr Ashton, were enclosed, was Anne
daughter and Co-Heiress of Sir Nathan Wright,
Bt of Tofts Hall who died 1777.

Ms Letters
from
Ashton to West
and
Walpole

† Lady Frankland Lewis was Harriet fourth daughter of
Sir George Cornwall B^t. married 11th March 1805 Rt Honble
Th^s. Frankland Lewis of Harpton Court, Radnor."

Next in interest to these in Mitford's Collection will be found the two letters from Miss
Speed, which he has preserved for us. I hope

there may be readers who will be glad to know how the 'Long Story' was received by those who were most concerned in it. If either of these letters from the only lady for whom Gray is supposed to have entertained any *penchant* have ever seen the light until now, the fact has escaped my notice.

I have never had the time completely to master the contents of these MS. volumes. I had to search them rapidly, in order to copy that which I thought would be most interesting; and this I hope I have succeeded in achieving. They contain MS. notes on Sophocles by Gray, and a sketch in Latin of an Inaugural Lecture on History, neither of which have been published. Mitford was working for himself, and therefore does not always indicate very clearly the sources or even the authorship of what he has transcribed. There are for example some slight French songs, which do not seem to me to be more than jottings by Gray of what he had read or heard, but which might, for all I know, be imitations either by himself or West. Other instances of a like perplexity, will be found in my notes. The 'Mason Papers' from which Mitford drew most of these materials are I believe those of which he speaks in the Preface to the 'Correspondence of Gray

and Mason' as having been placed in his hands
by Mr Penn, of Stoke Park. The fate of the
originals (though I have been kindly favoured
with all the information which Colonel Stuart
could give me), I am unable to trace; but it
is probable that they would have been quite
inaccessible to me even could I have discovered
where they were. This may, perhaps, be the
best place to mention that Mitford records a line
of Gray's in pencil,

'The rude Columbus of an infant world'—

where he found it, I am uncertain; perhaps
among these Mason papers; if it is in the Common
Place Books at Pembroke College, Cambridge,
whence I have gathered some other poetic jottings
of Gray, it escaped my notice in the search which
the kindness of Dr Searle, the Master of Pembroke,
allowed me to make there. It is obvious to
conjecture that this was a thought for the 'Elegy'
and that the 'rude Columbus' might have found
a place beside the 'village Hampden' and the
'mute inglorious Milton'.

The Common Place Books of Gray at Pembroke have given me much of West's; but offer,
as might be expected, of matter suitable to my
present purpose nothing *in extenso* that is new
of Gray's, except the two translations from the

Greek printed in this volume. Nor does an obliging letter which I have received from Mr R. A. Neil, Fellow and Librarian of Pembroke, encourage me to hope that more of Gray's is to be discovered there.

Though I honestly believe that the imperfections of this edition are not due to want of pains, I am well aware that even scanty opportunities are a poor excuse for faulty work, and therefore I would gladly have made my account of Mitford's MSS. more exact, and my references and annotations more complete, if I had had more time and more knowledge at my command. I cannot complain of want of assistance, and in addition to the obligations acknowledged already, or in the notes, I must here thank Mr R. F. Sketchley, the Librarian of the Dyce and Foster Libraries at South Kensington, and Mr J. W. Clark of Cambridge, for most useful communications; the Provosts of Eton and King's College, Cambridge, for the information which confirms my note on p. 80 *infra;* my friends Mr F. W. Cornish of Eton, Dr Henry Jackson and Mr E. S. Shuckburgh of Cambridge, for their encouragement and assistance; and Dr Porter, the Master of Peterhouse, for his kindly interest in this edition.

CONTENTS.

xvi CONTENTS.

INTRODUCTORY ESSAY.

EXPLANATORY AND CRITICAL.

My design in gathering these Papers has been
threefold. In the first place they are the records of
a remarkable and interesting friendship. The four
Eton friends Gray, Walpole, West and Ashton, known
to their schoolfellows as the Quadruple Alliance, are
here brought together once more. It has not indeed
been possible to reproduce their correspondence in
full, but something has now been added to the materials which are extant elsewhere in a printed form,
and if the present volume is in some respects a supplement, I have tried to give this part of it the interest
of a certain coherence. Of Gray and Walpole I have
given in full nothing but what is new to the world,
with the single exception of a Latin letter from Gray
to West, which, published by Mitford with the wrong
heading 'Mr West to Mr Gray', has been omitted by
Mr Gosse altogether. With this and another exception noted later on [1], whatever of theirs has been seen

¹ p. 18.

in print before, will only appear now in the form
of connecting links.

Although what is printed here of Ashton's is, all
but certain verses, entirely new, it has seemed ad-
visable to treat some of his letters in the same way.
To have given them in full would have been to add
to the heavier material of my volume, and I could
not persuade myself that I have in his case
the same kind of obligation as in the case of
Gray or West. Even West has a place (though a
very subordinate place) in literature; Ashton has
scarcely any. Letters are not interesting simply
because they are old; and distance lends no enchant-
ment to dulness. In transcribing Ashton's letters,
I came to the conclusion that he could be a very
ponderous young person, but I cannot convince
readers of this, except at their expense and that of
my volume, which might sink under his weight.
I am therefore contented to indicate where all these
letters are to be found[1]. Ashton was dubbed 'Plato'[2]
by his Eton friends; why, I cannot tell, except in
as far as he was supposed to have some skill in
Greek[3]; his temper, with a great affectation of

---

[1] Mitford's Common Place Books ad. fin. (Add. Mss. Brit.
Mus. 32,562.)

[2] See note infra p. 81.

[3] Walpole to West from Florence Oct. 2, 1740, suggests that
Ashton shall turn into Greek Buondelmonti's 'Spesso Amor
&c.' which Gray had Latinized.

equanimity at times, is the reverse of philosophic.
He is fitted however for the part of a δευτεραγωνιστὴς
and in this character he now appears. He was a
Fellow of King's, and subsequently of Eton, Rector
of St Botolph, Bishopsgate, and Preacher to the
Society of Lincoln's Inn[1]. Partly from the fact that
they were members of the same college at Cambridge,
but still more, I am inclined to think, from a certain
disposition to *toadyism*, he is in closer juxtaposition
with Walpole than with any other member of the
alliance. What part he played in the famous quarrel
between Gray and Walpole it is impossible now
exactly to determine, but it is probable that his
conduct in the matter caused an estrangement between himself and Gray. His interest in the case
appears from the Postscript to a letter (strangely
fulsome and exaggerated as I think) which he wrote
to Walpole on his recovery from his illness at Reggio.
This letter is given on p. 58. The Mrs — there

---

[1] Cunningham (H. Walpole's Letters, vol. I. p. 2). An
amusing letter from Walpole to Ashton dated from the
Christopher Inn at Eton has this " If I do not compose myself
a little more before Sunday morning, when Ashton is to preach
I shall certainly *be in a bill for laughing at church;* but how
to help it, to see him in the pulpit, when the last time I saw
him here, was standing up funking over against a conduct to
be catechized." But this letter is certainly misplaced between
one of 1737 and one of 1739, for Ashton was not ordained till
later. He was made Fellow of Eton Dec. 20, 1745, and probably never preached in the Chapel before that event.

spoken of who 'knows the whole' is perhaps Gray's
mother; but, if so, who is the Mrs Gr: mentioned
just before, to whom Ashton is 'infinitely obliged',
and with whom he is going 'to rejoice' over Walpole's
convalescence? This Mrs Gr: is undoubtedly the
lady to whom Walpole refers in the following from
Rome (infra p. 56).

"Mrs G. writes me word how much goodness she
met with in Hanover Sqre.[1] Poor Creature! You
know, how much it obliges me, my dear Ashton, &
if that can give you any satisfaction, as I well believe
it does, be assured, it touches me in the strongest
manner. *It obliges me in a Point that relates to my
mother*, & that is all I can say in this World!...
You must not tell that poor Woman, what I am
now going to mention. I fear we shall not see
Naples" &c. And then he proceeds to talk of the
malaria, and the roads infested by banditti, and
relates incidents likely to be disquieting to the
anxious female heart. It is certain that Walpole
is solicitous for some person inferior to him in rank,
who nevertheless has a claim upon his kindly interest.
—Whether "Mrs G." would be alarmed more on
Walpole's account, or on Gray's, the reader may
determine as he can[2]. The concern of Gray himself

---

[1] The residence of the Hon. Mrs Lewis, where Ashton was
living as Tutor to Lord Plymouth.

[2] See further the n. on p. 60.

at the death of Lady Walpole is manifested in a letter to West of Aug. 22, 1737, 'While I write to you, I hear the bad news of Lady Walpole's death on Saturday night last. Forgive me if the thought of what my poor Horace must feel on that account, obliges me to have done in reminding you that I am yours &c.' I should infer from this that Gray did not learn the 'bad news' from Walpole himself; yet as Lady Walpole died on the 20th of August, this speedy information must have come to Gray either through Ashton or from some domestic source. It should be remembered that in 1735 Mrs Gray submitted for the opinion of Counsel that remarkable 'case' in which are revealed the cruelties of her husband and the exertions she had made for her son, 'whilst at Eton School, and now he is at Peterhouse at Cambridge.' I should like to persuade myself, that the sufferings and struggles of this 'careful tender mother' had won for her the sympathy of Horace and Lady Walpole; and this may be true, whether or not these pages afford evidence pointing that way. We shall probably conclude that Mrs Gr: is *not* Mrs Gray; but whoever she may be, Walpole's thoughtfulness for her places him in a very amiable light. And whatever his offence against Gray himself may have been, there is manliness and good feeling in everything we know of Walpole's conduct in relation to this rupture—

As in this to his cousin the Hon. H. S. Conway[1] (London, 1741).

"Before I thank you for myself, I must thank you for that excessive good nature you showed *in writing to poor Gray.* I am less impatient to see you, as I find you are not the least altered, but have the same tender friendly temper you always had."

Evidently he is anxious to make peace. The first direct overtures towards a reconciliation came from him, as Gray acknowledges[2] in a letter to John

[1] Horace Walpole's Letters, ed. Cunningham, no. 42, vol. I. p. 731. Quoted, I discover, with the same intention, in Mitford's 2nd Life of Gray.

[2] But there are two facsimiles prefixed to the first volume of 'Walpoliana' which look as if they were connected with each other and with this reconciliation. The first is Gray's, the second Walpole's.

...do you mean to continue so, or shall You see me the less Willingly next Week, when I mean to call at your Door some Morning? I hope you are still in Town. believe me D[r] S[r] very sincerely yours

Cambridge, July 7   T Gray

I shall be very glad, S[r], to see you here again whenever it is convenient to you. Lest I should forget the time, be so good as to acquaint me three or four days beforehand when you wish to come, that I may not be out of the way, & I will fix a day for expecting you. I am

S[r]
yr obliged
humble Sert
Hor Walpole.

As far as my search can discover Gray's is not a fragment of

Chute of October 12, 1746 (wrongly assigned by Mr Gosse to 1750), "I find Mr Walpole then made some mention of me to you; yes, we are together again. It is about a year, I believe, since he wrote to me, to offer it, and there has been (particularly of late), in appearance, the same kindness and confidence almost as of old.   What were his motives, I cannot yet guess.   What were mine, you will imagine and perhaps blame me.   However as yet I neither repent, nor rejoice overmuch, but I am pleased."

The words ' It is about a year' &c. enable us with the aid of other evidence to fix the date of the reconciliation itself and of the letter of Gray's which gives an account of it to Nov. 1745[1].   In this letter Gray says,

" I wrote a note the night I came [to Stoke], and immediately received a very civil answer.   I went the following evening to see the *party* (as Mrs Foible says), was something abashed at his confidence ; he came

any extant letter.   I am not able to say as much about Walpole's.   If Gray is addressing Walpole, it looks as if he was reminding him of some friendly overtures, slighted at the time they were made ; if Walpole is addressing Gray *at all*, it is scarcely possible to doubt that he is replying to Gray's proposal of a visit, and that in a very reserved and formal manner.   But it is only the first document that is of importance.

[1] Walpole told Mason that in the year 1744 a reconciliation was effected between them by 'a Lady who wished well to both parties.'   I think he must be mistaken as to the year.

to meet me, kissed me on both sides with all the ease
of one, who receives an acquaintance just come out of
the country, squatted me into a Fauteuil, begun to
talk of the town and this and that and t'other, and
continued with little interruption for three hours,
when I took my leave very indifferently pleased, but
treated with wondrous good breeding.   I supped with
him next night (as he desired), Ashton was there,
whose formalities tickled me inwardly, for I found he
was to be angry about the letter I had wrote him.
However in going home together our hackney-coach
jumbled us into a sort of reconciliation : he hammered
out somewhat like an excuse ; and I received it very
readily, because I cared not twopence, whether it were
true or not.   So we grew the best acquaintance
imaginable, and I sat with him on Sunday some
hours alone, when he informed me of abundance of
anecdotes much to my satisfaction, and in short
opened (I really believe) his heart to me with that
sincerity, that I found I had still less reason to have
a good opinion of him, than (if possible) I ever had
before."

We know by a note of Mitford's to this letter,
that Mr Isaac Reed heard from Mr Roberts of the
Pell-office, in 1799, " That the quarrel between Gray
and Walpole was occasioned by a suspicion Mr Walpole
entertained, that Mr Gray had spoken ill of him to
some friends in England.   To ascertain this, he

clandestinely opened a letter, and resealed it, which Mr Gray with great propriety, resented."

I confess that I doubt whether Walpole ever opened Gray's letter and sealed it up again, although Mr Roberts of the Pell-office was 'likely to be well-informed', as Mr Isaac Reed assures us. I do not know how old Mr Roberts of the Pell-office was in 1799, but he told this story 58 years after the thing, whatever it was, happened, and before the original account reached his ears it must of necessity have been transmitted through a great number of persons, possibly at considerable intervals of time, and, it may be suspected, with the usual improvements and additions. What is certain is, that Ashton had something to do with the quarrel[1], and from the reference above 'I found he was to be angry about the letter I had wrote him', we may guess that something Gray wrote to Ashton about Walpole, either caused or increased the rupture. Gray's feeling about Ashton remained practically unabated, and he continues in every notice of him subsequently (except in writing to Walpole) to speak of him with irony or contempt. There was indeed one moment of *rapprochement*, caused by the death of West (see infr. Sect. II. let. 42), and I do not find that Gray ever took the

---

[1] As Mitford I find remarks in his *second* life of Gray; drawing the same inference from the Wharton correspondence.

trouble to manifest any strong resentment against
Ashton. But for the evidences of dislike we have
only to take some mentions of Ashton's name which
we find in Gray's letters to Wharton[1]. As in the
dream which he communicates to him, from which
we gather an exacter notion than adjectives will
supply:

"I thought I was in t'other world and confined in
a little apartment much like a cellar, enlightened by
one rush candle that burned blue. On each side
of me sate (for my sins) Mr Davie and *my friend
M^r A(shton)*; they bowed continually and smiled in
my face and while one filled me out very bitter tea,
*the other sweetened it with a vast deal of brown
sugar:* altogether it much resembled Syrup of Buck-
thorn. In the corner sat Tuthill very melancholy in
expectation of the tea-leaves."

If Walpole's offence was as grievous as the tale
above given would imply, we might well believe, with
Mr Isaac Reed, that there was "little cordiality afterwards between them". But how does this tally with
these words, written by Gray to Walpole (when

---

[1] See also *supra* and Gray's Works (ed. Gosse), ii. 144, iii.
86, 87. In the Index to this edition Thomas Asheton and Dr
Ashton are treated as different persons, and this misconception
may perhaps explain Mr Gosse's statement (Life of Gray,
p. 11) that 'Ashton, taking orders very early, dropped out of
the circle of friends.'

Walpole had some difference with another friend)
with obvious allusion to their own experience?—
"I always believed well of his heart and temper,
and would gladly do so still. If they are such as
they should be, I should have expected everything
from such an explanation; for it is a tenet with me
(a simple one, you'll perhaps say) that if ever two
people, who love one another come to breaking, it is
for a want of a timely eclaircissement, a full and
precise one, without witnesses or mediators, and without reserving any one disagreeable circumstance for
the mind to brood upon in silence."[1]

Is this the way men write to those who open other
people's letters and seal them up again? I cannot
reconcile the evidence of Gray's correspondence, or
any of the ascertained facts of his subsequent connection with Walpole either with the offence imputed,
or with Cole's statement that "when Walpole asked
Gray to Strawberry Hill, when he came, he without
any ceremony told Walpole that he came to wait on
him as civility required, but by no means would he
ever be there on the terms of his former friendship,
which he had utterly cancelled." Walpole's own
manly and candid account of the matter is that he
'treated' Gray 'insolently'. 'He loved me and I
did not think he did'. He was 'too serious a companion'. Gray was for antiquities &c. 'whilst I was

---

[1] Gray's Works (ed. Gosse), ii. 225.

for perpetual balls & plays;—the fault was mine'. And this passage from a letter to Ashton (Rome, May 28, 1740) betrays just the sense of growing discrepancy to which Walpole refers, an irksomeness against which better feelings were struggling :

"By a considerable volume of Charts & Pyramids which I saw at Florence, *I thought it threatened a Publication.* His travels have really improved him; I wish they may do the same for any one else."

The notes of foreign travel now published for the first time, which were set down in Gray's exquisite and careful handwriting with scarcely an erasure, must have taken him some time, and they are probably but a small part of his studious labours at this date. The eternal conflict between thoroughness and dilettantism is evidently being renewed between these young people. The strain must have been great; and they are both trying hard to keep their tempers. When nearly a year after this Gray writes to West from Florence that he has acquired in his two years absence from England 'a sensibility for what others feel, and indulgence for their faults and weaknesses', we can guess of whom he is thinking. Alas! he did but flatter himself. Only a few days after these words were written, the quarrel occurred. Whether the letter Gray wrote to Ashton was the bone of contention; or whether it only helped to make matters worse, the reader is now in as good a position

to judge as I am. Gray evidently believes that
Ashton was put up by Walpole to act a part about it,
and to pretend that it had made him indignant when
it did nothing of the sort. Perhaps again, Ashton
was one of those 'mediators' who, according to Gray's
experience, are best away. Cunningham tells us that
Ashton died at Bath in 1775, but that 'his friendship
with Walpole had ceased long before'. Walpole addressed to him the Poetical 'Epistle' from Florence;
and we learn from Gray's letters that he wrote a book
against Conyers Middleton, and that Gray thought it
had some things new and ingenious, but rather too
prolix, and the style here and there savouring too
strongly of sermon"[1].

The second part of my scheme is to collect all the
remains of the beloved and unfortunate Richard West.
This is an act of vicarious piety; it was designed, as
far as West's compositions are concerned, by Gray himself; and was also an unfulfilled project of Mitford's,
who writes (Correspondence of Gray and Mason,
Preface, p. xxvii) "Why Gray left his design unaccom-
plished is not known; but it may be endeavoured,
with the assistance of new materials, not indeed to
supply the office which he left unfulfilled, but to raise
the best monument to the memory of West from his
own works, which, at so late a period, can be done." I
am sorry that neither the plan of Mr Gosse's edition,

---

[1] Gray's Works (ed. Gosse), ii. 210.

nor that of the present volume has admitted of giving together in full the correspondence between Gray and West.   In Walpole's Correspondence as edited by Cunningham, West thus appears, to the great advantage of lucidity and interest.   If the editors of Cicero excluded from his works the letters of his correspondents, on the plea that they were not Cicero's, classical scholars would have cause to complain.   Letters, moreover, are more real and life-like when they can be read as dialogues ; the reader is more under the influence of the spirit in which they were composed.   Some figures are thus preserved in literature, engaging certainly, yet scarcely strong enough to stand alone ; I am not sure that West is not one of these.   The Englishman thinks as naturally of West in conjunction with Gray, as the Frenchman thinks of Etienne de la Boëtie in conjunction with Montaigne.   It is the light of friendship which glorifies these relics ; and the true devotee of literature, who is always something more than learned or critical, tries to look upon these unfulfilled promises of the early lost, with the eyes of those who once loved them.   We shall probably be unable to subscribe to Gray's estimate of West's Monody on the Death of Queen Caroline ; and we may be quite sure that if the unhappy line

     'And tho' not virtuous, virtuously inclin'd'

had been Mason's not West's, Gray would have said of it just what he did say to Mason in a similar

case, "All I can say is that your Elegy must not
end with the worst line in it; it is flat, it is prose;
whereas that above all ought to sparkle, or at least to
shine." To read these things in the right spirit we
must replace criticism by the emotional interest which
attaches to the sad story of this brief life. He was
the son of 'the Richard West, who' says Mr Gosse
'was made Lord Chancellor of Ireland when he was
only thirty-five, and who then immediately died.'
The mother of our West was the daughter of Bishop
Burnet. West died at the age of 26; and (to quote
from Mitford's Life of Gray) "It is said the cause of
his disorder, a consumption which brought him to an
early grave, was the fatal discovery which he made of
the treachery of a supposed friend, and the viciousness
of a mother whom he tenderly loved. This man,
under the mask of friendship to him and his family,
intrigued with his mother, and robbed him of his
peace of mind, his health and his life." The man in
question is said to have been secretary to West's
father[1]; Rogers was told that it was some person of

---

[1] 'A Mr Williams, whom she finally married when her son
was dead.' Mr Gosse (Life of Gray, p. 47). Gray's postscript to a letter from Walpole to West (Rome, April 16 N. S.
1740) has this 'We have sent you our compliments by a
friend of yours, and correspondent in a corner, who seems a
very agreeable man, one Mr Williams. I am sorry he staid
so little a while in Rome'. Is this the man? In any case we
may infer that Gray did not at this date know that there

inferior condition. A still more tragic colour is given to this strange story by what seems to have been a later discovery of Mitford's. "In a note hitherto unpublished," says Mr Gosse, "Dyce says that Mitford told him 'that West's death was hastened by mental anguish, there having been good reason to suspect that *his mother poisoned his father.*" These suspicions we can scarcely suppose were in West's mind before Sept. 28, 1739, on which day writing to Gray he speaks of his mother's health with filial anxiety, as the reason why they were then together at Tunbridge; and one cannot help wondering whether it was 'an honest ghost' that breathed into the young man's ear this tale of secret murder. Even in 1737 West describes himself as having been very ill, and it is probable that his feeble constitution was a legacy from his father. His own end was awfully sudden; both Gray and Ashton wrote to him when he was no more: Gray's letter is lost, but it enclosed the Ode on Spring for the eyes which were never to see it; Ashton's letter is given below; while it was being written, West was already two days dead. Always careless about his health, it is probable that the knowledge of his mother's guilt which came to him at some time within the last three years

was any sad story connected with the *name* Williams at all. He would have felt that in writing thus to his friend, he would be touching a wound.

of his life, made him more so; that it increased his
restlessness; that what he knew of bad made him
suspect worse, and connect some darker mystery with
his father's early death. I know not how this history
got abroad; if he told it to any one he told it to
Gray; we should never guess from the slightly-ruffled
surface of his correspondence, what deep sighs those
are

> Che fanno pullular quest' acqua al sommo.

But the reader should know that, beneath, a little
Hamlet-like tragedy is going on; perhaps not without
its good Horatio; and one thinks of Goethe's words
about "the lovely noble nature, without the strength
of nerve which forms a hero, sinking beneath a
burden which it cannot bear and must not cast
away." His last words to Gray 'Vale et vive paullisper cum vivis' were written in a cheerful and en-
couraging spirit; but as his friend thought upon
them in after days, they may have seemed like an
unconscious echo of the pathetic commission

> —Absent thee from felicity awhile
> And in this harsh world draw thy breath in pain
> To tell my story.

In the third place, there are here collected of
Gray's, whatever seemed of general interest, amongst
his hitherto unpublished relics. There are indeed
some evidences of his curious industry which have
not been included either in the edition of Mitford, or

G.   2

in that of Mr Gosse, and which are not printed here.
And it still remains true that in order to obtain the
whole of Gray's works, it is necessary to have recourse
to several distinct publications. If, for example, we
wish to read all Gray's notes of foreign travel we
must read one part of his Journal in France in Mr
Gosse's edition (vol. I. pp. 237—246), another part
in the present volume; the journal in Italy in the
present volume; and the Criticisms on Architecture
and Painting during a Tour in Italy in Mitford's
Aldine edition (vol. IV. pp. 225—305). Generally
speaking, I give nothing of Gray's which has been
before printed; the letters to John Chute which
will be found below, and which Mr Chaloner Chute
most kindly allows me to publish, have been recently printed by him in his 'History of the Vyne';
but none of these have appeared in any edition of
the poet's remains. In a search made under difficulties
and at rare intervals, it is likely that I have not seen
all that it would be worth while to edit; yet I do
not edit all that I *have* seen; there must be some
limit to what is called literature; for instance, there is
a copy in the British Museum of Verral's cookery[1],
with Gray's MS. notes; and these I did not transcribe.
I was indeed glad to discover from this book what
(such is the ignorance of man) I did not know before,

---

[1] It once belonged to Mitford. See his 'Correspondence
of Gray and Mason,' p. 252 n.

that Verral was a pupil of Clouet's, and that Clouet
was the Soyer of his age; because this enabled me to
understand the lines in the "Address of William
Shakespeare to M⁀ Anne, Regular servant to the
Rev. M⁀ Precentor of York"—

> "So York shall taste what *Clouet* never knew,
>   So from our works sublimer fumes shall rise;
> While Nancy earns the praise to Shakespeare due,
>   For glorious puddings and immortal pies."

His devotion to this branch of 'fair science' is a
quaint trait in our poet's character. Like Pope, a
weakling, he was probably more careful than Pope in
the matter of diet; but if not an epicure, he was at
least fastidious and epicurean. Samuel Rogers told
Mitford "that Gray in London saw little Society.
Had a nice dinner from the Tavern brought to his
lodgings, a glass or two of sweet wine, and as he
sippd it talked about great People[1]." This 'talking of
great people' is another little weakness, over which
one must pass lightly; Gray's temptations and opportunities lay in that direction; yet externals have
more to do with contemporary judgments than posterity is able to realise; social prejudices, the influence of cliques and coteries will cloud the strongest
minds; those who are forced to labour at the first
task that comes to hand, are not well-disposed to
their more fortunate brethren of the pen who can

[1] [Mitford, Add. Mss. Brit. Mus. 32,562, vol. III. p. 188.]

2—2

read or write at their leisure; there is always a Grub
Street in contrast with a Strawberry Hill; there are
always Johnsons and Grays. The man who had to
knock down the bullying Osborne with a folio was out
of sympathy with the man who thought it beneath
him to write for money, whose Odes Walpole printed
and to whom Dodsley stood hat in hand. This did
not affect Gray's estimate of Johnson's literary merit;
but surely some such feeling must explain Johnson's
utterly unworthy criticism of Gray. Gray's social
preferences did not betray him into fancies, except in
the case of novels, and the stage; his liking for the
younger Crébillon and his imperfect appreciation of
Fielding are in general contrast to his clear discern-
ment elsewhere; he agrees again with Walpole in dis-
paraging Garrick; a coincidence of opinion the more
noticeable, as the friends, estranged at this time, were
writing independently. But he disagrees with Walpole
over Johnson; praises 'London' and the 'Verses on
the opening of Garrick's Theatre'; and never seems to
have allowed his personal dislike to colour his opinion
of Johnson's real merits, whether as a writer or a
man. Walpole's aversion to Johnson on the contrary
is of that unreasoning and undiscriminating kind
which belongs to social and literary and political sets;
we may smile, we who see men in their right proportion or perspective, when, whilst coveting the acquaintance of Anstey and Mason, he excuses himself

for not desiring to know the 'bombastic' Johnson and the 'silly' Goldsmith, on the ground 'that he has seen Pope and lived with Gray'.

Our interest in Gray at this date seems indeed a little disproportionate to the scant and fragmentary nature of his positive achievements. But he fascinates us still, because he is one of us; because he shows himself, especially in his letters, a *modern;* because we feel that in his company we are at the sources of a familiar stream. We cannot indeed believe that when good Mr Brown said of Gray that 'he never spoke out' he had anything in his mind but the fact that Gray did not acknowledge to his friends how near he felt his end to be; and the comments which have been made upon the simple statement of *le petit bonhomme* read like fanciful homilies on an inappropriate text. Matthias, the 'Pursuer of Literature' (as Porson called him) whilst he tells us that at Gray

'Granta's dull abbots cast a side-long glance,
 And Levite gownsmen hugg'd their ignorance'

adds that he 'was his own exceeding great reward'— and Matthias here contrives to blunder very near the truth. Gray's melancholy has been much exaggerated. It was as he quaintly tells us 'a leucocholy'—and when he says of himself

'Fair science frown'd not on his humble birth
 And Melancholy marked him for her own'

he does but reproduce Milton's 'Il Penseroso'. Gray was the child of his own epoch, and never so much in advance of it, but that he could command many delighted readers when he pleased; and what happier lot could a man of letters crave than to combine freedom and leisure to follow his own bent, with that measure of success which Gray achieved in helping to give literature a new direction, amid much applause and homage in his life-time? His was not the type of mind, which an epoch of change, however momentous, could stimulate into production. He might have written letters or collected anecdotes about it; but there is no evidence whatever that it would have had any power to bring to the surface any latent springs of poetic thought and emotion. In his survey of contemporary events there is abundant curiosity and the keenest interest; there is never either much despondency or much enthusiasm. He lived through a period of great national depression, when as Cowper says

'The inestimable Estimate of Brown
Rose like a paper-kite and scared the town,'

by convincing, as Macaulay explains, its readers that "they were a race of cowards and scoundrels; that nothing could save them, that they were on the point of being enslaved by their enemies, and that they richly deserved their fate." He lived long enough to have been able, had he chosen, to say, before Cowper, that it was

"praise enough
To fill the ambition of a private man,

That Chatham's language was his mother tongue
And Wolfe's great name compatriot with his own."

Yet in his incidental treatment of public events
he has about as much 'high seriousness' as a George
Selwyn. One can compare his tone about them only
to a smile, in which there is nothing either very glad
or very sad; and yet no indifference or apathy. He
smiles in '46 over the defeat of Hawley at Falkirk;

"[At Cambridge] we talk of war, famine, and
pestilence, with no more apprehension than of a
broken head, or of a coach overturned between York
and Edinburgh."

Writing about the rebel Scotch Peers in the same
year, he is diverting and graphic over Balmerino and
Lovat and gently sympathetic over Cromartie; but I
question whether here or anywhere in his account of
contemporary politics the reader could separate his
manner or spirit from that of Walpole, by any generic
difference. He smiles again in '56 over Byng's loss
of Minorca;

" The British Flag, I fear, has behaved itself like
a trained-band pair of colours in Bunhill Fields...I
congratulate you on our glorious successes in the
Mediterranean. Shall we go in time, and hire a house
together in Switzerland? it is a fine poetical country
to look at, and nobody there will understand a word
we say or write."

Again, Wolfe, floating down the St Lawrence in

the still night, on his way to his heroic death, repeating in low tones to his brother officers the Elegy,
the tender pathos of which seemed to his heart an
achievement more glorious than victory, is a picture
for all time ; as often as it recurs to the memory, we
find it hard to call that a prosaic age, which produced
this most striking of all authentic testimonies to the
power of song.   This is the soldier's tribute to the
poet ; and what is the companion picture ?   Why,
briefly this; and if the contrast is a little shocking,
let us blame, not the unconscious Gray, gossiping with
a light heart, not knowing what would be expected of
him, but rather the last development of the higher
criticism :

    " [Pitt's] second speech was a studied and puerile
declamation on funeral honours (on proposing a
monument for Wolfe).   In the course of it he wiped
his eyes with one handkerchief, and Beckford (who
seconded him) cried too, and wiped with two hand-
kerchiefs at once, which was very moving."

    It was thus that Gray talked of ' Chatham's elo-
quence' in connection with ' Wolfe's great name.'
This is the Walpolean not the Wordsworthian spirit,
and what alchemy can convert the one into the other?
In this Gray is, as already said, the true child of his
epoch, and offers not a trace that he belonged, of
spiritual right, to earlier or later days.   A wise sentence
of Mr Lowell's should be written in large letters, to

warn us off by-paths in this matter. "It certainly was a comfortable time. If there was discontent, it was in the individual, not in the air; sporadic, not epidemic. Responsibility for the Universe had not yet been invented. A few solitary persons saw a swarm of ominous question-marks wherever they turned their eyes; but sensible people pronounced them the mere *muscae volitantes* of indigestion which an honest dose of rhubarb would disperse. Men read Rousseau for amusement, and never dreamed that those flowers of rhetoric were ripening the seed of the guillotine."

Gray read Rousseau; sometimes, as he confesses, 'heavily, heavily,' seeking that is, amusement, and finding it not; but for the signs of the times he consulted the weathercock. The last part of the letter to Wharton from which I quoted just now, is a weather and garden chronicle into which he slides from the statement that it is "a very critical time, an action being hourly expected between the two great Fleets, but no news as yet." It is as if we had Pepys and White of Selborne on the same page. But he has begun with a feeling account of the last illness of his friend Lady Cobham, and then has gone on to talk about house decoration in a very practical as well as aesthetic manner for the benefit of Wharton. Combine only this with a previous letter to the same correspondent in which he passes from Froissart to current political gossip, and we have abundant evi-

dence of a mind actively and wholesomely employed in
the offices of friendship, in literature, art, in the
'quidquid agunt homines' regarded with good humour-
ed amusement, and in the minute study of Nature[1].
In a correspondence so full and varied we are justified in declaring that the whole character of the
man stands revealed to us. Here at any rate 'he
speaks out' very plainly. And we shall find here
private affections, deep but limited, and wonderfully
little even of an invalid's despondency; we shall find
indeed local antipathies and prejudices, but to attribute *Weltschmerz* to him, or even any latent uneasiness pointing that way, is the merest anachronism.
Let us repeat once more Mr Lowell's golden phrase
"Responsibility for the Universe had not yet been
invented." We are speaking now of England and
Englishmen, and the most emphatic utterances which
I can recollect of Gray's breathe the buoyant and
cheerful public spirit of his age ; he reminds Horace
Walpole that 'desperare de Republicâ is a deadly sin
in politics'; and again, after quoting Gresset's

> Le cri d un peuple heureux est la seule éloquence
>   Qui sçait parler des rois,

he adds 'which is very true, and should have

---

[1] It may seem strange to associate Gray with Goethe; yet
it is certain that Gray and Goethe are demonstrative instances
that the scientific exploration of Nature is compatible with
a love of Nature on the imaginative side.

been a hint to him not to write odes to the King at all.'

"Born in the same year with Milton, Gray" we are told "would have been another man, born in the same year with Burns, he would have been another man." On the contrary, he would have been the same man, but a less finished artist, if he had been born in 1608. He would have been no more stirred by that eminently stirring time, than Sir Thomas Browne. In the year of Naseby Fight he might have been discussing with Browne whether the lion is afraid of the cock, and whether earwigs have wings. If he had loved young Edward King, we know already what sort of 'Lycidas' his would have been. The author would have bewailed his 'learned friend' but he would never 'by occasion, have foretold the ruin of our corrupted clergy then in their height.' In whatever age he had lived it was not *in* the man to link private sorrow with public calamity. When he feels most acutely he cannot even moralize, in that tenderly human spirit of his which never grows old; he can only complain. If we whose many conventionalisms are not only conventional but hideous, can forget for a moment that Gray in his Sonnet on the Death of West calls the sun 'Phœbus', it will be redeemed for us by this one touch of absolute sincerity, that it is only a cry of pain, real though disguised in music now a little trite to us. And

again he has the student's imagination, which does
not *feel* great events in the present, but needs distance and some obscurity to make them seem majestic.
On whatever times he might have fallen, if he had
attempted to sing of contemporary kings and battles,
Apollo would have twitched his ear. We may be
sure that he would have read and praised any immortal song; but his own soul would have rested
with L'Allegro and Il Penseroso and would never
have migrated into Samson Agonistes; and he might
admire, through his fine critical and artistic sense,
the insight and grand impartiality of Marvell's
Horatian Ode, and see with Marvell's eyes, the
tragedy at Whitehall, but he would be disposed to
rival the same Marvell only in the garden at Nun-
appleton

'Annihilating all that's made
To a green thought in a green shade.'

We have been looking backward, now let us look
forward from Gray's time. Coleridge, like Gray, produced too little poetry; but we agree to find the
explanation of this, not in the age, but in the man.
The age, we say, is inspiring; perhaps whatever of
enthusiasm there is in Coleridge is caught from it.
In his case a want of physical and moral energy
accounts for everything; a *vis inertiæ* which prevails
over the *momentum* which he has received from without. Gray's *momentum* comes from within; he writes

to please himself; publicity is with him always quite
a secondary matter, and his choice of subjects is
absolutely his own; at the same time his own age
welcomes him, and would gladly have had more from
him; Gibbon, a representative name, regrets that the
Poem on the Alliance of Education and Government
is but a fragment; in his life time Gray had less than
the common share of adverse criticism, and his incomplete designs were on themes which, whilst they
indicate his own taste and bias, were adapted to the
scope and comprehension of 'an age of prose and
reason.' Yet in his case, we are told, the age is
responsible for his want of production. It is my
conviction, though I have not space to develop it at
large, that 'born in the same year as Burns', Gray, if
he had lived at Cambridge (the Cambridge which we
know from Gunning's Reminiscences) would have
written even less great poetry, but perhaps more
satirical verses and more prose; what is certain is
that his real impediments to production were first
feeble health, next his boundless and discursive
curiosity, and next the extensive scale on which, like
a man who has abundant knowledge, and seems to
have abundant time before him, he formed his plans,
ever delaying, until the consciousness that the day is
far spent, makes him sad and silent about them. / To
these causes must be added his remoteness (by the
deliberate choice of one to whom books and comfort

were necessities of existence) from those inspiring scenes, the beauty of which he was amongst the first to realize. The much abused prosaic eighteenth century was hastening to give us those improved communications which make so many of us Wordsworthians once a year. Let us be just, amid our privileges, our raptures real or feigned over the sublimities of Nature, and our letters to the Times (bearing the unmistakeable accent of sincerity) on hotel bills and drainage, to the timid weakling who visited such scenes with difficulty and noted them lovingly, even though he brought to them or gained from them no emotions more abstruse than those which all men can share with him. Perhaps after all, he will survive by what *we* call his limitations, inasmuch as that poetry is the most securely immortal which has gained nothing and can lose nothing by the vicissitudes of sentiment and opinion. We may be all the merest Peter Bells some day over a yellow primrose, and yet retain just enough sense of the correspondence between the world within us and the world without to feel the truth of that rejected stanza of the Elegy :

'Hark how the sacred calm that broods around
  Bids every fierce tumultuous passion cease,
In still small accents whisp'ring from the ground
  A grateful earnest of eternal Peace.'

Wordsworth would never, let us add, have parted

with that stanza from any consideration of structure. But the nineteenth century, which has learnt from him that Poetry is an inspiration, will still return to Gray to learn that it is also an art. To Gray, it may be, rather than to Pope; because the character of Gray's thought and themes belongs less to the occasional and the transient. /

It is scarcely a paradox to say that he has left much that is incomplete, but nothing that is unfinished. His handwriting represents his mind; I have seen and transcribed many and many a page of it, but I do not recollect to have noticed a single carelessly written word, or even letter. The mere sight of it suggests refinement, order, and infinite pains. A mind searching in so many directions, sensitive to so many influences, yet seeking in the first place its own satisfaction in a manner uniformly careful and artistic, is almost foredoomed to give very little to the world; it must be content, as the excellent Matthias says, to be 'its own exceeding great reward.' But what is given is a little gold instead of much silver: a legal tender at any time, though it has never been soiled in the market. He claims our honour as one of those few who in any age have lived in the pursuit of the absolute best, and who help us to mistrust the glib facility with which we are apt to characterize epochs. In all that he has left, there is independence, sincerity, thoroughness; the highest exemplar of the critical

spirit; a type of how good work of any kind should
be done. He studied Greek when few studied it, and
when much that is now familiar to schoolboys was
unknown to scholars, yet he read with all the exact-
ness he could command as well as in the large fashion
of a man of letters.   He wrote with accents, generally,
I believe, rightly placed; though in this respect his
editors have declined to copy him.   His notes, designed for his own use, have been frequently quoted
by the late Master of Trinity; they prove very extensive reading and comparison of authorities; we
may infer that in the absence of adequate aids he
was often guided to the meaning more by the context
than by verbal scholarship.   To history he brought
the modern spirit of research, which, like the curiosity of Herodotus and Froissart, is a kind of
guarantee of impartiality, and virtually leaves to the
secure judgment of the world the task of pronouncing
sentence.   His critical opinions are safe, because they
are not controversial nor addressed to a public, but
the outcome of impressions gathered at leisure by a
mind at once comprehensive and exact.   We are no
losers by the circumstance that they were communicated only to his friends, for next in sincerity to the
good criticism which may be found in some poetry, is
that which we can extract from private letters[1].

[1] Gray's friends caught something of his power of pointed
expression.   Mason has not received many compliments of

And though Gray lived so much in the past, he is
receptive in the present, cognizant of new tendencies
and apt to resign himself to them, and to forego his
penetration when these are concerned; he would
willingly believe in Macpherson's Ossian; he is
perhaps the only Englishman of note whom it affects,
as it affected the Continentals; this is because his
sensitive genius has a little shudder of presentiment,
at this first breath of the reviving spirit of Romance.
It is these characteristics which make him, as I have
said, still modern for us in the best sense and justify
the curious and minute interest which some feel in
him now; it is at any rate the best account I am
able to give of a sort of homage which seems to
belong to much greater names, and yet which inclines
one who has given much time to Gray, whilst perhaps
half-smiling at his own enthusiasm, to repeat to his
fascinating shade the invocation

> Vagliami 'l lungo studio e 'l grande amore
> Che m' han fatto cercar lo tuo volume.

late; but Mr Lowell pays him a very great one in attributing
to Gray his saying "Jeremy Taylor is the Shakespeare of
divines."

SECTION I.

UNPUBLISHED LETTERS, CHIEFLY OF FOREIGN TRAVEL;

GRAY, WALPOLE AND ASHTON.

1. GRAY TO ASHTON.

To M[r] Ashton at the Honb[le] M[rs] Lewis's, in Hanover Square, London.

My dear Ashton,

It seems you have forgot the poor little tenement in which you so long lodg'd, and have set your heart on some fine Castle in the Air : I wish I were Master of the Seat you describe, that I might make yr Residence more agreeable, but as it is, I fear you'll hardly meet with common Conveniences.

I deserve you should be angry with me for haveing been so little punctual, in paying my Dues, & returning thanks for your advice some time since. All is at present, mighty well, that is just as you remember it, & imagin'd it would be : cool enough not to burn, and warm enough not to freeze one, but methinks the Counsel you gave me, was what you did not think proper to make use of in like Circumstances yrself ; perhaps you know why the same way of acting should be improper for you, & proper for me : I don't doubt but you have your reasons, & I trust you would not have me do anything wrong.

The account W: gives me of your way of Life is better than I expected. to be sure you must meet daily with little particulars enough to fill a letter, and I should be pleas'd with the most minute. Has M^{rs} L: a pimple upon her nose? does her Woman love Citron Water? &c: any of these would be a high regale for me. but perhaps you think it telling tales: you know best. Have you seen Madame Valmote[1]? naughty Woman! was you at the Christening? is the Princess with Child again? was you at the review? have you wrote e'er a Critique on the Accidence? is Despauterius[2] or Linacer most in your favor? but perhaps you think this tittle-tattle. Well! you know best. Pot-fair is at its height; there's old raffleing. Walpole is gone to Stamford, & to Lynn but returns in a day or two. I am gone to the Carrier's with this letter, and am

ever yrs

T. G.

June 30—Cambridge. [1738]

[1] Amelia Sophia, wife of the Baron de Walmoden, and mistress of George II. She came to England after the death of Queen Caroline in 1737. The christening referred to above is that of George Augustus, afterwards George III., which took place in June 1738.

[2] Jean Despautère, born at Ninove in Flanders, died 1520. His grammar was in vogue in France until superseded by that of the Port-Royal.

2. GRAY TO ASHTON.

Dear Ashton,

You and West have made us happy to night in a heap of letters, & we are resolvd to repay you twofold. Our English perhaps may not be the best in the World, but we have the Comfort to know that it is at least as good as our French. So to begin. Paris is a huge round City, divided by the Seine, a very near relation (if we may judge by the resemblance) of your old acquaintance, that ancient river, the river Cam. along it on either side runs a key of perhaps as handsome buildings, as any in the World. the view down which on either hand from the Pont Neuf is the charming'st sight imaginable. There are infinite Swarms of inhabitants and more Coaches than Men. The Women in general dressd in Sacs, flat Hoops of 5 yards wide nosegays of artificial flowers on one shoulder, and faces dyed in Scarlet up to the Eyes. The Men in bags, roll-upps, Muffs & Solitaires. Our Mornings have been mostly taken up in Seeing Sights: few Hotels or Churches have escapd us, where there is anything remarkable as to building, Pictures or Statues.

M[r] Conway[1] is as usual, the Companion of our

---

[1] Walpole's maternal cousin, the Mr Conway and General Conway of his correspondence, second son of the first Lord Conway, by Charlotte Shorter, his third wife, sister of Lady Walpole

travels, who, till we came, had not seen anything at
all; for it is not the fashion here to have Curiosity.
We had at first arrival an inundation of Visits
pouring in upon us, for all the English are acquainted,
and herd much together & it is no easy Matter to
disengage oneself from them, so that one sees but
little of the French themselves.   To be introduced to
the People of high quality, it is absolutely necessary
to be Master of the Language, for it is not to be
imagined that they will take pains to understand
anybody, or to correct a stranger's blunders.   Another
thing is, there is not a House where they do'nt play,
nor is any one at all acceptable, unless they do so too,
a professed Gamester being the most advantageous
character a Man can have at Paris.   The Abbés
indeed & men of learning are a People of easy access
enough, but few English that travel have knowledge
enough to take any great pleasure in this Company,
at least our present lot of travellers have not.   We
are, I think to remain here no longer than Ld^1
Conway stays, & then set out for Rheims, there to
reside a Month or two, & then to return hither again

...Commander in Chief 1782, Field Marshal 1793. He married
the Dowager Countess of Aylesbury, daughter of John D. of
Argyle; his only child by this marriage was Mrs Damer, the
sculptor, to whom Walpole left Strawberry Hill. [Cunningham.]

[1] Elder brother of the Conway mentioned before. [After-
wards Earl of Hertford, Marquis 1793; died 14th of June 1794.
Cunningham.]

& very often little hankerings break out, so that I am not sure, we shall not come back to-morrow.

We are exceedingly unsettled & irresolute, do'nt know our own Minds for two Moments together, profess an utter aversion for all manner of fatigue, grumble, are ill-natured & try to bring ourselves to a State of perfect Apathy in which [we] are so far advanced, as to declare we have no notion of caring for any mortal breathing but ourselves. In short I think the greatest *evil* could have happen'd to us, is our liberty, for we are not at all capable to determine our own actions.

My dear Ashton, I am ever

Yours sincerely

T: G:

Paris—Hotel de
Luxembourg, Rue
des petits Augustins
  April 21, N. S. [1739]

3. GRAY TO ASHTON.

My dear Ashton,

I shall not make you any excuses, because I ca'nt: I shall not try to entertain you with descriptions for the same reason; and moreover because I believe you do'nt care for them: so that you can

have no occasion to wonder at my brevity, when you
consider me as confind to the narrow bounds of We,
quatenus We, which I continue.

Our tête a tête Conversations that you enquire
after, did consist less in Words, than in looks
and signs, & to give you a notion of them, I ought
to send you our Pictures : tho' we should find it
difficult to sit for 'em in such attitudes as we naturally
fall into, when alone together.   At present Mr Conway
who lives with us, joins to make them a little more
verbose, & everything is mighty well.   On Monday
next we set out for Rheims, (where we expect to be
very dull) there to stay a Month or two, then we
cross Burgundy & Dauphiny, & so go to Avignon,
Aix, Marseilles &c. the Weather begins to be violently
hot already even here, and this is our ingenious Con-
trivance, as the Summer increases, to seek out cool
retreats among the scorchd rocks of Provence.   I
will not promise, but that if next Winter bid fair for
extreme Cold we shall take a trip to Muscovy.   You
in the mean time, will be quietly enjoying the temperate air of England, under yr own Vine, and under
your own (at least under Mrs Lewis's) Figtree and I
do'nt doubt but the fruits of your leisure will turn
to more account, than those of our laborious pere-
grination, and while our thoughts are rambling about
& changeing situation oftener than our bodies, you
will be fixing your attention upon some weighty

truth, worthy a Sage of yr honor's magnitude. The end of yr researches, I mean whatever your profound Contemplation brings to light, I shd be proud to be acquainted with, whether it please to be invokd under the appellation of Sermon, Vision, Essay or discourse ; in short, on whatever head, you may chuse to be loquacious (Wall on Infant Baptism excepted) a dissertation will be very acceptable, and receivd with a reverence due to the hand it comes from.

We have seen here your " Gustavus Vasa[1] " that had raisd the general expectation so high, long ago, a worthy piece of prohibited Merchandise, in truth ! The Town must have been extreme mercifully disposd ; if for the sake of ten innocent lines that may peradventure be pickd out, it had consented to spare the lives of the ten thousand wicked ones, that remain. I dont know what condition your Stage is in, but the French is in a very good one at present. Among the rest they have a Mad[lle] Dumenil[2] whose

---

[1] Walpole writing to West from Rheims June 18, 1739 N.S., describing his exercises in French says 'Besides this, I have paraphrased half the first act of your new 'Gustavus' which was sent us to Paris ; a most dainty performance, and just what you say of it.' Henry Brooke's 'Gustavus Vasa' was prohibited by Sir Robert Walpole's Act for Licensing Plays. The prohibition called forth Johnson's ironical ' Vindication of the Licensers of the Stage.' Brooke subsequently wrote 'The Fool of Quality,' a novel, by which he is better known.

[2] Marie Françoise Dumesnil, of the Comédie Française, born in 1711, retired from the stage 7 April 1776 and died in

every look and gesture is violent Nature, she is Passion itself, incarnate.

I saw her the other Night do the Phædra of Racine, in a manner which affected me so strongly, that as you see, I ca'nt help prattling about her even to you, that do not care two Pence.

You have got my Ld Conway[1] then among Ye: what do People think about him, & his improvements? You possibly see him sometimes, for he visits at Mrs Conduit's. is he charming, and going to be married like Mr Barrett? Pray write to me & persuade *West* to do the same, who, unless you rouse him, & preach to him, what a Sin it is to have the vapours, & the dismals, will neglect himself; I wont say his friends; that I believe him to be incapable of: I again recommend him to yr Care, that

1803, just after she had published her Memoirs under the editorship of M. Coste. There is an interesting article about her in the Biographie Universelle. Voltaire in an Essay "Des Divers Changements arrivés à l'art tragique"—written in 1761, says of her...'pour le grand pathétique de l'action, nous le vîmes la première fois dans Mademoiselle Dumesnil' (Works ed. 1832, vol. 65, p. 86). She seems to have shared the favour of the Parisian public with Mlle Clairon. Walpole thought her superior to Mrs Siddons. Writing to the Countess of Ossory 3 Nov. 1782, he says "All Mrs Siddons did, good sense or good instruction might give. I dare say that were I one and twenty, I should have thought her marvellous: but alas! I remember Mrs Porter and the Dumesnil" &c. &c. (Works ed. Cunningham, viii. 295.)

[1] See p. 40, n. 1.

you may nourish him, and cherish him & administer to him, some of that cordial Spirit of Chearfulness that you used to have the receipt of.

My Compliments to my Lord[1]. Good night
Yours ever
T. G.

4. GRAY AND WALPOLE TO ASHTON.

To
Mr Ashton
at Mrs Lewis's
Hanover Square
London
Franc à Paris

My dear Ashton,
The exceeding Slowness and Sterility of me, & the vast abundance & volubility of Mr Walpole & his Pen will sufficiently excuse to you the shortness of this little matter. He insists that it is not him but his Pen that is so volubility, & so I have borrowed it of him ; but I find it is both of 'em that is so volubility, for tho I am writing as fast, as I can drive, yet he is still chattering in vast abundance. I have desired me to hold his tongue, pho, I mean him, & his, but his Pen is so used to write in the first Person, that I have screwd my finger and

---

[1] Lord Plymouth, to whom Ashton was Tutor.

thumb off, with forcing it into the third.   After all
this confusion of Persons, & a little Stroke of Satyr
upon me the Pen returns calmly back again into the
old *I* and *me*, as if nothing had happened, to tell you
how much I am tired, & how cross I am, that this
cursed Scheme of Messrs Selwyn & Montague[1] should
have come across all our Measures, & broke in upon
the whole year, which, what with the Month we have
to wait for them, & the Month they are to stay
here, will be entirely slipt away, at least, the agreable
Part of it, and if we journey at all, it will be thro'
dirty roads and falling leaves.

The Man, whose arguments you have so learnedly
stated, & whom you did not think fit to honour with
a Confutation, we from thence conceive to be one,
who does us honour, in thinking us fools, & so you
see, I lay my claim to a share of the glory ;   we
are not vastly curious about his name, first because
it do'nt signify, 2dly because we know it already ; it
is either S^r T: G: himself, or yr friend Mr Fenton, if
it's them we do'nt care, & if it is not, we do'nt care

---

[1] Walpole to West, Rheims, July 20, 1739, writes 'This is
the day that Gray and I intended for the first of a southern
circuit; but as Mr Selwyn and George Montagu design us a
visit here we have put off our journey for some weeks.' [George
Augustus Selwyn the wit.   He was at Eton with Walpole, who
was about two years his senior.   Cunningham.]   Montagu is
of course Walpole's correspondent, concerning whom see Cunningham's ed. of Walpole's Letters, vol. I. p. 2, n. 4.

neither, but if you care to convince the Man, whoever
he be, that we are in some points not altogether
fools, you might let him know that we are most
sincerely

Yours

H W. ⅁

Rheims—July. [1739]

5. GRAY TO ASHTON.

Rheims. 25 Aug. N: S [1739]

My dear Ashton,

      I am not so ignorant of Pain myself as
to be able to hear of anothers Sufferings, without any
Sensibility to them, especially when they are those of
one, I ought more particularly to feel for : tho' indeed the goodness of my own Constitution, is in some
sense a misfortune to me, for as the health of everybody I love seems much more precarious than my
own, it is but a melancholy prospect to consider
myself as one, that may possibly in some years be
left in the World, destitute of the advice or Good
Wishes of those few friends, that usd to care for me,
and without a likelihood or even a desire of gaining
any new ones. this letter will, I hope, find you
perfectly recoverd, & your own painful experience
will, for the future, teach you not to give so much in
to a Sedentary Life, that has [I] fear been the Cause
of your illness. Give my duty to your Mind, & tell
her she has taken more care of herself, than of my

tother poor friend, your Body, & bid her hereafter remember how nearly *her* Welfare is connected with *his:* tell her too that she may pride herself in her great family, & despise him for being a poor Mortal, as much as she pleases, but that he is her wedded husband, & if he suffers, she must smart for it. my inferences you will say, do'nt follow very naturally, nor have any great relation to what has been said, but they are as follows. Messrs Selwin and Montagu have been here these 3 weeks, are by this time pretty heartily tired of Rheims, & return in about a Week. The day they set out for England, we are to do the same for Burgundy, in our way only as it is said to Province[1], but People better informd conceive that Dijon will be the end of our expedition. for me, I make everything that does not depend on me, so indifferent to me, that if it be to go to the Cape of Good Hope I care not: if you are well enough, you will let me know a little of the history of West who does not remember there is such a place as Champagne in the world.

Your's ever
T. G.

To

Mr Ashton at Mrs Lewis's	pour l'Angleterre
in Hanover Square	franc jusqu'a Paris
London	
franc a Paris.	

[1] *Sic* ap. Mitford.

6. WALPOLE AND GRAY TO ASHTON.

Rome, May 14, 1740 N. E.

Boileau's Discord dwelt in a College of Monks[1]. at present the Lady is in the Conclave. Corsini has been interrogated about certain Millions of Crowns that are absent from the Apostolic Chamber; He refuses giving an account, but to a Pope. However he has set several arithmeticians to work, to compose Summs, & flourish out expenses, which probably never existed. Cardinal Cibo pretends to have a Banker at Genoa, who will prove that he has received three Millions on the Part of the Eminent Corsini. This Cibo is a madman, but set on by others. He had formerly some great office in the government, from whence they are generally raised to the Cardinalate. after a time, not being promoted as he expected, he resigned his Post, and retired to a Mountain where he built a most magnificent Hermitage. There he inhabited for two years, grew tired, came back and received the Hat.

Other feuds have been between Card. Portia and the father of Benedict the Thirteenth, by whom he was made Cardinal. About a month ago, he was within three votes of being Pope; he did not apply to any Party, but went gleaning privately from all.

---

[1] 'Le Lutrin' chant 1.

G.   4

and of a sudden burst out with a Number, but too soon, and that threw him quite out. Having been since left out of their meetings, he askd one of the Benedictine Cardinals the reason, who replied that he never had been their friend and never should be of their assemblies, & did not even hesitate to call him Apostate. This flung Portia into such a rage that he spit blood, and instantly left the Conclave with all his baggage. But the great Cause of their antipathy to him, was, his having been one of the four, that voted for putting Coscia to death, who now regains his interest, & may prove somewhat disagreeable to his Enemies: whose honesty is not abundantly heavier than his own. He met Corsini t'other day, and told him, he heard his eminence had a mind to his Cell: Corsini answerd, he was very well contented with that he had. Oh! says Coscia, I do'nt mean here in the Conclave, but in the Castle St Angelo.

With all these animosities, one is near having a Pope[1]. Card. Gotto, an old, inoffensive Dominican, without any Relations, wanted yesterday but two voices, and is still most likely to succeed. Card. Altieri has been sent for from Albano, whither he

---

[1] Clement XII. had recently died. [Gray to his mother from Florence, March 19, 1740.] His successor was Benedict XIV. [amusingly described, same to the same from Florence, Aug. 21, 1740.]

was retird on acct of his brothers death, & his own illness, & where he was to stay till the Election drew nigh. There! There is a sufficient quantity of Conclave News I think…

We have miserable Weather for the season. Could you think I was writing to you by my fireside at Rome in the middle of May? the Common People say 'tis occasioned by the Pope's soul, which cannot find rest.

How goes your War? We are persuaded here of an additional one with France, Lord! it will be dreadful to return thro' Germany. I do'nt know who cooks up the news here, but we have some strange Peice every day. One that is much in vogue, & would not be disagreeable for us, is, that the Czarina[1] has clapt the Marquis de la Chétardie in Prison; one must hope till some months hence, 'tis all contradicted.

[1] The Czarina was Anne, who died on the 28th of October of this year. The Marquis de la Chétardie had been Ambassador at Berlin. Carlyle (Frederick the Great, vol. III. p. 180 People's ed.) under year 1734 describes him as "a showy restless character, of fame in the Gazettes of that time; who did much intriguing at Petersburg some years hence, first in a signally triumphant way, and then in a signally untriumphant." The Crown Prince (afterwards Frederick the Great) 'took a good deal to him' at this date. He was the lover of the Princess Elizabeth and intrigued with "a Surgeon called L'Estoc" to set her on the throne of Russia, Dec. 5th, 1741, displacing the Regent Anne (Princess Catherine of Mecklenburg. Carlyle, Ib. IV. 180—183).

4—2

I am balancing in great uncertainty, whether to go to Naples, or to stay here. You know 'twould be provoking to have a Pope chosen just as one's back is turnd: and if I wait, I fear the heats may arrive. I do'nt know what to do. We are going to night to a great assemblee at one of the villas just out of the City, whither all the English are invited; amongst the rest Mr Stuard[1] and his two Sons. There is one lives with him calld Lord Dunbar[2], Murray's brother who would be his Minister, if he had any occasion for one—I meet him frequently in Public Places & like him. He is very sensible, very agreable, & well bred.

Good night Child; by the bye, I have had no letters from England these two last Posts.

Yrs ever.——

I am by trade a finisher of Letters. don't you wonder at the Conclave? Instead of being immur'd, every one in his proper hutch as one us'd to imagine, they have the Liberty of scuttling out of one hole

[1] The Old Pretender. Gray describes this ball in a letter to West of May 21 (Works, ed. Gosse II. 76 lett. 32). There "Il Serenissimo Pretendente (as the Mantova gazette calls him) displayed his rueful length of person, with his two young ones, and all his ministry around him."

[2] See also Gray's letter to his Father July 16, 1740. The ball was given by Count Patrizii to the Prince and Princess Craon.

into another, ...

. . I do assure you, every thing one has heard say of Italy, is a lye, & am firmly of opinion, that no mortal was ever here before us. I am writeing to prove that there never was any such a People as the Romans, that this was antiently a Colony of the Jews, and that the Coliseum was built on the model of Solomon's temple. Our People have told so many Stories of them, that they do'nt believe any thing we say about ourselves. Porto Bello[1] is still said to be impregnable and it is reported the Dutch have declar'd War against us. The English Court here, brighten up on the news of our Conquests, and conclude all the Contrary has happen'd. You do not know perhaps, that we have our little good fortune in the Mediterranean, where Adm[l]. Haddock[2] has over-

[1] It was of course already taken, by Admiral Vernon with his six ships, Nov. 21, 1739.

[2] Walpole writing to West from Rome, May 7 of this year, says 'We heard the news last night from Naples that Admiral Haddock had met the Spanish convoy going to Majorca, and taken it all, all; three thousand men, three colonels, and a Spanish grandee. We conclude it is true, for the Neapolitan Majesty mentioned it at dinner.' On which Wright notes "This report, which proved unfounded, was grounded on the fact that on the 18th April his Majesty's ships Lennox, Kent, and Orford, commanded by Captains Mayne, Durell, and Lord Augustus Fitzroy, part of Admiral Balchen's squadron, being on a cruise about forty leagues to the westward of Cape Finisterre, fell in with the Princessa, esteemed the finest ship of war in the Spanish navy, and captured her after an engage-

turnd certain little boats carrying Troops to Majorca,
drown'd a few hundred of them, and taken a little
Grandee of Spain, that commanded the Expedition.
at least, so they say at Naples. I'm very sorry. but
methinks they seem in a bad Condition. Is *West*
dead to the world in general, or only so to me? for
you I have not the impudence to accuse, but you
are to take this as a sort of reproof, and I hope you
will demean yourself accordingly. You are hereby
authoriz'd to make my particular Compliments to
my Ld Plymouth[1], and return him my thanks de
l'honneur de son Souvenir. So I finish my Postcript
with

Your's ever

T. G.

7. WALPOLE TO ASHTON.

Rome. May 28[2] 1740 N.S.

Dear Child,

I have just received your Letter of news; I
had heard before of Symphony's affair, with Lady —.
but they calld it a report; but I find like many
stories of that kind 'tis true. What?[3] are We to be

ment of five hours." (Letters of Horace Walpole ed. Cunningham, vol. I. pp. 46, 47, lett. 29.)

[1] Ashton was Tutor to the Earl of Plymouth. [Mitford.]

[2] Possibly 23, for Mitford's MS is doubtful here.

[3] Written by Mitford without this note of interrogation, but
it is necessary for clearness.

to appear before the H: of Lords? are there to be damages? or is it to be blown over, with only a separate Maintenance for the Fair One? I am sorry he has obviously established such a Character. 'Tis too soon to be arrived at one's *ne plus ultra.* I doubt 'tis all the fame he will ever be master of, & tis horrid to begin where one must end.

By a considerable volume of Charts and Pyramids which I saw at Florence, I thought it threatend a Publication. His travels have really improvd him; I wish they may do the same for any one else.

West has sent me a letter of Fragments, which not being antique, I am extremely angry, are not compleat.

> 'Nor cease the Maiden Graces from above
> To shower their fragrance on the fields[1] of Love.'

I desire' you will set him to digging in the same Spot, where he found these verses, for the other parts of the Poem. I took them for his own; but upon showing them to a great virtuoso here, he assures me they are undoubtedly ancient, by one of the best hands, & in the true greek Taste.

This is the first day, we have had, that one can call warm; they say, in England you have not a leaf yet on the Trees.

I have made a Vow against Politics, or I w^d wish

---

[1] ? field or fields,—doubtful in ms.

you joy of your W.^t Indian Conquests. One shall not know you again. You will be so martial all. Here one should not know, if there had ever been such a thing as War, if it were not now and then from seeing a Scrap[1] of a Soldier on an old Bas-relief. 'Tis comical to see a hundred & twenty thousand inhabitants in a City where you scarce ever see one that has not taken a vow never to propagate; But they say there are larger Parsley beds here than in other Countries. Dont talk of our Coronation; 'tis never likely to happen. The divisions are so great between the Albani and Corsini factions, that the Conclave will probably be drawn out to a great length. With Albani are his Uncle's Creatures, the Spanish & Neapolitan factions, and the Zelanti; a set of Cardinals, who always declare agst any Party, and profess being solely in the interest of the Church. With *Corsini* are the late Pope's Creatures, and the Dependents of France.

Mrs G.[2] writes me word how much goodness she met with in Hanover Sqre. Poor Creature! You know, how much it obliges me, my dear Ashton, & if that can give you any Satisfaction, as I well believe it does, be assurd, it touches me in the strongest Manner. It obliges me in a Point that relates to my Mother, & that is all I can say in this World! You

---

[1] *Sic* apparently.

[2] pp. 3—5, 60.

must make my particular[1] to Mrs Lewis ; her kindness to M^rs^ G : is adding to the severall great obligations I have to her.   'Tis a pleasure to receive
such from one who acts from no Motives, but innate
goodness and benevolent virtue.   You must not tell
that poor Woman, what I am now going to mention.
I fear we shall not see Naples.   We have been setting
out for some time ; and if we do not[2] to be back by
the end of this month, it will be impraticable from
the heats, and the bad air, in the Campania· but we
are prevented by a great body of banditti, Soldiers
deserted from the King of Naples, who have taken
Possession of the roads, & not only murderd several
Passengers, but some Sbirri who were sent agst them.
Among others was a poor Hermit, who had a few old
Medals which he had dug up, that they took for
Money.   The Poverty of the Roman States and the
mutinous humor of the inhabitants who grow des-
perate for want of a Pope, thro' decay of trade, & a
total want of Specie are likely to encrease the bands,
while the Conclave sits, so that I fear we are Prisoners
at Rome, till the Election.   I should not at all dislike my Situation, if I were entirely at Liberty & had
nothing to call me to England.   I shall but too soon
miss there the Peace I enjoy here ; I do'nt mention

---

[1] *Sic* ap. Mitford.

[2] I think this is the reading, the meaning being, 'if we do
not set out, so as to return &c.'

the pleasures I enjoy here, which are to be found in
no other City in the World, but them I could give up
to my friends with satisfaction.   But I know the
Causes that drove me out of England, and I do'nt
know that they are remedied.   But adieu! when I
leave Italy, I shall launch out into a Life, whose
Colour I fear, will have more of black than of White.

Yrs—

ever.

8. [1]ASHTON TO WALPOLE.

My dearest. Walpole

Since the last letter I received from you
which tho' it gave me the Pleasure of yr Recovery[2]
did not however rid me from the fear of a Relapse I
have not been able this Week to pick up one Syllable
relating to you….Judge you what I have felt.   an
interval of 7 weeks, without one word of intelligence
after so dangerous an indisposition, in so remote a
place unattended, as I feard, with Physician or
friend.   I went from Somerset House to Downing St.
& from Downing Str. to Somerset House, but still
nothing.   I would fain have persuaded poor Mrs Gr:
and myself that if any thing ill had happend we
must have heard.   My apprehensions would have it,

---

[1] Mitford Add. mss. 32,562, p. 210.

[2] For Walpole's illness at Reggio see sect. II. lett. 33 n. 1.

that that was at best conjecture. It might be so,
but it might be otherwise. So dextrously did we
impose a cruel deceit upon ourselves, by admitting
no Probability that would make for us, and by
stretching[1] every Possibility of the Contrary into a
Demonstration. In short we feard and felt the worst.
If one had told me you were actually dead, it would
have been no news to me. I had already attended
you to the grave & had become as lifeless as if I
had been laid there with you. I do solemnly protest
to you that I would not feel again what I have done
on this occasion, no, not for the inexpressible satisfaction of knowing the contrary. My senses are so
bemumbd, with so long a concern, that it was almost
beyond the Power of any Pleasure to recall 'em. Dear
M^{rs} G, I thank her, did all she could; indeed I am
infinitely obligd to her. She enclosd yr letter to me
the moment she receivd it. I trembled when I opend
hers, but when I saw the jewel within, I do not know
or cannot tell you what I did This is the third
Letter I have wrote to you, since I have had yrs. My
dear Walpole, I speak sincerely to you. I would not
for the World go over that time again, which I have
passd since you left England. I would not, I do
assure you....I am like a Man who has been tossd
about a long Winter's Night in uneasy dreams. I
have been draggd thro rivers and thrown down

[1] Possibly 'straining', for Mitford's ms is difficult here.

Precipices. Oh! it has been a weary Night. Come dear Walpole and bring the day. I would say a thousand things to you, but I will think of nothing but yrself. Tell me for Gods sake all yr intended Motions and let em be homeward all. Trifle not with a Constitution which carries more lives in it than your own.

Acton (?) July 5. 1741.

[P.S.]

I have not been able to see M^rs Gr: since your letter; I will go [on?] perhaps next Week to rejoice with her. Believe me, I am much obliged to her.

West is hic & ubique...at Paris[1], at London, in the Country. I never see him. He talks of the Army[2], the Law & the Ministry. He suspects some disagreement between you and ——[3] I hope the broken bone will be stronger when set. M^rs —— came to me in such a Manner as makes me believe she knows the whole[4].

---

[1] Vide sect. ii. lett. 32 *infra*.
[2] Sect. ii. lett. 33 *infra*.
[3] '*Sic* MS.' [Mitford.]
[4] The objections to identifying M^rs Gr: or G. with the mother of the poet are (1) that she seems to be a different person from the M^rs—— of this Postscript, (2) that there is no *proof* of her solicitude about Gray himself. The second difficulty may be to some extent explained. For Mason tells us that "When Mr Gray left Venice, which he did in the midst of July, he returned home through Padua, Verona, Milan, Turin and

Lyons. From all which places he writ either to his Father or
Mother with great punctuality: but merely to inform them of
his health and safety: about which (as might be expected) they
were now very anxious, as he travelled with only a 'Laquais de
Voyage'." It is uncertain whether Mason had seen any letters
of Gray from Venice; but it is most improbable that Gray left
his mother unacquainted with his movements at any time after
his separation from Walpole. Mr C. Vade Walpole obligingly
informs me that he knows of no Mrs G. connected in any way
with his family at this date, who fulfils the conditions of this
correspondence. I leave this perplexing problem *in medio*.

SECTION II.

CORRESPONDENCE AND REMAINS OF RICHARD WEST.

[Letters &c. marked * have not before been published. The text of the other letters is from Mason's 'Gray' and Cunningham's 'Letters of Walpole', Vol. I.]

SECTION II.

WEST.

THE famous singer Carlo Broschi (who probably took the name Farinelli from his uncle the composer) was in England during the years 1734, 5 and 6. What Ashton means *infra* is, I think, that Gray has left London, where Farinelli is singing, and that Walpole has gone thither.

1. * ASHTON TO WEST.

Jan[y] 29. (1735 or 6)[1].

...Gray is happily escap[d] from the Sirens' song tho' Farinelli[2] joined in the concert. Walpole has now left us with a full resolution to taste of every fruit in that Paradise, except the forbidden tree. I hope you will see him often while he stays in Town...

I fancy I have told you that a wild young Poet of Trinity College has taken a mad flight out of a garret Window[3]: but finding no Castle in the air to rest at, his wings failed him and so he dropt. His

---

[1] It must be 1736 if we can be *certain* that Walpole was not in Cambridge before March 11, 1735. Cf. p. 72 *infra*, n. 1.

[2] For Farinelli in England see Grove's Dict. of Music and Musicians, and the 4th Plate of Hogarth's 'Marriage à la mode.'

[3] No record of this exploit exists at Trinity, as Dr Aldis Wright, the Vice-Master, has kindly ascertained for me.

G.   5

Life is not despaird of.   If I have not told you this before 'tis news.   If I have, you may toss this stupid letter by as an old Evening Post.

Yrs ever

Ashton.

The incident referred to in the following letter, fixes the date to October 1735.

"The matter related to the attempt of the Heads to nominate the persons who were to be Proctors, and the Vice-Chancellor admitted Trant (Chr.) as Proctor instead of Caryl (Jes.), who had more votes than the other in the Senate.   Against this Caryl appealed.[1]"

2.   * ASHTON TO WEST.

Thrice-highest Zephyrille,

The substance of yr last letter was a complaint for the loss of three friends, and an enquiry after them.   What intelligence concerning them may be collected from my information, hear shortly.

To begin with the last, first.   I can answer for one.   The other Two are almost strangers to me.   I have seen neither of them these 4 months.   Walpole I have not heard from this fortnight, nor Gray this Age.   The Papers say Walpole is for Italy instantly. this Piece of News does but ill correspond with the

---

[1] Kindly communicated by Dr Luard, the University Registrary.

last letter I had from him; but what reasons he may have since to alter his resolution, is to me a mystery.

Lord Conway[1] is in this Part of the World—a fall from his Horse at New Market has bruisd his arm, but I hope, not dangerously. We have had some bustle here about the election of Proctor, the heads of Colleges have chosen one, whom the White Hoods declare unduly elect: the affair may be of Service to Innkeepers & Lawyers. I am surprizd to hear such poor paltry harangues as are utterd once a week from the Rostra of this Nurse of Science. a good Sermon would be a great novelty. Pray are they as rare with you? I dont know what they may be now. What they were 230 years agon I can tell. You shall have a specimen. The University had, says my Historian, three gentlemen, and three only, capable of Preaching. It so happend that in the absence of these three Concionators, Mr Taverner of Woodeaton, a gentleman of great repute for learning, & Sheriff for the County entered the Pulpit, with Sword by his side and gold Chain round his Neck, & thus from his Stone-Tub begunn. 'Arriving at the Mount of St. Maries, in the Stony (?)[2], where I now stand, I have brought you some fine biskets baked in the oven of Charity, carefully conserved for the Chickens of the Church, the Sparrows of the Spirit &

[1] See p. 40, n. 1. [2] Word illegible.

5—2

the Swallows of Salvation &c. Now to God the Father &c. I heartily commend you.'   T. ASHTON.

Received yr letter at Lancaster and answerd it, as you know, I am sure by this time.

When I have any further intelligence from the lost men, you shall certainly know—till then, & after then,   I am yrs—

entirely.

3. WEST TO GRAY.

You use me very cruelly: you have sent me but one letter since I have been at Oxford, and that too agreeable not to make me sensible how great my loss is in not having more. Next to seeing you is the pleasure of seeing your hand-writing; next to hearing you is the pleasure of hearing from you. Really and sincerely I wonder at you, that you thought it not worth while to answer my last letter. I hope this will have better success in behalf of your quondam school-fellow; in behalf of one who has walked hand in hand with you, like the two children in the wood,

> Through many a flowery path and shelly grot,
> Where learning lull'd us in her private maze.

The very thought, you see, tips my pen with poetry, and brings Eton to my view. Consider me very seriously here in a strange country, inhabited by things that call themselves doctors and masters of arts; a country flowing with syllogisms and ale, where Horace & Virgil are equally unknown; consider me, I say, in this melancholy light, and then think if something be not due to

Yours.

Christ Church. Nov. 14. 1735.

P.S. I desire you will send me soon, and truly and positively, a History of your own time.

To this Gray replied 'When you have seen one of my days you have seen a whole year of my life; they go round and round like the blind horse in the mill.... I must not send you the history of my own time, till I can send you that also of the reformation.' This is from Letter II. in Mr Gosse's edition (vol. II.), and is obviously in answer to the above letter of West's, and carries on, as Mason remarks, the allusion to the writings of Bishop Burnet, West's grandfather. With Letter I. (ed. Gosse) which is subsequent to Letter II., and to which alone the date May 8, 1736 belongs, Gray sends to West a portion of his translation from Statius, with the words 'For this little while last past I have been playing with Statius; we yesterday had a game of quoits together. You will easily forgive me for having broke his head, as you have a little pique to him.' It is probable that Mason has garbled West's reply to this by fusing, *more suo*, separate letters together, for the line which West selects for comment was not included (*teste* Mitford) in that part of the translation which was sent to him on May 8th by Gray. It is just possible of course that another letter of Gray's has been lost.

4. WEST TO GRAY.

I agree with you that you have broke Statius's head, but it is in like manner as Apollo broke Hyacinth's, you have foiled him infinitely at his own weapon. I must insist on seeing the rest of your translation, and then I will examine it entire, and compare it with the Latin, and be very wise and severe, and put on an inflexible face, such as becomes the character of a true son of Aristarchus, of hypercritical memory. In the mean while,

> And calm'd the terrors of his claws in gold

is exactly Statius—Summos[1] auro mansueverat ungues. I never knew before that the golden fangs on hammercloths were so old a fashion. Your Hymeneal[2]

---

[1] 'extremos' in Statius.

[2] On the Marriage of Frederic, Prince of Wales. See Works of Gray ed. Gosse, vol. i., p. 168 sq. Ashton writes to West April 11th, 1736:

* "My dear Zephyrille

Have you composd yr Epithalamium? and in what Shape will it appear? do you dart(?) yourself above the Clouds on a Pindaric Wing, or do you chant Ovidian Strains upon a Sprig of Myrtle? does your happy-daring Muse aspire to the aery (*sic*) tracts of the Mantuan Swan, or will she humbly condescend to hop from spray to spray with the Sparrow of Catullus?...My dear, I am confident that in whatever manner she come, she will be perfectly wellbred...Master Gray seems to touch upon the manner of Claudian. My own Lady closes her lips on this occasion. I hardly know whether she is more apprehensive of interrupting their Highnesses

I was told was the best in the Cambridge collection before I saw it, and indeed, it is no great compliment to tell you I thought it so when I had seen it, but sincerely it pleased me best. Methinks the college bards have run into a strange taste on this occasion. Such soft unmeaning stuff about Venus and Cupid, and Peleus and Thetis, and Zephyrs and Dryads, was never read. As for my poor little Eclogue, it has been condemned and beheaded by our Westminster judges; an exordium of about sixteen lines absolutely cut off, and its other limbs quartered in a most barbarous manner. I will send it you in my next as my true and lawful heir, in exclusion of the pretender who has the impudence to appear under my name.

As yet I have not looked into sir Isaac. Public disputations I hate; mathematics I reverence; history, morality, and natural philosophy have the greatest charms in my eye; but who can forget poetry? they call it idleness, but it is surely the most enchanting thing in the world, "ac dulce otium et pæne omni negotio pulchrius."

I am, dear sir, yours while I am

R. W.

Christ Church, May 24, 1736.

happiness, or unwilling to make her appearance in any such honourable Company, and fearful to open her Mouth in so polite an Assembly. Though in truth, her feet have been of late so cramped up in Logical fetters, that she knows not how to form her Steps to Poetick Measure."

In a letter from Ashton to West of March 4th, 1736[1], from King's he excuses himself, in answer I think to a polite remonstrance of West's, for not having written before. "A violent fit of adverse valetude" he says "has for some time chained my thoughts." He then discourses in somewhat dreary fashion in reply to some remarks of West's on Letter Writing and concludes "I intended to have filled a sheet & Walpole's Italian coming in makes me finish before I come to the bottom of a page." This Italian is I suppose Piazza, who also taught Gray and perhaps Ashton too. See Gray's letter to Mr Birkett of Peterhouse which made that gentleman so angry (letter III. ed. Gosse vol. II. and Mr Gosse's note there. Also Mr Gosse's Life of Gray p. 18).

The following letters from Ashton throw so much light upon elections to King's in those days, that I am tempted to give them at some length. It will be seen by West's letter of Aug. 1736, p. 82, that the efforts for Prinsep, *alias* 'Quid', were unavailing.

I am indebted to the Provost of Eton for the substance of the following explanation of Ashton's scheme. Prinsep was fourth on the Register for King's. Ashton hoped that Prinsep might get King's by the opportune occurrence of at least *four* vacancies. *One* was to be made by Thomas Lane reported (wrongly) to be dead—a *second* by William Willymott, who was to resign under Dr Berriman's influence, whatever that was—a *third* by John Ewer "by means of the Duke of Rutland" (Ewer had been Lord Granby's travelling Tutor, *Alumni Etonenses* p. 314)—and

---

[1] 1735 in Mitford's transcript; perhaps to be understood as 1735-6. Walpole tells us that he went up to King's, March 11th, 1735, and before the date of this letter he has apparently already been in residence, and studying Italian at Cambridge.

the fourth by Mr Sleech under the influence of the Bishop
of Exeter.   This was Stephen Weston, Sleech's uncle by
marriage, who was Bishop of Exeter 1724—1743.   This
Sleech is not the future Provost of Eton but his younger
brother John.

This scheme of Ashton's did not 'come off", for
(1) Thomas Lane did not die then, but vacated his
Fellowship by marriage in the next year.   In 1748 he
was 'practising Physic' at Sevenoaks (*Alumni* p. 316).
(2) Only two vacancies occurred and these not till Aug. 2,
1736.   William Willymott's vacancy was taken by Sparkes,
Edward Green's by Hall.   Wagstaff and Prinsep never
went to King's.

Ewer became Rector of Bottesford in 1735.   He enjoyed a year of grace.   This explains Ashton's statement
that he "is obliged to resign within the year".   Willymott
was presented to the Rectory of Milton, Cambridgeshire,
in 1735.   It is possible that Berriman was to use his influence with Willymott not to avail himself of his year of
grace, or at least not to press his tenure to the uttermost.

5.   *ASHTON TO WEST.   (No date.)

(Extract.)

Tho' I am not insensible to the beautys that
occur in every part of yr Epistle, yet no place of it
made so deep an impression on my mind as that
which relates to *Quid*.   Poor *Quid!* if his cheek
had burnt every time I thought of him, he would
wish I had chose another subject for my thoughts.   I
hope you think not I want any instigation to exert

myself in behalf of so good a man. The recollection
of what I have felt will represent his misfortunes to
me in the justest light. Non ignaru' mali miseris
succurrere disco. Fortune has learnt me to pity the
distress'd, but has put it out of my Power to relieve
them. What I can, I will. Prinsep should be happy,
if I could say, What I will, I can. He is most
powerfully recommended by two very prevailing
advocates, Great merit & small fortune.

I went immediately to Horatio & acquainted him
with the Case. He seemd extremely willing to do
anything he could; but as he has no acquaintance
with any of the Gentlemen who are likely to hasten
the succession from Eton, I really cannot see how he
can be of any service to *Quid.* Whatever is or may
be in my Power to oblige him, he may infallibly
depend upon, as upon many accounts, so because he
is approved by you, who are most dear to

ASHTON.

6. *ASHTON TO WEST.

[Probable date June 1736.]

I am in raptures, my dearest West, at the de-
scription of *Oxford.* If it exceeds my idea, it must
exceed every thing. I can imagine nothing less than
Heaven top'd Towers, Hesperian groves, & Gates of
Chrysolite. if it sh^d answer my expectation it is the
Place in the World the most improper for what it is

designd, unfitt for any Study, but Architecture &
Botany. Yet Philosophical insensibility clouds the
eyes of y^r elders, and Aristotle is permitted to fix his
throne, in a City too noble for the Court of Alexander.
Well! but do they not pay adoration to the steps of
Newton? is not Lock[1] reverd among you? I am
sure my dear, you must admire the human wits
divine, who have so artfully unravelld the intricate
Maze of thought, so curiously explaind the grand
Simplicity of the works of Nature. But pray, have
you laid out any Plan for Study, or do you rove at
large in the field of literature? I am at a loss here,
my dear Zephyrille, I travell in an unknown region
without a guide & if I err in my first step my expedition will only serve to carry me further from my
way. But of this hereafter. I have just received a
little intelligence which I will communicate to you
instantly. It relates to Prinsep. We have heard
that Mr Lane a fellow of our Society is dead. If it
is true, tho' it is not yet confirmd, Prinseps Succession is by no means impossible. Bid him look
about him. What he does should be done quickly. I
take it for granted that if the Captain take advantage
of Mr Lane's death, the two next Seniors will make
sufficient (?) interest for their own Election. Hall
we hear is secure of Mr Green, and Dr Berriman will
undoubtedly (prevail upon?) Willymot.... Prinsep

---

[1] sic.

then will stand first upon the roll. What I would
propose then is to make personal interest with M^r
Ewer, or Mr Sleech (who are both oblig'd to resign
within the year) or if he can more conveniently
engage these by means of the Duke of Rutland & the
Bishop of Exeter. He will say, this is proceeding
upon supposition. 'Tis true, Mr Lane's death is not
yet certain, but consider, it will be suff^t for him to
engage a conditional Promise, that if his seniors shall
be all...before the Election bills are closd : either
of the Gentlemen I mentiond (who will be both of
them on the spot) would make (way?) for his
succession. And in the meantime alarm Hall and
Wagstaffe with the news of Lane's death, to set
their friends at work, but be as silent as may
be of his own design. What think you? is the
scheme impracticable? I profess I don't think it is.
Let him make sure, in case he comes to be senior,
for it is here confidently believed he will be, and if
he is but a moment so, it will be enough if Ewer
and Sleech are upon the Place. Only upon the
supposition of the certainty of this intelligence, lett
us substitute

in the room of Mr Lane	Sparkes
Mr Greene	Hall
Dr Willymott	Wagstaffe
Mr Ewer	Prinsep
Mr Sleech	

I vow I see no cause of Despair, but all the reason in the world to attempt some difficulty in the hopes of so great advantage. I am his & yrs sincerely[1]

T: ASHTON.

7. *ASHTON TO WEST.

My dear West,

The reason of entertaining you with this intelligence is, that I am uncertain where to find out Prinsep, which I hope you will do, if he is in Terra Cognita, and because to one of yr humanity, I am confident nothing can be more agreable than any Proposal which may tend to the advancement of Learning and Sincerity, both which qualities, I think, are inherent in Prinsep. We had a public Commencement voted, but the decree is now reversd. Gray has left us a good while I have not yet wrote to him. I love you and long to see you.

ASHTON

June 24. 1736 King's Coll.

[1] In the suggestions of doubtful words above, I have not been guided so much by the *ductus literarum* of Mitford's extremely minute transcript, which I had not before me, when the explanation of this letter came to hand; but rather by the probable sense.

8. WEST TO ASHTON.

...Arethusa mihi concede laborem
Pauca meo Gallo—

You may see, by what I wrote to Gray that I intend you a visit the latter end of next month. I long to compare Colleges. I must absolutely take measure of King's College, Chapell. Have you any such walks as Maudlin? and then I want much to see Dr Bentley the ὁ πάνυ Commentator: what is he about? I hear your Dr Middleton is about obliging us with Cicero's Life.

> Esse nihil dicis quidquid petis improbe Cinna
> Si nil Cinna petis, nil tibi Cinna nego[1].

> Whenever Cinna asks a favor
> O 'tis nothing Sir he'll say;
> Cinna, you are too modest rather—
> Is't really nothing?—take it, pray.

[This letter probably belongs to July, 1736.]

9. ASHTON TO WEST.

Thursday 12 Aug. 1736.

My dear Zephyrille,

When I reflect that this is the anniversary of my arrival at Cambridge, the 2nd Anniversary[2]; this

---

[1] Martial iii. 61.

[2] Ashton was *elected* to King's in 1733. It would appear from the above that he did not go up to Cambridge until 1734. He was in fact admitted a Scholar of King's on the evening of Aug. 11, 1734, as the Provost of King's kindly informs me.

agreeable thought suggests to me one of a very different complexion; videlicet that it is now above two years since I saw you: but the Promise with which you conclude yr letter, gives me hope, that in much less time I shall see you again.

Return, thou wandring Child, return to thy father's house, and accept the fatted Calf which I am determind to sacrifice to thy arrival.

> Come, my swain and bring with thee
> Jest & youthful jollity
> Quirks[1] and cranks & wanton wiles
> Nods and becks and wreathed smiles
> Sport that wrinkled Care derides
> And Laughter holding both her[1] sides.

I showd Horatio yr letter; he hopes for yr coming as well as I. We neither of us leave College till the beginning of September. Make haste, my dear, I am tired of old, musty Philosophy & learned Dust. You are the only author I would care to read. Prithee come and bring with you a new edition of yrself multo auctior & emendatior, Oxford printed anno Domini 25 & 26[2]. The vivacity of yr agreeable Page will be some relief to a Soul half extinguishd with the suffocating fume of Jargon and Nonsense.

Yrs

eternally

ASHTON.

[1] 'Quips' and 'his' ap. Milton.

[2] Sic, I believe, ap. Mitford. But perhaps it should be '35 & '36, years of West's residence at Oxford.

My hearty Service to Prinsep. I think him much injurd. pray determine instantly & let us know yr resolutions.

Walpole wrote to West from King's College, Cambridge, Aug. 17, 1736 : 'Gray is at Burnham, and what is surprising has not been to Eton....'Tis the head of our genealogical table, that is since sprouted out into the two branches of Oxford and Cambridge. You seem to be the eldest son, by having got a whole inheritance to yourself ; while the manor of Granta is to be divided between your three younger brothers, Thomas of Lancashire [Ashton] Thomas of London [Gray] and Horace[1]...I hope you are a mere elder brother, and live upon what your father left you...poetry ; but we are supposed to betake ourselves to some trade, as logic, philosophy, or mathematics....I tell

---

[1] In a previous letter to West, dated Nov. 9, 1735, Walpole says

"Tydeus rose and set at Eton ; he is only known here to be a scholar of King's ; Orosmades and Almanzor are just the same ; that is, I am almost the only person they are acquainted with, and consequently the only person acquainted with their excellencies. Plato improves every day ; so does my friendship with him. These three divide my whole time, though I believe you will guess there is no quadruple alliance ; that was a happiness which I only enjoyed while you was at Eton. A short account of the Eton people at Oxford would much oblige " &c.

It should be obvious enough that this is an account of ' the Eton people ' at Cambridge and therefore that West at Oxford is not Almanzor, as Cunningham thinks. Nor is Walpole Tydeus ; for Walpole never was a Scholar of King's, and it is utterly inconceivable that an Etonian writing from King's to a brother Etonian would use this term in any but its exactest

you what I see ; that by living amongst mathematicians, I write of nothing else : my letters are all parallelograms, two sides equal to two sides ; and every paragraph an axiom, that tells you nothing but what every mortal almost knows.'

10. WEST TO WALPOLE.

Aug. 1736.

My dearest Walpole :

Yesterday I received your lively—agreeable— gilt—epistolary—parallelogram, and to-day I am preparing to send you in return as exact a one as my little *compass* can afford you. And so far, sir, I am sure we and our letters bear some resemblance to parallel lines, that, like them, one of our chief pro- perties is, seldom or never to meet. Indeed, lately

sense. Plato is certainly not Henry Coventry as Mr Gosse conjectures ; witness the way in which in a letter to George Montagu, himself an Etonian, this Henry Coventry is spoken of (May 30, 1736) by Walpole :

" There is lately come out a new piece called A Dialogue between Philemon and Hydaspes on false Religion, by one Mr Coventry, A.M. and fellow, formerly fellow commoner, of Magdalen. He is a young man, but 'tis really a pretty thing."

Plato I am nearly certain is Ashton. In evidence of this, I would refer to sect. ii. let. 23, *infra*, written by West at a time when Ashton was in his company. Orosmades is certainly Gray ; though I know no other *proof* of this, than the letter of West (sect. ii. let. 27, *infra*) to Walpole, when Gray and Walpole were travelling together abroad. Who Tydeus and Almanzor were does not much concern us ; they were not, it is clear, members of the Quadruple Alliance.

G. 6

my good fortune made some *inclination* from your
university to mine; but whether I can reciprocate or
no, I leave you to judge from hence—

I sent Ashton word that I should more than
probably make an expedition to Cambridge this
August; but Prinsep, who was to have been my
fellow-traveller, and would have gone with me to
Cambridge, though not to King's, is unhappily dis-
appointed; and therefore my measures are broke, and
I am very much in the spleen—else by this time
I had flown to you with all the wings of impatience

> Ocyor cervis, et agente nimbos
> Ocyor Euro[1].

But now, alas! as Horace said on purpose for me to
apply it,

> Sextilem totum mendax desideror—

This melancholy reflection would certainly infect all
the rest of my letter, if I were not revived by the
sal volatile of your most entertaining letter. I am
afraid the younger brother will make much the better
gentleman, and so far verify the proverb; and indeed
all my brothers[2] are so very forward, that like the
first and heaviest element, I shall have nothing but
mere dirt for my share:—and really such is the case
of most of your landed elder brothers, while the
younger run away with the more fine and delicate

---

[1] In playful allusion to his own name of Favonius.
[2] Of the Quadruple Alliance. [Cunningham.]

elements. As for my patrimony of poetry, my dearest Horace, *ut semper eris derisor!* what little I have I borrowed from my friends, and like the poor ambitious jay in the trite fable, I live merely on the charity of my abounding acquaintance. Many a feather in my stock was stolen from your treasures; but at present I find all my poetical plumes moulting apace, and in a small time I shall be nothing further than, what nobody can be more, or more sincerely,

Your humble servant, and obliged friend,

R. WEST.

Gray at Burnham, and not see Eton? I am Ashton's ever, and intend him an answer soon —I beg pardon for what's over leaf; but as I am moulting my poetry, it is very natural to send it you, from whom and my other friends it originally came. I translated[1], and now I have ventured to imitate the divine lyric poet.

Ode—TO MARY MAGDALENE.

Saint of this learned awful grove,
While slow along thy walks I rove,
The pleasing scene, which all that see
Admire, is lost to me.

---

[1] This version is lost; he sent another, of Hor. Carm. 1. 5 to Walpole July 12, 1737 (sect. ii. let. 15).—Bryant, in his interesting, but perplexing, letter of Reminiscences to an unknown correspondent (given in Mitford's 2nd Life of Gray), says that there survives of West's 'a curious parody upon the fourth ode of the fourth book of Horace.' Where?

The thought, which still my breast invades,
Nigh yonder springs, nigh yonder shades
Still as I pass, the memory brings
 Of sweeter shades and springs.

Lost and inwrapt in thought profound,
Absent I tread Etonian ground;
Then startling from the dear mistake,
 As disenchanted, wake.

What though from sorrow free, at best
I'm thus but negatively blest:
Yet still, I find, true joy I miss;
 True joy's a social bliss.

Oh! how I long again with those,
Whom first my boyish heart had chose,
Together through the friendly shade
 To stray, as once I stray'd!

Their presence would the scene endear,
Like paradise would all appear,
More sweet around the flowers would blow,
 More soft the waters flow.

       Adieu!

In December, 1736, Gray writes to West: "You must know that I do not take degrees, and, after this term, shall have nothing more of college impertinences to undergo.... Surely it was of this place, now Cambridge, but formerly known by the name of Babylon, that the prophet spoke when he said 'The wild beasts of the desert shall dwell there...' You see here is a pretty collection of desolate animals, which is verified in this town to a tittle, and perhaps it may also allude to your habitation...however I defy your owls to match mine." An undated letter of Ashton's to West has this: *'perhaps the fame of our young Refiners[1] may not yet have reached your Ears, a congress of young Gentlemen, enemies to Prejudice and contracted notions, upon a thoro' examination of their Powers and Properties have found that our ancestors for 6000 years past, have laboured under the Servile State of unnecessary dependence, which intolerable yoke these public spirits, for the honor of themselves and advantage of Posterity, have resolvd to shake off, and in consequence of this noble resolution, have declared themselves Independent. Now the Revd Doctors have called some Privy Councillors to examine it, peradventure they may be able to find a flaw in this Demonstration. Since a corollary immediately deducible from this Proposition will strike at the root of Preferment & be destructive of the glorious expectation of a Lawn Sleeve & Crosier.' Mitford interprets these young Refiners or Reformers to be Gray, Walpole &c. Whether Ashton's not very excellent fooling refers to any real circumstance, it is perhaps impossible to determine ; it is inserted here as descriptive of the attitude of these young people. He concludes 'I sh[d] be glad to hear from Prinsep' who was possibly then at Oxford with West.

11. WEST TO GRAY.

I congratulate you on your being about to leave college[2], and rejoice much you carry no degrees with you. For I would not have You dignified, and I not,

---

[1] Or 'Reformers' for Mitford is scarcely decipherable here.

[2] I suspect that Mr West mistook his correspondent ; who in saying he did not take degrees, meant only to let his friend know that he should soon be released from lectures and disputations. [Mason.]

for the world, you would have insulted me so. My
eyes, such as they are, like yours, are neither meta-
physical nor mathematical; I have, nevertheless, a
great respect for your connoisseurs that way, but am
always contented to be their humble admirer. Your
collection of desolate animals pleased me much; but
Oxford, I can assure you, has her owls that match
yours, and the prophecy has certainly a squint that
way. Well, you are leaving this dismal land of
bondage, and which way are you turning your face?
Your friends, indeed, may be happy in you, but what
will you do with your classic companions? An inn of
court is as horrid a place as a college, and a moot
case is as dear to gentle dulness[1] as a Syllogism. But
wherever you go, let me beg you not to throw poetry
"like a nauseous weed away:" cherish its sweets in
your bosom; they will serve you now and then to
correct the disgusting sober follies of the common
law, misce stultitiam consiliis brevem, dulce est
desipere in loco; so said Horace to Virgil, those sons
of Anac in poetry, and so say I to you, in this
degenerate land of pigmies,

> Mix with your grave designs a little pleasure,
> Each day of business has its hour of leisure.

In one of these hours I hope, dear sir, you will

---

[1] Pope's expression, already become a commonplace,
['And *gentle Dulness* ever loves a joke.'
Dunciad, Bk ii. l. 34, anno 1728.]

sometimes think of me, write to me, and know me yours,

'Εξαύδα, μὴ κεῦθε νόῳ, ἵνα εἴδομεν ἄμφω·

that is, write freely to me and openly, as I do to you, and to give you a proof of it I have sent you an elegy of Tibullus translated. Tibullus, you must know, is my favourite elegiac poet; for his language is more elegant and his thoughts more natural than Ovid's. Ovid excels him only in wit, of which no poet had more in my opinion. The reason I choose so melancholy a kind of poesie, is because my low spirits and constant ill health (things in me not imaginary, as you surmise, but too real, alas! and, I fear, constitutional) "have tuned my heart to elegies of woe;" and this likewise is the reason why I am the most irregular thing alive at college, for you may depend upon it I value my health above what they call discipline. As for this poor unlicked thing of an elegy[1], pray criticise it unmercifully, for I send it with that intent. Indeed your late translation of Statius might have deterred me; but I know you are not more able to excel others, than you are apt to

---

[1] This elegy, the sapient Mason tells us, he omits 'because' (among other reasons) 'it is not written in alternate but heroic rhyme: which I think is not the species of English measure adapted to elegiac poetry.' We may have suffered little loss; but the same principle would have justified the suppression of Pope's 'Eloisa to Abelard'.

forgive the want of excellence, especially when it is
found in the productions of

Your most sincere friend.

Christ Church, Dec. 22. 1736.

12. WEST TO WALPOLE.

Christchurch Jan. 12. 1736–7.
Dear Sir:

Poetry, I take it, is as universally con-
tagious as the small-pox; every one catches it once
in their life at least, and the sooner the better; for
methinks an old rhymester makes as ridiculous a
figure as Socrates dancing at fourscore. But I can
never agree with you that most of us succeed alike;
at least I'm sure few do like you: I mean not to
flatter, for I despise it heartily; and I think I know
you to be so much above flattery, as the use of it is
beneath every honest, every sincere man. Flattery
to men of power is analogous with hypocrisy to God,
and both are alike mean and contemptible; nor is
the one more an instance of respect, than the other
is a proof of devotion. I perceive I am growing
serious, and that is the first step to dulness: but I
believe you won't think that in the least extraordinary, to find me dull in a letter, since you
have known me so often dull out of a letter.

As for poetry, I own, my sentiments of it are
very different from the vulgar taste. There is hardly

anywhere to be found (says Shaftesbury) a more
insipid race of mortals, than those whom the moderns
are accustomed to call poets—but methinks the true
legitimate poet is as rare to be found as Tully's
orator, *orator qualis adhuc nemo fortasse fuerit.*
Truly, I am extremely to blame to talk to you at
this rate of what you know much better than myself:
but your letter gave me the hint, and I hope you will
excuse my impertinence in pursuing it. It is a
difficult matter to account why, but certain it is that
all people, from the duke's coronet to the thresher's
flail[1] are desirous to be poets: Penelope herself had

[1] A hint at Stephen Duck the Thresher-poet, then an
object of Queen Caroline's bounty, and of Pope's satire.
[Cunningham.] Later in this year, after the death of Caroline,
West writes of him

> 'Mean time thy rural ditty was not mute,
> Sweet bard of Merlin's cave.'

Merlin's Cave was a fancy or folly of Queen Caroline's at
Richmond; in it she had a library, of which Duck was
custodian.

> How shall we fill a library with wit
> When Merlin's Cave is half unfurnish'd yet?

says Pope in his 'Epistle to Augustus.' He was angry, as
Mr Pattison explains, because his own writings had no place
in the royal collection—

> 'Call Tibbald Shakespear, and he'll swear the nine
> Dear Cibber! never match'd one ode of thine.
> Lord! how we strut thro' Merlin's Cave, to see
> No poets there, but *Stephen*, you and me.'
>
> (Sat. and Ep. vi. 140.)

not more suitors, though every man is not Ulysses
enough to bend the bow. The poetical world, like
the terraqueous, has its several degrees of heat from
the line to the pole—only differing in this, that
whereas the temperate Zone is most esteemed in the
terraqueous, in the poetical it is the most despised.
Parnassus is divisible in the same manner as the
mountain Chimaera

> —mediis in partibus hircum,
> Pectus et ora leae, caudam serpentis habebat.

The medium between the rampant lion and the
creeping serpent is the filthy goat—the justest
picture of a meddling poet, who is generally very

Stephen bore his honours meekly, if we may trust the
testimony of ' unfastidious Vinny Bourne '—

> 'Nec mutantur adhuc mores; sed et ille modestus
> Ille verecundus, qui prius, usque manes.'
> [V. Bourne, Ad Stephan. Duck, Ἐγκωμιαστικόν. 1743.]

"The destruction of Merlin's Cave is commemorated by
Mason, Heroic Epistle l. 55—

> '...for see untutor'd Brown
> Destroys those wonders which were once thy own.
> Lo, from his melon-ground the peasant slave
> Has rudely rush'd and level'd Merlin's Cave,
> Knock'd down the waxen wizard, seiz'd his wand,
> Transform'd to lawn what late was fairy-land,
> And mar'd with impious hand each sweet design
> Of Stephen Duck and good Queen Caroline.'"
> [Pattison.]

Duck was gardener as well as librarian. 'Te Curatorem
Regius Hortus habet' says Vincent Bourne l. c.

bawdy and lascivious, and like the goat, is mighty
ambitious of climbing up mountains, where he does
nothing but browse upon weeds. Such creatures as
these are beneath our notice. But whenever some
wondrous sublime genius arises, such as Homer or
Milton, then it is that different ages and countries all
join in an universal admiration. (Poetry (I think I
have read somewhere or other) is an imitation of
Nature : the poet considers all her works in a
superior light to other mortals ; he discerns every
secret trait of the great mother, and paints it in its
due beauty and proportion. \ The moral and the
physical world all open fairer to his enthusiastic
imagination : like some clear-flowing stream, he
reflects the beauteous prospect all around, and like
the prism-glass, he separates and disposes nature's
colours in their justest and most delightful appear-
ances. This sure is not the talent of every dauber :
art, genius, learning, taste, must all conspire to
answer the full idea I have of a poet ; a character
which seldom agrees with any of our modern mis-
cellany-mongers—But

Quid loquor? aut ubi sum? quae mentem insania mutat?

I have got into enchanted ground, and can hardly
get out again time enough to finish my letter in a
decent and laudable manner Dear sir, excuse and
pardon all this rambling criticism—I writ it out of

pure idleness ; and I can assure you, I wish you idle
enough to read it through.

>I am, my dear Walpole,
>
>>Yours most sincerely,
>
>>>R. WEST.

I wish you a happy new year.

13.   WEST TO WALPOLE.

ChristChurch February 27, 1736–7.

My dear Walpole :

It seems so long to me since I heard from
Cambridge, that I have been reflecting with myself
what I could have done to lose any of my friends
there. The uncertainty of my silly health might
have made me the duller companion, as you know
very well; for which reason Fate took care to remove me out of your way : but my letters, I am sure,
at least carry enough sincerity in them to recommend
me to any one that has a curiosity to know something concerning me and my amusements. As for
Ashton, he has thought fit to forget me entirely; and
for Gray, if you correspond with him as little as I do
(wherever he be, for I know not) your correspondence
is not very great.—   Full in the midst of these re-
flections came your agreeable letter.   I read it, and
wished myself among you.   You can promise me no
diversion, but the novelty of the place, you say, and
a renewal of intimacies.   Novelty, you must know, I

am sick of; I am surrounded with it, I see nothing
else. I could tell you strange things, my dear
Walpole, of anthropophagi, and men whose heads do
grow beneath their shoulders. I have seen Learning
drest in old frippery, such as was in fashion in Duns
Scotus' days: I have seen Taste in changeable, feeding
like the chameleon on air: I have seen Stupidity in
the habit of Sense, like a footman in the master's
clothes: I have seen the phantom mentioned in The
Dunciad[1], with a brain of feathers and a heart of
lead: it walks here, and is called Wit. Your other
inducement you suggested had all its influence with
me: and I had before indulged the thought of
visiting you all at Cambridge this next spring—But
Fata obstant—I am unwillingly obliged to follow
much less agreeable engagements. In the mean
time I shall pester you with quires of correspondence,
such as it is: but remember, you were two letters in
my debt—though indeed your last letter may fully
cancel the obligation. You may recollect my last
was a sort of criticism upon poetry; and this will
present you with a sort of poetry[2] which nobody ever
dreamt of but myself.

I am, dear sir,

Yours very sincerely,

R. WEST.

[1] Book ii. l. 42.
[2] This poetry does not appear. [Berry.]

On the 5th of April 1737 Ashton sends to West from King's a critique or panegyric of Glover's Leonidas which has a Postscript— * "M[r] Walpole is gone as far as Hockrell[1] with Dodd & Whalley[2] (*sic*) who are coming

[1] Chesterfield writes to his godson 'you put me in mind of that great man mentioned by Homer, and afterwards by Horace, *qui mores multorum hominum* (*sic*) *vidit et urbes*, for you have not only seen Cambridge, but also Clare Hall and Hockrel.' (let. CLVIII.) 'The Fly for Four Passengers at 12*s.* each goes to London every day by Chesterford, Hockerill and Epping.' (*Cantabrigia Depicta* 1763 p. 112.) It was a suburb of Bishop's Stortford. [Ld. Carnarvon.]

[2] 'My public tutor [at Cambridge] was Mr John Smith; my private Mr Anstey; afterwards Mr John Whaley was my tutor.' [Short Notes of my Life. Walpole, Letters, I. p. lxii. ed. Cunningham.]

'Mr Dodd was my fellow-collegian and school-fellow at Eton, a man universally beloved, lively, generous and sensible. I think his father kept an inn at Chester; but a Judge Dodd, of that county, related to him, left him his large fortune. He had a wretched tutor at College, John Whaley, who would have ruined most other people; but Mr Dodd's natural good sense got the better of his vile example. Mr Walpole and Mr Dodd, while at College were united in the strictest friendship.' Cole, *Athenæ Cantabrigienses*. MS. [Walpole's Letters, Cunningham vol. IX. App. p. 522.] Dodd is perhaps 'Tydens', p. 80 n.

Cole's antipathy to Whaley is manifested in another MS. He has transcribed a Tour through England in 1735 by Whaley, who records that he dined at Shrewsbury 'with much pleasure, at finding a large collection of honest Whigs met together in Shropshire.' On which Cole notes 'Whatever this honest collection of Salopian Whigs may have been on the whole, I am as well satisfied as of any thing I know, that there was one *rascal, duly and truly* in the company.' [vid. Murray's *Johnsoniana* 1836 p. 417.]

to Town, he has Leonidas with him & will be home to-night. I paid y[r] compliments to Dodd & Whaley Gray longs to hear from you."

14. WEST TO GRAY.

I have been very ill, and am still hardly recovered. Do you remember Elegy 5th, Book the 3rd, of Tibullus, Vos tenet &c. and do you remember a letter of M[r] Pope's, in sickness, to M[r] Steele? This melancholy elegy and this melancholy letter I turned into a more melancholy epistle of my own, during my sickness, in the way of imitation; and this I send to you and my friends at Cambridge, not to divert them, for it cannot, but merely to show them how sincere I was when sick: I hope my sending it to them now may convince them I am no less sincere, though perhaps more simple, when well.

AD AMICOS.

While you, where Camus rolls his sedgy tide,
Feel every joy, that friendship can divide;
Now, as each art and science you explore,
And with the ancient blend the modern lore,
Studious to learn alone whate'er may tend
To raise the Genius—or the heart to mend:
Now pleased along the cloister'd walk to rove,
And trace the verdant mazes of the Grove,
Where social oft, & oft alone you use
To catch the Zephyr, or to court the Muse.
At me meantime (while e'en devoid of art
These lines give back the image of my heart)

At me the power, that comes or soon or late,
Or aims, or seems to aim the dart of fate.
From you remote—methinks alone I stand
Like some sad exil in a dreary land;
Around no lenient friend, no friend to join
In mutual warmth, or mix his heart with mine.
Or real pains, or those which spleen can raise
For ever blot the Sunshine of my days.—
To sickness still, & still to grief a prey,
From me Health turns her rosy face away.
. Just Heaven! what sin, ere life begins to bloom,
Devotes my head untimely to the tomb?
Did e'er this hand against a brother's life
Drug the dire bowl, or point the murd'rous knife?
Did e'er this tongue the Slanderer's tale proclaim,
Or madly violate the Maker's name?
Did e'er this heart betray a friend, or foe
Or know a thought, but all the world might know?
As yet just started from the lists of time
My growing years have scarcely told their prime;
Useless as yet, through life I've idly run,
No pleasures tasted, and few duties done.
Ah! who, ere autumn's mellowing Suns appear,
Would pluck the promise of the vernal year?
Or ere the grapes their purple hue betray,
Tear the crude cluster from the mourning Spray?
Stern power of Fate, whose Ebon Sceptre rules
The Stygian desarts, & Cimmerian pools,
Ah spare, nor rashly smite the youthful heart,
A victim yet unworthy of thy dart!
Then, when late age shall blast my withering face,
Shake in my head, and falter in my pace;
Then aim the Shaft, then meditate the blow
And to the dead my willing Shade shall go.
    How weak is Man to Reason's judgeing eye!
Born in this moment, in the next we dye.

Part mortal clay, and part ethereal fire,
Too proud to creep, too humble to aspire;
In vain our Plans of happiness we raise:
Pain is our lot, and patience is our praise
Wealth, birth or honours, Conquest or a Throne
Are, what the wise would fear to call their own,
Health is at best a vain precarious thing,
And fair-faced youth is ever on the wing.
[1]'Tis like the stream, beside whose watry bed
Some blooming plant exalts his flowry head;
Nursed by the wave the spreading branches rise,
Shade all the ground, & blossom to the skies,
The waves the while beneath in secret flow,
And undermine the hollow bank below;
Wide and more wide the waters urge their way,
Bare all the root, and on the fibres prey,
Too late the plant bewails his foolish pride
And sinks untimely in the whelming tide.

But why these thoughts, or what's my death to me?
Few will lament perhaps whene'er it be.
[2]For those the wretches I despise, or hate,
I neither envy nor enquire their fate.
For me, whene'er almighty Death shall spread
His wings around my unrepineing head,
[3]I care not tho' this face be seen no more,
The world will pass as chearful as before;

[1] "Youth, at the very best, is but the betrayer of human life in a gentler and smoother manner than age: 'tis like the stream that nourishes a plant upon a bank, and causes it to flourish and blossom to the sight, but at the same time is undermining it at the root in secret." Pope's Works, vol. VII. p. 254, 1st edition. Warburton. [Mason's note.]

[2] "I am not at all uneasy at the thought that many men whom I never had any esteem for, are likely to enjoy this world after me." Ibid. [Mason.]

[3] "The morning after my exit the sun will rise as bright as ever, the flowers smell as sweet, the plants spring as green." Ibid. [Mason.]

G.   7

Bright as before the Day-Star will appear
The fields as verdant, and the skies as clear:
Nor storms, nor comets will my doom declare,
Nor signs on earth, nor portents in the air;
Unknown and silent will depart my breath,
Nor Nature e'er take notice of my death.
Yet some there are (ere sunk in endless night)
Within whose breasts my monument I'd write:
Loved in my life, lamented in my end,
Their praise would crown me, as their precepts mend:
To them may these fond lines my name indear,
Not from the Author but the Friend sincere[1].

Christ Church, July 4, 1737.

15. *WEST TO WALPOLE.

Tuesday July 12 1737

My dearest Walpole,

I have writ Ashton a long serious letter, for which reason I intend to be very witty in this, I tell you so beforehand, for fear you should mistake me; you must expect a Similie in every letter, and a Metaphor in every syllable. Nay, you'll find a je ne sçay, in every Comma, and something very surprizing in every full Stop.[2] I don't intend to think neither, for I've heard your great Wits never think—

---

[1] The text above, is taken from Gray's Common Place Books at Pembroke, I. 91, Gray's handwriting, subscribed Fav: 1737.

[2] Marks like those above (} *) seem to indicate some playful eccentricities of writing here transcribed by Mitford.

Critics indeed prescribe it as a rule
That you must think before you write.
But I who am you know, no fool
Aver their judgment is not right
Now if you ask the reason why
I'll tell you truly by and bye
Meantime if you should rashly think
My Pen will drop a word of Sense
Pray read no more, but with the rest dispense
For faith, I send you nought but Ink,
But if you deem the want of thought
A tolerable fault,
Prithee, proceed
On that condition you may read.

I think these lines very much a la Française you can tell why? and now I'll give you some in the English fashion

To thee my thoughts magnetically roll
My heart the Needle is, and thine the Pole
Since thou art gone, no Company can please,
They rather show my Want, than give me Ease.
When Sol resigns our Hemispheres to night
Ten thousand Stars, but ill supply his light
Tho' to repay thy loss, enough there be
They're all a poor Equivalent of thee.
Like Ovid thus I stand, whose lines declare
No inspiration like our native air
Banished from thee, I feel my notes decay
And miss the Muse, to animate the lay.

Now, what Muse do you like the best, French or English? in my opinion the first is in a Consumption, & the latter in a dropsy. The French one is a pale

Slammekin without any color in her Skin ; and
the English drab[1] is a flush'd[1] Dowdy as full of
pimples as she can stare. Had I time, I w^d rifle
all Petrarca, but I would send you some

> Sonnetti, madrigalletti
> Versi sciolti, vezzozetti[2]
> Per signor, mio Valpoletti.

I would send you some Spanish too, not plain but
mighty ampullated, were I suff^ly vers'd in the obras
del Poetas Castellanos; and then I'd tell you that
the Italian and Spanish Muse both us'd a great deal
of Paint, only the last laid on in higher colors.

I dare say, after all, you'll tell me this is nothing
to you, and yet so far it is, that I intended all this
to divert you, & if it does not, at least the intention
was good. If I knew as many languages as Briareus
had hands, I should tell you a hundred Ways only,
how much I am—

I know I might end my letter here, very conveniently, and end very prettily, but I wont ; I'll
write as far as my Paper will let me, & then as
Alexander wept heretofore, that he had no more to
conquer, or as the wild Indian that gallop'd with full
speed, till he came to the sea, & then wonder'd that
he could gallop no further, so I—. à propos, an ode
of Horace lies before me, which I translated about 3
months ago—here it is

---

[1] 'dab' and 'flusd' in Mitford's ms.   [2] *sic*.

AD PYRRHAM.

Say what dear Youth his amorous rapture breathes
Within thy arms beneath some Grott reclind?
  Pyrrha, for whom dost thou in wreathes
    Thy golden tresses bind
In plainness elegant? how oft shall he
Complain alass! upon the fickle skies
  And suddenly astonishd see
    The blackning tempest rise:
Who now enjoys thee, happy in Conceit
Who fondly thinks thy love can never fail
  Never to him—unmindful yet
    Of the fallacious Gale.
Wretch! to whom thou untryd seemest fair,
For me, I've scapd the Wreck; let yonder fane
  Inscrib'd my gratitude declare
    To him that rules the Main.

I am, dear Sir, with all sincerity, your most
humble Servant & affectionate friend

                       RICH. WEST

  P.S. I am afraid I cannot see you this Summer,
but I long to hear from you
    To
        Horace Walpole Esqr
           at King's College
               Cambridge
  (from Oxford)

  To the letter enclosing 'Ad Amicos' (*supra*) Gray replied Aug. 22, 1737 'If what you sent me last be the pro-
duct of your melancholy, what may I not expect from your
more cheerful hours?......But while I write to you I hear
the sad news of Lady Walpole's death on Saturday night

last.' A letter from Ashton to West, undated but placed
by Mitford among those of 1737, has * 'Mʳ Walpole is now
with us & his Sense will soon get the better of his misfortune.' Ashton continues ' Dʳ Barnard's determination
of me for Eton is an honor I have no inclination to accept.
My friend Horace has disposd of me in a way more to my
Satisfaction. I am engagd to Lᵈ Plymouth. When I
leave Cambridge I am not certain.'

By comparison with the letter which follows it, and
in the absence of other evidence I am disposed (but very
doubtfully) to assign to the year 1737 this letter of Ashton's
to West.

16. *ASHTON TO WEST.

King's Coll: Camb: Nov 16 (?)

Dear West,

If you judge my esteem for you by the number
of my letters, you err in yr judgment. 'Tis true I am
very dilatory in my remittances; at which you will
less wonder, when I acquaint you with the Cause.
You must know then that for the three months past
I have constantly laboured under the intolerable
fatigue of having nothing to do, & it is my misfortune (excuse my infirmity) always to be most busy
when I have least business. This to you will seem
a Paradox: but my Case is much the same as Charles
Lyttleton's, who staid 2 years at Oxford, without
seeing the Musaeum, because he might have seen it
every day. When I had so much time upon my
hands, I could not see one hour more convenient for

writing than another, and therefore I did not write at all. Now I am engaged in a constant & necessary round of eating, reading & praying, I find that if I do not write to you this Minute, I cannot write to you the next. So my multiplicity of business supplies me with an opportunity, of which my want of any has long deprivd me.

I could wish to have had Gray's fortune; but I often see you by him at second hand. I find by his Picture of you that there is a different sameness in you, an improved resemblance of what you was, but this Pleasure I receive from the copy, only makes me desirous to see the originall-

I am

Dear West

Y^{rs} most sincerely

ASHTON.

17. WEST TO GRAY.

Receiving no answer to my last letter, which I writ above a month ago, I must own I am a little uneasy. The slight shadow of you which I had in town, has only served to endear you to me the more. The moments I passed with you made a strong impression upon me. I singled you out for a friend, and I would have you know me to be yours, if you deem me worthy. Alas, Gray, you cannot imagine how miserably my time passes away. My health and

nerves and spirits are, thank my stars, the very worst,
I think, in Oxford. Four-and-twenty hours of pure
unalloyed health together, are as unknown to me as
the 400,000 characters in the Chinese vocabulary.
One of my complaints has of late been so over-civil
as to visit me regularly once a month—jam certus
conviva. This is a painful nervous headache, which
perhaps you have sometimes heard me speak of
before. Give me leave to say, I find no physic com-
parable to your letters. If, as it is said in Eccle-
siasticus "Friendship be the physic of the mind,"
prescribe to me, dear Gray, as often and as much as
you think proper, I shall be a most obedient patient.

Non ego
Fidis irascar medicis, offendar amicis.

I venture here to write you down a Greek epigram,
which I lately turned into Latin, and hope you will
excuse it.

[ΠΟΣΕΙΔΙΠΠΟΥ.]

Τὸν τριετῆ παίζοντα περὶ φρέαρ Ἀστυάνακτα
    Εἴδωλον μορφᾶς κωφὸν ἐπεσπάσατο.
Ἐκ δ' ὕδατος τὸν παῖδα διάβροχον ἥρπασε μάτηρ,
    Σκεπτομένα ζωᾶς εἴ τινα μοῖραν ἔχει.
Νύμφας δ' οὐκ ἐμίηνεν ὁ νήπιος, ἀλλ' ἐπὶ γούνων
    Ματρὸς κοιμηθεὶς τὸν βαθὺν ὕπνον ἔχει.

Perspicui puerum ludentem in margine rivi
    Immersit vitreae limpidus error aquae:
At gelido ut mater moribundum e flumine traxit
    Credula, & amplexu funus inane fovet;
Paullatim puer in dilecto pectore, somno
    Languidus, aeternum lumina composuit.

Adieu! I am going to my tutor's lectures on one Puffendorff, a very jurisprudent author as you shall read on a summer's day.

Believe me, yours &c.

Christ Church Dec. 2, 1737.[1]

In the interval between the preceding letter and the Latin reply of Gray, Ashton writes from King's to West Dec. 6th, 1737 (Founder's Day at King's and Eton): "'Only think that I am just risen from a fat Founder's feast and then guess what kind of a letter you are to receive from me...With respect to the little insults that have been levelled at you, I would not have you perceive them." Then follows sage advice, throwing however but little light on the nature of the insults in question, of which West nowhere makes mention in his extant correspondence.

18. GRAY TO WEST.

Literas, mi Favoni! abs te demum, nudiustertius credo, accepi plane mellitas, nisi forte quâ de ægritudine quâdam t:â dictum : atque hoc sane mihi habitum est non paulo acerbius, quod te capitis morbo implicit·um esse intellexi; oh morbum mihi quam odiosum! qui de industriâ id agit, ut ego in

---

[1] The date in Mason and Mitford is Dec. 2, 1738. As however the letter of West's on p. 108 is expressly dated Feb. 21 1737-8 it is plain that the year of *this* letter is 1737. It is possible also that the day of the month is wrongly given. The letter was not received by Gray till Jan. 20th. Gray's '*demum*' shows that there was *some* delay, but an interval of 49 days is difficult to account for.

singulos menses, Dii boni, quantis jucunditatibus
orbarer! quam ex animo mihi dolendum est, quod

> Medio de fonte leporum
> Surgit amari aliquid!

Salutem, mehercule, nolo tam parvipendas, atque
amicis tam improbe consulas: quanquam tute for-
tassis aestuas angusto limite mundi, viamque (ut
dicitur) affectas Olympo, nos tamen non esse tam
sublimes, utpote qui hisce in sordibus et fæce diutius
paululum versari volumus, reminiscendum est: illæ
tuæ Musæ, si te ament modo, derelinqui paulisper
non nimis ægre patientur: indulge, amabo te, plus
quam soles corporis exercitationibus: magis te campus
habeat, aprico magis te dedas otio, ut ne id ingenium
quod tam cultum curas, diligenter nimis dum foves,
officiosarum matrum ritu, interimas. Vide, quæso,
quam ἰατρικῶς tecum agimus,

> ἠδ᾽ ᾽πιθήσω
> φάρμαχ᾽ ἅ κεν παύσῃσι μελαινάων ὀδυνάων.

Si de his pharmacis non satis liquet, sunt festivitates meræ, sunt facetiæ et risus; quos ego
equidem si adhibere nequeo, tamen ad praecipiendum
(ut medicorum fere mos est) certe satis sim:
id quod poeticè sub finem epistolæ lusisti, mihi
gratissimum quidem accidit; admodum Latine coc-
tum et conditum tetrastichon, Græcam tamen illam
ἀφέλειαν mirifice sapit: tu quod restat, vide, sodes,
hujusce hominis ignorantiam; cum, unde hoc tibi sit

depromptum, (ut fatear) prorsus nescio : sane ego equidem nihil in capsis reperio quo tibi minimæ partis solutio fiat. Vale, et me ut soles, ama.

A. D 11 Kalend. Februar. [1738]

19. WEST TO GRAY.[1]

I ought to answer you in Latin, but I feel I dare not enter the lists with you—cupidum, pater optime, vires Deficiunt. Seriously, you write in that language with a grace and an Augustan urbanity, that amazes me : your Greek too is perfect in its kind. And here let me wonder that a man, longe Graecorum doctissimus, should be at a loss for the verse and chapter whence my epigram is taken. I am sorry I have not my Aldus with me, that I might satisfy your curiosity; but he, with all my other literary folks, are left at Oxford, and therefore you must still rest in suspense. I thank you again and again for your medical prescription. I know very well that those "risus, festivitates, et facetiæ" would contribute greatly to my cure, but then you must be my apothecary as well as physician, and make up the dose as well as direct it ; send me, therefore, an electuary of these drugs, made up secundum artem, 'et eris

[1] This was written in French, but as I doubted whether it would stand the test of polite criticism, so well as the preceding would of learned, I chose to translate so much of it as I thought necessary in order to preserve the chain of correspondence. (Mason.)

mihi magnus Apollo' in both his capacities, as a god
of poets and god of physicians. Wish me joy of
leaving my college, and leave yours as fast as you
can. I shall be settled at the Temple very soon.

Dartmouth-Street. Feb. 21. 1737–8.

Mitford says, "In Walpole's Works vol. I. p. 204, is a
well known epigram which was written by West, 'Time
and Thomas Hearne,' which was printed by Mr Walpole
in a paper intended for the 'World' but not sent, and
which is commonly attributed to Swift." But this is not
exact. On turning out the reference I find it is only the
Answer by Mr Polyglot that is attributed to West. The
authorship of the original epigram is not there discussed
it is only called 'the known distich'.

> Pox on't, quoth Time to Thomas Hearne,
> Whatever I forget, You learn.

> Answer by Mr Polyglot.
> †Damn it, quoth Hearne, in furious fret,
> Whate'er I learn, You soon forget.

† It was written at Christ-Church, Oxford, by Richard
West, esq. a young gentleman of great genius, who died at the
age of twenty-six. He was son of Mr West, lord Chancellor of
Ireland, by Elizabeth, daughter of bishop Burnet. [Note in
Walpole's Works *l.c.*]

If this note is correct West wrote this 'Answer' before
the date of the above letter, though at what time during
his college residence I have no means of determining. I
am inclined to attribute the following verses also to some
time during West's stay at Christchurch. They are I
think the basis of the Latin Verses attributed by me to
Gray among the Latin poems *infra*, 'Gratia magna tuæ
fraudi' &c. The 'Monody' was probably written in
December 1737. Queen Caroline died on the 20th of Nov.
in that year.

From A Collection of English Songs by Dalrymple.[1]

Thanks, Chloe, thy coquetting Art
At length hath heal'd my love-sick heart,
    At_length Thy-Slave is free :
I feel no Tyrant's proud control!
I feel no Inmate in my Soul
    But Peace and Liberty.

Put on thy Looks of cold disdain,
Or speak respectful, 'tis in vain,
    Nor Frowns nor Smiles can move,
Those Lips no more have words to bind,
Those Eyes no more have light to find
    The Path that leads to Love.

But still I hear You, smiling, say
"'Tis sign You've flung your chains away
    You take such pains to shew 'em"
Why, Chloe, there's a fond delight
Our former dangers to recite,
    And let our Neighbours know 'em.

After the thunder of the Wars,
The Vet'ran thus displays his Scars,
    And tells You of his Pains;
The Galley-Slave, enslav'd no more,
Shews You the Shackles which he wore,
    And where their mark remains.

For me, I quit a fickle fair;
Chloe, has lost a heart sincere;
    Who first should sing Te Deum?
You'll never find so true a Swain:
But Women full as false and vain,
    By dozens One may see 'em.

                              RICHARD WEST.

[1] (Brit. Mus. $\frac{992 \text{ h}}{4}$ 23).

From Dodsley's Collection Vol. 2, London 1758 p. 274[1].

A MONODY ON THE DEATH OF QUEEN CAROLINE.

By RICHARD WEST ESQ.; SON TO THE CHANCELLOR OF IRELAND, AND GRANDSON TO BISHOP BURNET.

I.

Sing we no more of Hymeneal lays,
Nor strew the land with myrtles and with bays:
The voice of joy is fled the British Shore
For Caroline's no more:
And now our sorrows ask a sadder string;
Come, plaintive goddess of the Cyrrhan Spring,
Pour thy deep note, and shed thy tuneful tear,
And, while we lose the memory of pain
In thy oblivious strain,
—Ah! drop thy cypress on yon mournful bier!
Begin: nor more delay
The sacred meed of gratitude to pay:
Begin: whate'er immortal song can do,
To the dear name of Caroline is due:
Who loves the Muse, deserves the Muse's love:
Then raise thy numbers high,
Sound out her glory to the throne of Jove,
Spread the glad voice thro' all the ambient sky,
From the dull marble vindicate her praise,
And waft it down to lighten future days.

II.

Ye bards to come, the song of truth attend:
This, this is she, the Muse's judge and friend!
The royal female! whose benignant hand
Throughout fair Albion's land
Dealt every useful, every decent part,
Each Memphian science, and each Attick art:

---

[1] [Brit. Museum, 992 d 131.]

Within the Muse's bower
She oft was wont to lose the vacant hour,
Or underneath the sapient grot reclin'd,
Her soul to contemplation she resign'd,
And for a while laid down
The painful, envied burthen of a crown:
Mean time thy rural ditty was not mute,
Sweet bard of Merlin's cave![1]
Tho' rude, thy ditty was of her, who gave
Thy voice to sing, and tun'd thy oaten flute
In strains unwonted to the ear of swain:
As when the lark, ambitious of the skies,
Quits the low harvest of the golden plain,
Taught by the sun's inspiring warmth to rise,
Sublime in air he spreads his dappled wings,
Mounts the blue aether, and in mounting sings.

III.

But whither wander the licentious song?
Such joyous notes to happier days belong!
Ah me! our happier days are now no more:—
Return, sad Muse: see pale Britannia weep,
See all the sisters of the subject deep
Their sovereign's loss deplore!
See fond Ierne give her sorrow vent,
And as she tunes her brazen lyre to woe,
Indulge her grief to flow!—
See even the northern Orcades lament!
Nor ends the wailing here:
Where-e'er beneath our flag wild Ocean roars,
From furthest Orient to Hesperia's shores,
From torrid Affrick to the world's cold end
The British woes extend:
And every colony has dropt a tear.

[1] Stephen Duck. See note p. 89.

IV.

O honour'd flood! with reeds Pierian crown'd
Isis! whose argent waters glide along
Fair Bellosite's Lycaean shades renown'd,
Now aid my feeble song;
And call thy chosen sons, and bid them bring
Their lays of Dorick air,
With lenient sounds to steal awhile from care
Th' inconsolable King:
Oh! sooth his anguish, and compose his pains
With artful unimaginable strains,
According sweetly to the golden lyre,
Such as might half inspire
The iron breast of Hades to resign
Our lost, lov'd Caroline.
These are thy glorious deeds, almighty Death!
These are thy triumphs o'er the sons of men,
That now receive the miserable breath,
Which the next moment they resign again!
[1] Ah me! what boots us all our boasted power,
Our golden treasure, and our purpled state?
They cannot ward th' inevitable hour,
Nor stay the fearful violence of Fate;[1]
—Virtue herself shall fail:
Else now, if virtue ever could prevail,
Death had not dar'd to violate the throne,
Nor had Britannia heard her sovereign groan.
—Ye nymphs! recall the Song:
For heaven-born virtue does to heaven belong,
And scorns the meanest of her sons should die,
But opens him a passage to the sky;

---

[1] Ah me...Fate. The suggestion of the stanza in the elegy,
The boast of heraldry the pomp of pow'r &c.

Her rod ay-pointing to th' eternal goal,
From the brute earth she frees the ardent soul;
Swift from the vulgar herd aloft she springs,
Spurns the moist clay, and soars on azure wings.

V.

Then hence with sorrows vain:
Ye Theban Muses! elevate the strain:
Search o'er the records of immortal fame,
And high refulgent on the female line,
Imblaze in starry characters the name
Of British Caroline:
While sacred story rings with Sheba's praise,
While Berenice's virtues still inspire
The Cyrenean lyre,
And Gloriana blooms in Spenser's lays:
Thy name, great Queen, shall glow in every page,
Shall dwell in every clime, and live in every age.
When George shall go, where William went before,
And all the present world shall be no more;
When the fond factions of unjust mankind,
The mean, the mad, the envious, and the blind
Shall turn to worms and dust;
Then Time, impartial judge, that states the price
Of each man's virtue, and of each man's vice
From thy bright fame shall clear the cank'ring rust;
And O! the Muses ever shall be just.

VI.

But lo! what sudden radiance gilds the skies?
'Tis Gratitude descending from above,
Known by the sweetness of her dove-like eyes,
Daughter of truth and universal love!
To Henry's sacred dome she wafts along,
And on thy tomb she pours
Celestial sweets and amaranthine flowers:

G. 8

The old, the young, the rich, the wretched crowd
Numerous around her, and with accents loud
Raise the mix'd voice, and pour the grateful song
"Hail Queen! adorn'd by nature and by art!
Thine was each virtue of the head and heart
Thy people blest thee, and thy children lov'd
And thy King honour'd, and thy God approv'd."

VII.

But here my labours cease:
'Tis time the foaming courser to release.
And thou, O royal Shade
Forgive the Muse that these vain honours paid
A Muse as yet unheeded and unknown;
That dares to sacrifice to truth alone,
Not prone to blame, not hasty to commend,
No foe unjust, no mercenary friend,
No sensual bosom, no ungenerous mind,
And, tho' not virtuous, virtuously inclin'd.[1]

[1737]

In June, 1738 Gray sent West another Latin letter commencing with the Sapphic ode

'Barbaras ædes aditure mecum
Quas Eris semper fovet inquieta'

from which it would appear that he at that time was himself contemplating a career at the Bar. The ode proceeds to say how much pleasanter it were to spend the hours with books and the Muse under the shady elm,—and describes Gray's enjoyment of the spring and sunshine.

---

[1] This follows, in Dodsley's collection, the Ode on a Distant Prospect of Eton College, the Ode on the Spring 'Lo where the rosy-bosom'd hours,' and that on the Death of Walpole's Cat.

Then follows prose, and then the Alcaic stanza 'O lacry-marum fons' &c. To which West replies *infra*.

20. WEST TO GRAY.

I return you a thousand thanks for your elegant ode, and wish you every joy you wish yourself in it— But, take my word for it, you will never spend so agreeable a day here as you describe : alas ! the sun with us rises only to show the way to Westminster-Hall.—Nor must I forget thanking you for your little Alcaic fragment. The optic Naiads are infinitely obliged to you.

I was last week at Richmond Lodge, with Mr Wal-pole, for two days, and dined with Cardinal Fleury[1] : as far as my short sight can go, the character of his great art and penetration is very just, he is indeed

nulli penetrabilis astro.

I go to-morrow to Epsom, where I shall be for about a month. Excuse me, I am in haste, but believe me always &c.

August 29, 1738[2].

---

[1] Sir Robert Walpole. (Mason.) Fleury, the contemporary French minister, was, like Walpole, credited with a love of Peace. In 1733, Pope had written

'Peace is my dear delight—not Fleury's more :
But touch me, and no minister so sore.'

[2] I am again perplexed at the long interval between this letter and that to which it is the answer.

8—2

21. *ASHTON TO WEST.

Sep. 9. 1738 Hanover Sq.

My dear West,

Why must you vent all your dear Spleen at a
Coffee House to deprive me of a pleasure which it is
not often in your Power to give, of seeing you out of
humor? I shall go to the Temple to-morrow, & I
am determind to visit yr door, tho' I am afraid it
will not open its Eyes upon me. I shall however
enjoy the happiness (the loss of which old Adam
most regretted at his expulsion from Paradise)[1] of
saying to myself

> 'In this room he appeard: behind this door
> Stood visible: among those books his voice
> I heard: here with him on this Staircase talk'd.'

I thank you, my dear for your invitation to Epsom
or Oxford, I am sorry I am not a free agent to comply
with it....a small Piece of Paper light at this House
to day with *Gray's* name attachd to it, & declares
he is very well, that Stourbridge fair is full blown &
that he will go to bed at Cambridge but 14 nights
more.

You know that the alarm of Sir Robert's Danger
had set many hearts a beating with hopes and fears,
which are now equally dispersd—our friend Horace

---

[1] Par. Lost, xi. 320 sq.

has received good advantages by Tunbridge Wells.
He will be in Town next Tuesday.

Yrs very sincerely

ASHTON.

Write soon—oro, obsecro, obtestor.

In Sept. 1738 Gray writes to West:

"I am at this instant in the very agonies of leaving
college....If you knew the dust, the old boxes, the bed-
steads and tutors that are about my ears, you would look
upon this letter as a great effort....I fill up my paper with
a loose sort of version of that scene in Pastor Fido that
begins, Care selve beati."

"This Latin version" says Mason "is extremely elegiac,
but as it is only a version I do not insert it." Accordingly
it has disappeared, as far as I know, altogether. To it
West refers in the *Elegia* which follows *infra*.

22. WEST TO GRAY.

I thank you again and again for your two[1] last
most agreeable letters. They could not have come
more à-propos; I was without any books to divert
me, and they supplied the want of every thing; I
made them my classics in the country; they were
my Horace and Tibullus—Non ita loquor assentandi
causâ, ut probe nôsti si me nôris, verum quia sic mea
est sententia. I am but just come to town, and, to
show you my esteem of your favours, I venture to

---

[1] Those of June and September, 1738.

send you by the penny-post, to your father's, what you will find on the next page : I hope it will reach you soon after your arrival, your boxes out of the waggon, yourself out of the coach, and tutors out of your memory.

Adieu, we shall see one another, I hope, to-morrow.

ELEGIA.

Quod mihi tam gratæ misisti dona Camenæ
   Qualia Maenalius Pan Deus ipse velit,
Amplector te, Graie, & toto corde reposco,
   Oh desiderium jam nimis usque meum!
Et mihi rura placent, et me quoque sæpe volentem
   Duxerunt Dryades per sua prata Deæ;
Sicubi lympha fugit liquido pede, sive virentem,
   Magna, decus nemoris, quercus opacat humum :
Illuc mane novo vagor, illuc vespere sero,
   Et, noto ut jacui gramine, nota cano.
Nec nostrae ignorant divinam Amaryllida silvæ :
   Ah, si desit Amor, nil mihi rura placent.
Ille jugis habitat Deus, ille in vallibus imis,
   Regnat et in Cælis, regnat et Oceano ;
Ille gregem taurosque domat, saevique leonem
   Seminis; ille feros, ultus Adonin, apros :
Quin et fervet amore nemus, ramoque sub omni
   Concentu tremulo plurima gaudet avis.
Duræ etiam in silvis agitant connubia plantae,
   Dura etiam et fertur saxa animâsse Venus.
Durior et saxis, et robore durior ille est,
   Sincero siquis pectore amare vetat :
Non illi in manibus sanctum deponere pignus,
   Non illi arcanum cor aperire velim ;
Nescit amicitias, teneros qui nescit amores :
   Ah! si nulla Venus, nil mihi rura placent.

Me licet a patriâ longe in tellure juberent
  Externâ positum ducere Fata dies;
Si vultus modo amatus adesset, non ego contra
  Plorarem magnos voce querente Deos.
At dulci in gremio curarum oblivia ducens
  Nil cuperem præter posse placere meæ:
Nec bona fortunae aspiciens, neque munera regum,
  Illa intra optarem brachia cara mori.
Sep. 17. 1738.

᛫IMITATION OF HORACE. Lib: I: Ep: 2.[1]

While haply You (or haply not at all)
Hear the grave Pleadings in the Lawyers' Hall
Or, while you haply Littleton explore,
Turning the learned leaden Pages o'er.
Think me again transported to peruse
The golden Rhapsodies of Milton's Muse:
Who shews us in his high Seraphic Song,
What just, what unjust, what is Right, what Wrong,
With Sense at least, and Evidence as true,
As all our Judges of the Bench could do.
Why thus I think (to Hardwick no Offence)
Give Ear, and with your Coke awhile dispense.
  The Tale disastrous You remember well,
How Satan tempted and how Adam fell;
And how he tasted the forbidden Tree,
Induced by female Curiosity;
How thus our Paradise we lost, & all
The Children perish'd in the Fathers' Fall
Nor be that other Tale forgotten here
More moral, tho' less pleasing to the Ear

[1] From Pemb. Common Place Books, vol. I. p. 273.

How in the Desart Wild with Hunger spent
Full forty Days our patient Saviour went
Then spurning back to Hell the wily Fiend
Taught us on Heaven (Heaven only) to depend,
Hence us redeem'd at our Messiah's cost:
The Cross regaining, what the Apple lost.
Thus while I read our Epic Bard divine,
My Mind intent with Pleasure Use to joyn,
From either Poem this Instruction draws,
To trust in God, and to obey God's Laws.
    Enough of Sermon: I perceive you nodd.
You think me mighty wise, & mighty odd:
Your Lips, I see, half verge upon a Smile—
Dear Sir, observe the Horace in my Style.
Just such to Lollius, his misguided Friend,
He knew with decent Liberty to send
Beneath the Critique dext'rous to convey
Advice conceal'd, in the best-natured Way.
But you're no Lollius, and no Horace I:
Here is no Room sage Maxims to apply.
Would you not burst outright to hear me say
Satan, my friend, may lead the best astray;
By Nature ill, by Habit worse inclined,
Add Pride, add Envy, add the willful Mind
Still prone to disobey & to deceive,
All men are Adam, & all women Eve.
Thus bad, thus all corrupted, much I fear
Morality sounds painful to the Ear.
    The Dogs of Night, that murder & that steal,
Outwatch the Watchmen of the publick Weal:
Fools, that we are! less Labour to employ
To save ourselves, than Villains to destroy.
Suppose your Body sick; at any Price
You run to Mead or Hollings for Advice:
This for thy Body: but suppose thy Mind,
For that what Mead or Hollings will you find?

Rise, Sluggard, rise & quit thy Morning-Bed
E're yet Aurora lifts her rosy Head:
Take Plato down, take Tully, take Bruyère[1],
Make honest Things, & Studies all thy Care:
At sight of Industry Vice flies away,
As Spectres vanish at the Face of Day.
If ought offensive to the Eye appear
Not long You let the Object be too near:
What hurts the Mind more patient to endure,
For Years together we delay the Cure.
Meanwhile the Time irrevocable flies:
Begin, & have the Spirit to be wise:
Begin, nor do, as did the Rustick Ass
Who stood, & waited till the Stream should pass
The Stream, Poor fool! you little seem to know
Flows, as it flow'd, and will for ever flow.
The gay Town-house, the pleasant Country-Seat,
The fertile Meadow, & the Garden neat,
The fruitful Nursery, the tender Wife,
Are Joys Men almost value with their Life:
Yet all these Joys, and more (could more be sent)
Make not the total of one Word, Content.
Not all the Gold of the Peruvian Mine,
Not all the Gems that blaze beneath the Line
Can cure a Fever, or one Care expell:
Possessions make not the Possessour well.
The Man, who lives in Hope, or lives in Fear,
In nougt he has can tast the Joy sincere.
Sooner shall Handel give the deaf delight,
And Rafael's Pencil charm the Blind to Sight.

---

[1] Norton Nicholls falls into a curious error about this line. He says (Reminiscences of Gray) '…I remember part of a line among some juvenile MS. verses in his commonplace book *of advice to West*, in which he recommends him to rise early, and

—read Plato, read Bruyère.'

First cleanse the Vessel, e're the Wine you pour
T'will else be Vinegar, and Wine no more.
Obvious to Sense the Allegory lies:
Would you be happy, be but only wise
Reject all Pleasures of the Sense; they're vain.
Each Hour of Pleasure has it's Hour of Pain.
Bound thy mad Wishes: fix on something sure:
The Harpy Avarice is ever poor.
May none but Vilain's[1], be with Envy curst!
Of all the Vices 'tis the Vice the worst:
Scarce all the Tortures of the Damn'd in Hell
The Pangs of wretched Envy can excell.
Sore shall He smart & most severely pay,
Who lets his Passion o'er his Reason sway:
Oft, to his Scorn, shall his unguarded Rage
Act o'er the Part of Cassius on the Stage
Reprove his Friend, upbraid, insult, resent,
Rave like one wild, grow sorry, & repent
Oh! if you'd live in gentle Peace with all
Restrain the boiling Fury of thy Gall:
Oh! early wise it's growing force restrain
Like the Steed, curb it: like the Lyon, chain.
    Youth, Youth's the Season for Instruction fit.
The Colt's young Neck is pliant to the Bit.
The young Hawk listens to the Master's sound,
The Whelp unlash'd was never yet a Hound.
Now, Boy, 's the time, my gentle Boy, draw nigh:
Come with thy blushing Front. & open Eye
Now, while thy Breast is, as the Current, clear,
Unruffled, unpolluted, & sincere:
Now fair and honest all thy Hours employ,
For know, the Man is grafted on the Boy.
The Cask once season'd keeps the Flavour long,
Adieu! thus ends my moralizeing Song.

[1] sic.

Abrupt I finish: my hard Task is o'er:
Forgive me, Pope! I'll imitate no more.

> Fav: from Epsome, before I went
> to France in 1739[1].

Walpole writes to West from Rheims June 18, 1739
N.S.: "I had prepared the ingredients for a description
of a ball, but Gray has plucked it from me...to stay your
stomach, I will send you one of their vaudevilles or
ballads, which they sing at the comedy after their *petites
pièces.*" He then mentions Henry Brooke's 'Gustavus
Vasa.'[2]

23.   WEST TO WALPOLE.

Temple, June 21. 1739

Dear Walpole :

Your last letter puts me in mind of
some good people, who, though they give you the
best dinner in the world, are never satisfied with
themselves, but—wish they had known sooner—quite
ashamed—a little unprepared—hope you'll excuse,
and so forth : for you tell me, you only send me this
to stay my stomach against you are better furnished,
and at the same time you treat me, *ut nunquam in
vitâ melius.* Nor is it now alone that I have room
to say so, but 'tis always : and I know I had rather
gather the crumbs that fall from under your table,

---

[1] Gray's note.   [2] See p. 43 *supra* and note.

than be a prime guest with most other people. Sincerely, sir, nobody in Great Britain, nor, I believe, in France, keeps a more elegant table than yourself: mistake me not, I mean a metaphorical one, for else I should lie confoundedly: for you know you did not use to keep a very extraordinary one, at least when I had the honour to dine with you:—boiled chickens and roast legs of mutton were your highest effort. But with the metaphor, the case is quite altered: 'tis no longer chapon toujours[1] bouilli: 'tis *varium et mutabile semper* enough, I am sure: 'tis *Italo perfusus aceto:* 'tis *tota merum sal:* you see too, it has a particularity, which perhaps you did not know before, that it is of all genders, and is masculine, feminine, or neuter, which you please. Your feasts are like Plato's: one feeds upon them for two or three days together, *et è convivio sapientiores resurgimus quàm accubuimus.* So it is with me; and I never receive any of your tables, or *tabulæ,* for you know 'tis the same thing, but I exclaim to myself

Di magni! salicippium[2] disertum!

If you don't understand this line, you must consult with Doctor Bentley's nephew, who thinks nobody can understand it without him; when after all it does not signify a brass farthing whether you understand it or no. But, sir, this is not all: you not

---

[1] [toujours chapon?]　　　[2] vid. Catullus 53. 5.

only treat me with a whole bushel of attic salt, and
a gallon of Italian vinegar, but you give me some
English-French music -a vaudeville in both languages!

Docte sermones utriusque linguae

But now I talk of music at a feast; I'll tell you of a
feast and music too. About a fortnight ago, walking
through Leicester-fields, I ran full-butt against somebody. Upon examination, who should it be but Mr
A— ? I mean the nephew of the lord of ——. So
we saluted very amicably, and I engaged to sup with
him Thursday next. To his lodgings I went on
Thursday, and there I found Plato, Puffendorf, and
Prato (can't you guess who they be?) A very good
supper we had, and Plato gave your health. I believe
he is in love. Did you ever hear of Nanny Blundel?
But I forget our music. We had sir, for an hour or
two, an Ethiopian, belonging to the Duchess of Athol,
who played to us upon the French-horn. A— made
me laugh about him very much. I said, I suppose
you give this Ethiopian something to drink? Upon
which he ordered him half-a-crown. I said, So *much*?
Oh! he's only a Black, answered he. Puffendorf
(who you know says good things sometimes) said, not
amiss, Oh, sir, if he had been a White, he'd have
given him a crown. I don't pretend to compare our
supper with your partie de cabaret at Rheims; but

at least, sir, our materials were more sterling than
yours. You had a goûté forsooth, composed of des
fraises, de la crême, du vin, des gateaux, &c. We,
sir, we supped à l'Angloise. Inprimis we had buttock
of beef, and Yorkshire ham; we had chickens too, and
a gallon bowl of sallad, and a gooseberry pye as big as
anything. Now, sir, notwithstanding (do you know
what this notwithstanding relates to? I'll mark the
cue for you—'tis) notwithstanding, I say, I am neither
solers citharae, neque musae deditus ulli, as you are;
yet, as I am very vain, and apt to have a high opinion
of my own poetry, I have a mind to treat you as
elegantly as you have treated me—as you remember
a certain doctor at King's College did the Duke of
Devonshire—and so have prepared you a little sort
of musical accompagnamento for your entertainment.
'Tis true I said to myself very often—

> An quodcunque facit Maecenas, Te quoque verum est,
> Tanto dissimilem, et tanto certare minorem?

Then I reflected—

> Ut gratas inter mensas symphonia discors,
> Et crassum unguentum, et Sardo cum melle papaver,
> Offendunt, poterat duci quia cœna sine illis;
> Sic animis natum inventumque poema juvandis,
> Si paulum summo discessit, vergit ad imum.

Yet in spite of these two long quotations (which I
made no other use of than what you see) I still

determined to scrape a little, and accordingly have
sent you, in lieu of your vaudeville, a miserable
elegy[1].

* Imitated from Propertius El: 15: Lib. 3:

Nunc, oh Bacche tuis &c.

Now prostrate Bacchus at thy Shrine I bend:
This once be gracious Father and attend!
Thine great Lyaeus is the power confest
To chase our sorrows, & restore our rest:
'Tis thine, each joy attendant on the bowl,
Thine each gay Lenitive that glads the Soul.
God of the rosey cheek, & laughing eye,
To thee from Cynthia and from love I fly:
If ever Ariadne was thy Care,
Now shew thy pity, & accept my prayer.
　Then, Bacchus, if by thee renew'd I find,
As once, my old serenity of mind,
My Umbrian hill shall flourish with the vine
Thine Bacchus, all my labours shall be thine
With my own hands the generous growth I'll rear,
Rank the young shoots, & watch the riseing year,
Till all my boughs with the red Autumn bend,
And the large Vintage in my Vats descend.
　Hail, mighty Bacchus, to my latest hour
In grateful strains I'll celebrate thy power;
And as I strike the Dithyrambic string,
Thy name, thy glory, & thy power I'll sing:
Thy birth I'll sing, thy mother's fatal fires,
Thy Indian trophies, & Nysaean choirs:

[1] This elegy does not appear. [Berry.] I think it must be
the Imitation of Propertius which I find in Gray's Common
Place Books at Pembroke with date of this month and year.

I'll sing Lycurgus by his Pride undone :
The dire disaster of Agave's son :
And the false Tuscans hurl'd into the Main.
I'll sing the wonders of the Naxian plain
Thy lakes of honey & thy floods of wine ;
Such blessings, father, are reserved for thine!
Now, Io Bacchus! to the general Song.
Bacchus, to thee I'll lead the pomp along :
O'er thy white neck the vivid Ivy spread,
The Lycian mitre nodding on thy head :
Divine with oil thy honest face shall glow,
And to thy feet the dauncing robe shall flow.
Meantime thy Orgies in procession come :
Dircæan Thebes shall beat the hollow Drum,
Th' Arcadian reed shall give a softer sound,
And Phrygian cimbals rattle hoarse around :
High at thy shrine the Flamen Priest shall stand
White-robed, with Ivy crown'd, and in his hand
The golden Vase : th' inferiour throng shall sing :
Io ! again shall thro' the Temple ring.
   And I thy Bard these wonders will rehearse,
And sound thy glories in no common verse :
Of thee this only recompense I ask,
A slight reward for such a toilsome task,
'Tis but to ease my bosom of its pain,
And never may I feel the pangs of love again.[1]

I dare say you wish you could shake the pen out
of my hand. But I do'nt know how it is ; I am at
present in a vein to make up for the dryness of most
of my former letters since you have been abroad ;
and I can't tell but that I may fill up this sheet, if
not another, with more such trumpery. I forgot all

[1] 'Fav: June 1739'—Gray's note.

this while to thank for the packet[1] which I have received, and which was more welcome to me than an Amiens-pye; for I can't help running on with the metaphor I set out with; and you know I always was a *heluo librorum*. The first thing I pitched upon was Crebillon's love-letters, allured by the garnishing, I fancy; that is, the red leaves and the blue silk kalendar. 'Tis an ingenious account of the progress of love in a very virtuous lady's heart, and how a fine gentleman may first gain her approbation, then her esteem, then her heart &c. But do'nt you think it ends a little too tragically? For my part, I protest, I was very sorry; the last letter made me cry. But the passions are charmingly described all through, and the language is fine. After this I would have read the Amusement Philosophique; but Asheton has run away with it—

Callidus, quicquid placuit jocoso
Condere furto.

Very jocose indeed to rob a body! So I ha'n't seen it since. Gustave is no bad thing, as far as I can judge. One may see the author was young when he wrote it, and it looks to me like a first play of an

---

[1] 'We are making you a little bundle of petites pieces: there is nothing in them, but they are acting at present; there are too Crebillon's letters, and Amusemens sur le langage des Bêtes, said to be of one Bougeant, a Jesuit; they are both esteemed, and lately come out.' Gray to West, from Paris, May 22, 1739.

author. But the language is natural, and in many places poetical. The plot is very entertaining, only I do'nt like the conclusion. It ends abrupt, and Leonor comes in at last too much like an apparition. The rest of the pieces I have not read; but from what I can discover by a transient view, I fancy they are better seen than read.

I am now at the eigth page : 'tis time to have done, and wish you adieu. I hear Sir Robert is very well. My Lord Conway[1] is reckoned one of the prettiest persons about town.

Yours ever
R. WEST.

24. *ASHTON TO WEST.

London. Aug. 25. 1739.

Friend[2],

The kind Message thou didst leave with my servant John raisd my Appetite of seeing thee to a very great Pitch, in so much that my bowells did yearn, yea verily I did hunger & thirst for thy Company many days. I would have devourd thy Sayings, & would have hung upon thy Mouth, as an infant hangs on the Nipple of the breast. I would have suckd in thy words, as the warm new Milk, but thou

---

[1] See *supra* p. 40 n. 1 and p. 44.
[2] This Letter is in a large regular assumed Hand, to imitate the Quakers' Manner of Penmanship. (Mitford.)

hast defrauded my Soul, & withdrawn thyself un-
kindly from me.

The exhortation I gave thee was good, tho' clothd
in the language of the Profane. Feed thy Soul with
such food, and truly thou wilt be fat & well liking.

Our friend Whitfield is too hard for Edmund
Gibson[1]. Perhaps thou hast seen his Answer it is
wrote in the meek Spirit of Satyr, in all the humility
of religious Sneer. I doubt the Spirit of Truth had
no hand in the Controversy.

Our friends on the other side of the Water salute
thee, but they complain as much of the want of thy
letters as I do of the want of thyself.

Fare thee well.

The following is in answer to a letter from Gray dated
Lyons, Sept. 18 N.S. 1739, in which he reproaches West
for having let him reside three months at Rheims without
writing more than once. Gray describes in pretty and
humorous fashion the junction of the Rhône and Saône
and says "All yesterday morning we were busied in
climbing up Mount Fourvière where the ancient city stood
perched at such a height that nothing but the hopes of
gain could certainly ever persuade their neighbours to
pay them a visit." He concludes by saying that there are
at Lyons "a thousand matters that you shall not know
till you give me a description of the Païs de Tombridge,
and the effect its waters have upon you."

[1] Bp of London. He wrote a Pastoral Letter against
Lukewarmness and Enthusiasm (1739), to which Whitefield
replied in the same year.

25. WEST TO GRAY.

Temple, Sep. 28. 1739.

If wishes could turn to realities, I would fling-down my law books, and sup with you to-night: But, alas! here I am doomed to fix, while you are fluttering from city to city, and enjoying all the pleasures which a gay climate can afford. It is out of the power of my heart to envy your good fortune, yet I cannot help indulging a few natural desires; as for example, to take a walk with you on the banks of the Rhône, and to be climbing up mount Fourviere:

> Iam mens praetrepidans avet vagari:
> Iam laeti studio pedes vigescunt.

However, so long as I am not deprived of your correspondence, so long shall I always find some pleasure in being at home. And, setting all vain curiosity aside, when the fit is over, and my reason begins to come to herself, I have several other power-ful motives which might easily cure me of my restless inclinations. Amongst these, my mother's ill state of health is not the least, which was the reason of our going to Tunbridge; so that you cannot expect much description or amusement from thence. Nor indeed is there much room for either; for all diver-sions there may be reduced to two articles, gaming

and going to church.' They were pleased to publish
certain Tunbrigiana this season; but such ana! I
believe there were never so many vile little verses put
together before. So much for Tunbridge. London
affords me as little to say. What! So huge a town
as London? Yes, consider only how I live in that
town. I never go into the gay or high world, and
consequently receive nothing from thence to brighten
my imagination. The busy world I leave to the
busy; and am resolved never to talk politics till
I can act at the same time. To tell old stories, or
prate of old books, seems a little musty; and toujours
chapon bouilli, won't do. However, for want of
better fare, take another little mouthful of my
poetry.

O meæ jucunda comes quietis!
Quæ fere ægrotum solita es levare
Pectus, et sensim, ah! nimis ingruentes
       Fallere curas:

Quid canes? quanto Lyra die furore
Gesties quando hûc reducem sodalem
Glauciam[1] gaudere simul videbis
       Meque sub umbrâ?

Walpole to West from Turin Nov. 11, 1739, N.S. relates
how on the passage of Mont Cenis his spaniel 'Tory' was
seized by a young wolf[2]. He sends a copy of an inscription

---

[1] He gives Mr Gray the name of Glaucias frequently in his
Latin verse, as Mr Gray calls him Favonius. [Mason.]

[2] Letters of Walpole ed. Cunningham, vol. 1. no. 18.
Gray to his Mother, Works vol. 11. let. xxi. ed. Gosse.

recording how Charles Emmanuel II., duke of Savoy 'viam regiam...dejectis scopulorum repagulis, æquata montium iniquitate, quæ cervicibus imminebant præcipitia pedibus substernens, æternis populorum commerciis patefecit. A.D. 1670...'. Among the English at Turin he mentions 'a Mr C***, a man that never utters a syllable. We have tried all stratagems to make him speak. Yesterday he did at last open his mouth and said *Bee.* We all laughed so at the novelty of the thing that he shut it again, and will never speak more.'

26. WEST TO WALPOLE.

Temple, Dec. 13, 1739.

Dear Walpole:

Bee! for I have not spoke to-day, and therefore I am resolved to speak to you first. Asheton is of opinion you have read Herodotus; but I imagine no such thing, and verily believe the gentleman to be a Phoenician[1]. I can't forgive Mont Cenis poor Tory's death! I can assure her I'll never sing her panegyric, unless she serves all her wolves as Edgar the Peaceable did. It did touch a little upon the traveller. What do you think it put me in mind of?

[1] See Herodotus II. 2. West here makes a slip. The experiment of Psammetichus discovered that the *Phrygians* were the oldest nation, βέκος being the Phrygian name for bread.

Not a bit like, but it put me in mind of poor
Mrs Rider in Cleveland[1], where she's tore to pieces
by the savages. I can't say I much like your Alps by
the description you give; but still I have a strange
ambition to be where Hannibal was: it must be a
pretty thing to fetch a walk in the clouds, and to
have the snow up to one's ears. But I am really
surprised at your going two leagues in five hours:
a'n't it prodigious quick, to go down such a terrible
descent? The inscription you mention is very pretty
Latin. I see already you like Italy better than
France and all its works. When shall you be at
Rome? Middleton, I think, says, you find there
everything you find everywhere else. I expect
volume upon volume there. Do you never write
folios as well as quartos? You know I am a *heluo* of
everything of that kind, and I am never so happy as
when—*verbosa et grandis epistola venit.*—We have
strange news here in town, if it be but true: we hear
of a sea-fight between six of our men of war and ten

---

[1] Probably the *Histoire de M. Cleveland, fils naturel de
Cromwel; ou, le Philosophe Anglais. Écrite par Lui-même.*
Utrecht (Paris) 1732-9. It appeared almost at the same time
in English, being published by Nicholas Prevost in the Strand.
It was written by the Abbé Prévost, the author of *Manon
Lescaut.* (The editor finds these particulars of *Cleveland*,
which he has never read, in Notes and Queries 1885 vol. i.
pp. 370, 371, contributions by Mr Edward Solly and Mr Henri
van Laun.)

Spanish; and that we sunk one and took five. I should not forget that Mr Pelham[1] has lost two only children at a stroke: 'tis a terrible loss: they died of a sort of sore-throat. To muster up all sort of news: Glover[2] has put out on this occasion a new poem, called London, or The Progress of Commerce; wherein he very much extols a certain Dutch poet, called Janus Douza, and compares him to Sophocles; I suppose he does it to make interest upon 'Change. Plays we have none, or damned ones. Handel has had a concerto this winter. No opera, no nothing. All for war and Admiral Haddock. Farewell and adieu!

Yours,

R. WEST.

Walpole at Bologna had been reading the 2nd Georgic. He says that ll. 461—466 are exactly like Martial: that ll. 495—498 resemble Claudian; ll. 501—506, Juvenal; ll. 523—534, Horace.

He does not intend, he says, to send West an account of what he has seen. "Only think what a vile employment 'tis making catalogues. And then one should have

---

[1] The Right Honourable Henry Pelham, brother of the Minister Duke of Newcastle, and Prime Minister himself at the time of his death in 1754. [Cunningham.]

[2] Richard Glover, author of Leonidas, died 1785. West's father was the maternal uncle of Glover, and in the Inner Temple Hall is a portrait of Lord Chancellor West, presented by Glover. [Cunningham.]

that odious Curl[1] get at one's letters, and publish them like Whitfield's Journal, or for a supplement to the Traveller's Pocket-companion." (Letters I. p. 31 ed. Cunningham.) Meanwhile the winter in England, as will be seen, has been very severe.

* Ipse Pater Thamisinus aquas jam frigore vinci
  Ingemit, hostilemq a magno corpore frustra
  Connisus glaciem, & sævas relevare catenas,
  Indignans imo cursum eluctatur in alveo:
  Ingruit interea, & toto se flumine sternit
  Torpida Vis hyemis: lympharum agitabilis humor
  Deperit, & solidi mutatur imagine campi.
  Nec jam usquam ratibus locus, ut prius; omnia duris
  Irrita substiterunt vinclis, lateque rigescunt
  Relliquiæ cymbarum, & fracto robore palmæ,
  Velaq et antennæ: tristis stat navita ripâ
  Ingratasque rates artemq reponit inanem.
      At populum tota certatim ex urbe ruentem
  Migrare in fluvium cernas, durumque per æquor
  Huc illuc volitare: omnes uno impete gaudent
  Immixti pueriq leves, timidæq puellæ
  Nymphæq, juvenesq & gressu tardior ætas.
  Quin subitis etiam constructa mapalia tignis
  Ædificant: Thamisisq suo consurgere dorso
  Miratur, scenamque fori, stabilesque tabernas   .
  Insuetosq Lares, & non navalia tecta.

                                   Fav: the hard Winter 1740[2].

---

[1] Walpole was of course not aware that Curll was tricked by Pope into publishing his correspondence. See Courthope's Life of Pope, pp. 283.—290.

[2] Gray's note in Pembr. Common Place Books, whence the above is transcribed.

27. WEST TO WALPOLE.

Jan. 23. 1740.

It thaws, it thaws, it thaws! A'n't you glad of it? I can assure you we are: we have been this four weeks a-freezing: our Thames has been in chains, our streets almost unpassable with snow, and dirt, and ice, and all our vegetables and animals in distress. Really, such a frost as ours has been is a melancholy thing. I don't wonder now that whole nations have worshipped the sun; I am almost inclined myself to be a Guebre: tell Orosmades[1]. I believe you think I'm mad, but you would not if you knew what it was to want the sun as we do: 'tis a general frost delivery. Heaven grant the thaw may last! for 'tis a question.

Your last letter, my dear Walpole, is welcome. I thank you for its longitude, and all its parallel lines. You have rather transcribed too many lines out of Virgil: but your criticism I agree with, without any hesitation. Whimsical, quotha: 'tis just and new. You might have added Ovid—

> Quos rami fructus, quos ipsa—[2]

and Statius:

> At secura quies—[3]

and what follows down to

> Non absunt—

But what do you think? Your observations have set

---

[1] Gray, see n. pp. 80, 81.

[2] Georg. ii. 500.   [3] Ib. 467—471.

me a-translating, and Ashton has told me it was worth
sending.   Excuse it, 'tis a tramontane.   I shall certainly publish your letters.   But now I think on't, I
won't; I should make Pope quite angry.   Addio, mio
caro, addio!   Dove sei? Ritorna, ritorna, amato bene!

Yours from S. Paul's to St Peter's!

R. WEST.

I believe you must send my translation to the
academy of the Gelati.

My love to Gray, and pray tell him from me

ψῦχος δὲ λεπτῷ χρωτὶ πολεμιώτατον.[1]

28. WEST TO WALPOLE.

March 29, 1740.

My dear Walpole:

Since I have finished the first act[2], I send you
now the rest of it.   Whether I shall go on with it is
to me a doubt.   I find you all make the same objections to my style: but change my manner now I

[1] A fragment of Euripides quoted by Cicero, Ep. ad Fam.
xvi. 8. [Berry.]

[2] Of his tragedy of Pausanias. Gray wrote from Florence
more than a year after this to West (April 21, 1741): "I
must defer giving my opinion of Pausanias till I can see the
whole, and only have said what I did in obedience to your
commands." That West may have his revenge he sends him
the first 53 lines of his 'De Principiis Cogitandi'. 'Pausanias'
is lost, or at least evades search.

ca'nt, for it would not be all of a piece, and to begin afresh goes against my stomach; so I believe I must even break it off and bequeath it to my grandchildren to be finished with other old pieces of family work. I have another objection to it, and that is, the unlucky affair of an impeachment in the play. For, supposing the thing public, which it was never intended to be, every blockhead of the faction would swear Pausanias was Greek for Sir Robert, though it may as well stand for Bolingbroke. But the truth is, the Greek word signifies neither one nor t'other, as you may find in Scapula, Suidas, and other lexicographers.

R. W.

Gray writes to West from Florence, Jan. 15, 1740, recounting the places which he has visited since leaving Genoa, but refusing to give him a detailed account even of Florence itself. 'Before I enter into particulars' he says 'you must make your peace both with me and the Venus de Medicis, who, let me tell you, is highly and justly offended at you for not inquiring, long before this, concerning her symmetry and proportions.' Mason tells us that the letter which accompanied West's Elegy in reply 'is not extant: probably it was only enclosed in one to Mr Walpole.'

ELEGIA.

Ergo desidiæ videor tibi crimine dignus;
    et merito: victas do tibi sponte manus.
Arguor & veteres nimium contemnere Musas
    irata et nobis est Medicaea Venus.

Mene igitur statuas & inania saxa vereri!
 Stultule! marmoreâ quid mihi cum Venere?
Hic veræ, hic vivæ Veneres, et mille per urbem
 quarum nulla queat non placuisse Iovi.
Cedite Romanae formosae, et cedite Graiæ,
 sintq oblita Helenae nomen, et Hermionae!
Et quascunq refert aetas vetus, Heroinae:
 unus honos nostris jam venit Angliasin.
Oh quales vultus! Oh quantum numen ocellis!
 i nunc, et Tuscas improbe confer opes.
Ne tamen haec obtusa nimis praecordia credas,
 neu me adeo nullâ Pallade progenitum:
Testor Pieridumq umbras & flumina Pindi,
 me quoque Calliopes semper amasse choros;
Et dudum Ausonias urbes, & visere Graias
 cura est, ingenio si licet ire meo:
Sive est Phidiacum marmor, seu Mentoris aera,
 Seu paries Coo nobilis e calamo;
Nec minus artificum magna argumenta recentûm
 Romaniq decus nominis, & Veneti:
Qua Furor & Mavors & saevo in marmore vultus,
 quaq et formoso mollior aere Venus;
Quaq loquax spirat fucus, viviq labores,
 et quidquid calamo dulcius ausa manus:
Hic nemora et sola maerens Meliboeus in umbrâ,
 lymphaq muscoso prosiliens lapide;
Illic majus opus, faciesque in pariete major
 exsurgens[1], Divûm et numina Coelicolûm.
O vos felices[1], quibus haec cognoscere fas est,
 et totâ Italiâ qua patet usque frui!
Nulla dies vobis eat injucunda nec usquam
 nôritis[1] quid sit tempora amara pati.[2]

[1] Gray's transcript has 'exurgens', 'fœlices', noritis.
[2] [Gray notes on Pemb. mss. "Fav: sent from London to Florence. April — 1740."]

29. WEST TO GRAY.

Bond-street, June 5, 1740[1].

I lived at the Temple till I was sick of it: I have just left it, and find myself as much a lawyer as I was when I was in it. It is certain, at least, I may study the law here as well as I could there. My being in chambers did not signify to me a pinch of snuff. They tell me my father was a lawyer, and, as you know, eminent in the profession; and such a circumstance must be of advantage to me. My uncle[2] too makes some figure in Westminster-hall; and there's another advantage: then my grandfather's name would get me many friends. Is it not strange that a young fellow, that might enter the world with so many advantages, will not know his own interest? &c. &c. What shall I say in answer to all this? For money, I neither dote upon it nor despise it; it is a necessary stuff enough. For ambition, I do not want that neither; but it is not to sit upon a bench. In short, is it not a disagreeable thing to force one's inclination, especially when one's young? not to mention that one ought to

[1] A letter of Ashton's partly badinage, partly flattery, and neither in good taste, (belonging I think to this time approximately), was directed to Mr Richard West at Mrs Sherard's in Prince's Court near Story's gate, Westminster.

[2] Sir Thomas Burnet.

have the strength of a Hercules to go through our
common law; which I am afraid, I have not. Well!
but then, say they, if one profession does not suit
you, you may choose another more to your inclination.
Now I protest I do not yet know my own inclination,
and I believe, if that was to be my direction, I should
never fix at all. There is no going by a weathercock. I could say much more upon this subject;
but there is no talking tête-à-tête cross the Alps.
Oh the folly of young men, that never know their
own interest! they never grow wise till they are
ruined! and then nobody pities them, nor helps
them. Dear Gray! consider me in the condition of
one that has lived these two years without any person
that he can speak freely to. I know it is very seldom
that people trouble themselves with the sentiments of
those they converse with; so that they can chat
about trifles, they never care whether your heart
aches or no. Are you one of these? I think not.
But what right have I to ask you this question?
Have we known one another enough, that I should
expect or demand sincerity from you? Yes, Gray, I
hope we have; and I have not quite such a mean
opinion of myself, as to think I do not deserve it.
But, signor, is it not time for me to ask something
about your future intentions abroad? Where do you
propose going next? an in Apuliam? nam illo si
adveneris, tanquam Ulysses, cognosces tuorum nemi-

nem. Vale. So Cicero prophesies in the end of one of his letters[1]—and there I end.

Yours &c.

Of the preceding letter Mason says that it is 'written apparently in much agitation of mind which Mr West endeavours to conceal by an unusual carelessness of manner.' To it Gray replies in a letter from Florence (July 16, 1740): "You do yourself and me justice, in imagining that you merit, and that I am capable of sincerity....Why did you change your lodging? Was the air bad, or the situation melancholy? If so, you are quite in the right." He then tries to reconcile him to the study of the law. "Are you sure, if Coke had been printed by Elzevir, and bound in twenty neat pocket volumes, instead of one folio, you should never have taken him for an hour, as you would a Tully, or drank your tea over him[2]?...Do you really think, if you rid ten miles every morning, in a week's time you should not entertain much stronger hopes of the Chancellorship...than you do at present?"

On August 13th 1740 Ashton sent to West a tedious (but happily incomplete) letter on the Sublime. The following replies are only given *in extenso* to make the collection of West's work as complete as possible. Ashton's letter was directed "To be left at Morley's Coffee House, Tunbridge Wells, Kent."

---

[1] Cicero to L. Valerius (Ad Diversos i. 10), but with more point 'Neque in Apuliam *tuam* accedas' &c.

[2] Cf. Henry Mackenzie's 'Man of Feeling' chap. xii. 'One of his guardians indeed, who in his youth had been an inhabitant of the Temple, set him to read Coke upon Littleton, a book which is very properly put into the hands of beginners in that science, as its simplicity is accommodated to their understandings, *and its size to their inclination.*'

30. * WEST TO ASHTON.

To
    Thomas Ashton Esqr
      at the Honble Mrs Lewis's
        in Hanover Square
          London

No more of your civil Prefaces, dear Ashton; I am sorry we can't agree, but who can help it? I shall never be of your opinion, till you can convince me ; and I beg you'll never be of mine, but upon the same Condition. Our controversy, I find, is reduced to this one question. Whether your definition of the Sublime is a just and comprehensive definition or not?

The Sublime, say you, is a just and lively representation of the grand objects and Circumstances of Nature. Now, I humbly propose another question first i.e. whether your definition is a clear and expressive definition or not?

This question indeed is of little importance to yrself, who made the definition & consequently must know yr own Meaning when you made it: but to me, who did not make it, and only guess yr Meaning from the Words, I read in the definition itself, it is of great importance. For how should I know whether the Meaning of a Definition is just,

G.   10

unless the Words are clear to me? How should I judge whether 'tis comprehensive, unless I comprehend it?

I had no doubts about my comprehension till your last letter; but now I have: for you seem there to give a greater latitude of meaning to some of your Words, than I think the Words will bear.

I shall be in Town very soon & then you shall explain to me, if you'll give yourself the trouble: for I hate all explanations but oral explanations.

Besides if you send any more letters I shall miss them: for the Company is all gone from here & the Consequence is, that the Post brings us no more letters.

Yours internally

R. W.

Tunbridge Wells. Sept. 31. 1740.

31. * WEST TO ASHTON.

[Imperfect.][1]

I mean; 'tis like that Picture of a handsome man, which, at the same time 'tis very well executed, yet owes its Principal beauty to its prototype.

2ndly.   I am afraid I talk both superficially & unintelligibly: but I'll proceed, tho' I waste another

---

[1] Mitford,—who seems to make this the second of these two letters on the Sublime.

sheet of paper. The Sublime therefore which I
mean, I place neither in the object, nor in the idea
immediately rising from it. I must place it therefore
at last either in the Sentiment or expression, or both:
and now methinks I am returnd to what occasiond
the debate, between the Lord and the Doctor. Were
I to place it in either singly, I should certainly place
it in the Sentiment—for there is the Principium
& fons. Unless you think nobly, I defy you to talk
so, or even to look so, much less to act so. Noble
thoughts are the common Substratum of noble
actions & discourses, the orator and the hero are both
derived from hence. But I place it in both, tho'
more in the Sentiment, than in the Expression. And
this perhaps is the reason, why a great Sentiment
expressd even in the simplest words, will nevertheless appear sublime. The true sublime is like true
Beauty 'Induitur formosa est; exuitur, ipsa forma
est'—it rather looses[1] than gains by ornament. It
thunders, it lightens, it bursts immediately from the
mind of the Orator upon his Hearers, it convinces
them, it amazes them, its authority is irresistible.
Such are (?was) the Speech of Henry the IVth of
France to his Soldiers—There are your Ennemyes—
remember you are Frenshmen'—and that Henry is
your General— Supposing these words accompanied

_____

[1] sic in Mitford's transcript.

10—2

with their proper emphasis and Fire, in Speaking, do
you think there was any Frenshman[1], there, who
would not have fought to the last drop in his veins?
and so much, Sirs, for the Sentiment.

3. I come now to the Expression, which is all,
that is further requisite in the writer; but in the
Orator there would be pronunciation, gesture &c.
which it would be foreign to talk of here: nor have I
room to talk much more about its Expression, I shall
only make this one observation i.e.—That in the
description of the Sublime, objects such [as ?] are so
naturally 'tis usual to give into sounding Phrases and
noble Metaphors—but when the Sublime is in the
Sentiment itself, 'tis generally cloathd in simple
expressions.

If I may give the Preference, I should prefer the
last kind, but I doubt—and you are tired I see,
& think I have been talking nonsense for a good
while together—so—Finis

R. WEST.

Δόξα μόνῳ τῷ Θεῷ

P.S. Alexander[2], the Great, Banquier à Paris,

---

[1] *sic* in Mitford's transcript.

[2] Walpole writes to West, Nov. 1740, 'Direct to me
addressed to Monsieur Selwyn, chez Monsieur Alexandre, rue
St Apolline, à Paris. If Mr Alexandre is not there, the street
is, and I believe that will be sufficient."

is in the Bastile. Pray how are we to send our letters.

To Thomas Ashton Esq[1]
        at Mrs Lewis's, at her house
            in Hanover Square, London.

32. * WEST TO ASHTON.

To
    Mr Ashton
        at M[rs] Lewis's in
            Hanover Square
                London
    pour
        Angleterre

Dear Ashton,

West at Paris? would you believe it? and yet 'tis so. How it came about, is another Story. Some time or other, you may know it, but be assur'd, I did not come to divert myself. Expect therefore no letters of entertainment from me, I am taken up with something else, and consider myself at Paris, just as I did at London. Nevertheless, if you have a mind to hear from an old friend now and then, you shall; have pity too on me, in a strange Country, and write to me sometimes. Be so good as to call or send to Dick's Coffee house, and if there are any letters for

[1] Ashton it will be noted was not ordained in 1740. Introductory Essay, p. 3, n. 1.

me, I shd be glad to have them sent me. My address is racomandè a Messrs Lubhard & Vernil, Banquiers, rue de St Martin a Paris.

Excuse me, I am in haste, as everything here is. Adieu! & do'nt forget me.

Paris, May 8, N. S. [1741].

A Postscript of Gray's (Florence, July 31, N. S. 1740) to a letter from Walpole to West, throws some light upon the following application from West to Walpole. Gray says: "We shall never come home again; a universal war is just upon the point of breaking out; all out-lets will be shut up. You do'nt tell me what proficiency you make in the noble science of defence. Do'nt you start still at the sound of a gun? Have you learned to say Ha! ha! and is your neck clothed with thunder? Are your whiskers of a tolerable length? And have you got drunk yet with brandy and gunpowder? Adieu, noble Captain!"

The criticism of Pausanias to which West refers *infra*, was sent from Reggio on the 10th of May N.S. 1741. From it we gather that there were two characters in the play named Cleodora and Argilius, who according to Walpole 'do not talk laconic but low English'; and that Cleodora was a Persian, and might be expected to speak more heroically.

33. WEST TO WALPOLE.

London, June 22, 1741.

Dear Walpole:

I have received your letter from Reggio, of the 10th of May, and have heard since that you fell

ill[1] there, and are now recovered and returning to
England through France. I heard the bad and good
news both together; and so was afflicted and com-
forted both in a breath. My joy now has got the
better, and I live in hopes of seeing you here again.
The author of the first act of Pausanias desires his
love to you; and, in return for your criticism, which
seems so severe to him in some parts and so prodigious
favourable in others, that if he were not acquainted
with your unprejudiced way of thinking, he should
not know what to say to it, has ordered me to acquaint you with an accident that happened to him
lately, on a little journey he made. It seems he
had put all his writings, whether in prose or rhyme,
into a little box, and carried them with him. Now,

---

[1] There is no mention of Gray in Walpole's letter of the
10th of May, and it is probable that the quarrel and the de-
parture of Gray for Venice, had already taken place. From a
letter of Gray to West of the 21st of April from Florence it
seems that Gray and Walpole had planned to visit Venice
together by the 11th of May, in time to see the Doge wed the
Adriatic. Walpole says (Short Notes of my Life) 'Mr Gray
left me, going to Venice, with Mr Francis Whithed and Mr
John Chute, for the festival of the Ascension. I fell ill at
Reggio of a kind of quinzy and was given over for five hours,
escaping with great difficulty.' Spence, (the Oxford Professor
of Poetry and friend of Pope, author of the 'Anecdotes' &c.)
whose acquaintance Walpole had made at Florence, fortunately
found himself at Reggio, and his opportune assistance probably
saved Walpole's life. (See Walpole's Letters ed. Cunningham,
vol. 1. p. 64 n.)

somebody imagining there was more in the box than there really was, has run away with them; and, though strict inquiry has been made, the said author has learnt nothing yet, either concerning the person suspected, or the box. Since I am engaged in talking of this author, and as I know you have some little value for him, I beg leave to acquaint you with some particulars relating to him, which perhaps you will not be so averse to hear.

You must know then, that from his cradle upwards he was designed for the law, for two reasons : first, as it was the profession which his father followed, and succeeded in, and consequently there was a likelihood of his gaining many friends in it : and, secondly, upon account of his fortune, which was so inconsiderable, that it was impossible for him to support himself without following some profession or other. Nevertheless, like a rattle as he is, he has hitherto fixed on no profession: and for the law in particular, upon trial he has found in himself a natural aversion to it: in the meanwhile he has lost a great deal of time, to the great diminution of his narrow fortune, and to the no little scandal of his friends and relations. At length, upon serious consideration, he has resolved that something was to be done, for that poetry and Pausanias would never be sufficient to maintain him. And what do you think he has resolved upon? Why, apprehending that a general war in Europe was

approaching, and therefore, that there might be some
opportunity given, either of distinguishing himself,
or being knocked of the head: being convinced,
besides, that there was little in life to make one over
fond of it—he has chosen the army; and being told
that it was a much cheaper way to procure a commission by the means of a friend, than to buy one, to
do which he must strip himself of what fortune he
has left, he desired me to use what little interest I
had with my friends to procure him what he wanted.

At first I objected to him the weakness of his
constitution, which might render him incapable of
military service, and several other things; but all to
no purpose. He told me, he was neither knave nor
fool enough to run in debt, and that he must either
abscond from mankind, or do something to enable him
to live as he would upon a decent rank, and with
dignity; and that what he chose was this.

I perceived there was nothing to reply; so I
submitted; and as I have some sort of regard for the
man, I promised him I would use what interest I had,
and frankly told him, I would venture to ask for him
what I should hardly ask for myself.

Excuse my freedom, dear Walpole; and whether
I succeed or not, assure yourself that I shall always be,

Yours most affectionately,

R. WEST.

34. *GRAY TO WEST.

(date uncertain)[1]

As I know you are a lover of Curiosities, I send you the following, which is a true and faithful Narrative of what passed in my study on Saturday the 16th, instant. I was sitting there very tranquil in my chair, when I was suddenly alarmed with a great hubbub of Tongues. In the Street, you suppose? No! in my Study, Sir. In your Study say you? Yes & between my books, which is more. For why should not books talk as well as Crabs & Mice & files & Serpents do in Esop. But as I listend with great attention so as to remember what I heard pretty exactly, I shall set down the whole conversation as methodically as I can, with the names prefixed.

Mad. de Sevigné. Mon cher Aristote! do get a little further or you will quite suffocate me.

Aristotle. Οὐδέποτε γυνή...I have as much right to this place as you, and I sha'nt remove a jot.

M. Sevigné. Oh! the brute! Here's my poor Sixth tome is squeezed to death: for God's sake, Bussy, come & rescue me.

[1] I incline to assign it to London, 1742; although Mitford writes 1740. I cannot think it is from abroad; and Gray was abroad during the whole of 1740. From the fact that the letter is a fragment, I infer, but with some hesitation, that Mitford's date is conjectural.

Bussy Rabutin. Ma belle Cousine! I would fly to your assistance. Mais voici un diable de Strabon qui me tue, and I have no one worth conversing with here but Catullus.

Bruyere. Patience! You must consider we are but books, and so ca'nt help ourselves. for my part I wonder who we belong to. We are a strange mixture here. I have a Malebranche on one side of me, and a Gronovius on t'other.

Locke. Certainly our owner must have very confused ideas, to jumble us so strangely together. He has associated me with Ovid and Ray the Naturalist.

Virgil. 'Me vero primum dulces ante omnia Musæ Accipiant !'

H. More. Of all the Speculations that the Soul of Man can entertain herself withall there is none of greater moment than this of her immortality.

Cheyne. Every man after fourty is either a fool or a Physician.

Euclid. Punctum est cujus nulla est....

Boileau. Peste soit de cet homme avec son Punctum! I wonder any man of sense will have a Mathematician in his Study.

Swift. In short, let us get the Mathematics banishd first, the Metaphysicks and Nat: Philosophy may follow them.

Vade Mecum. Pshaw! I and the Bible are enough for any one Library.

This last ridiculous egotism made me laugh so heartily that I disturbd the poor books & they talk'd no more.

35. WEST TO GRAY.

I write to make you write, for I have not much to tell you. I have recovered no spirits as yet, but, as I am not displeased with my company, I sit purring by the fire-side in my arm-chair, with no small satisfaction. I read too sometimes, and have begun Tacitus, but have not yet read enough to judge of him; only his Pannonian sedition in the first book of his annals, which is just as far as I have got, seemed to me a little tedious. I have no more to say, but to desire you will write letters of a handsome length, and always answer me within a reasonable space of time, which I leave to your discretion.

Popes[1], March 28, 1742.

P.S. The new Dunciad![2] qu'en pensez vous?

To West's of March 28 Gray replies: "I trust to the country, and that easy indolence you say you enjoy there, to restore you your health and spirits; and doubt not but, when the sun grows warm enough to tempt you from your fire-side, you will like all other things) be the better for his influence. He is my old friend, and an excellent nurse I assure you." Then follows an excellent criticism

[1] David Mitchell's Esq., at Popes near Hatfield, Hertfordshire.
[2] This is the 4th Book of the Dunciad published in 1742.

of Tacitus. Gray proceeds: "As to the Dunciad, it is greatly admired; the Genii of Operas and Schools, with their attendants, the pleas of the Virtuosos and Florists, and the yawn of dulness in the end, are as fine as any thing he has written.` The Metaphysicians' part is to me the worst: and here and there a few ill-expressed lines. and some hardly intelligible." He sends West the concluding speech of the first scene of his Agrippina, which he acknowledges to be much too long, and begs West to retrench.

36. WEST TO GRAY.

Popes, April 4, 1742.

I own in general I think Agrippina's speech too long; but how to retrench it, I know not: but I have something else to say, and that is in relation to the style, which appears to me too antiquated. Racine was of another opinion: he nowhere gives you the phrases of Ronsard: his language is the language of the times, and that of the purest sort; so that his French is reckoned a standard. I will not decide what style is fit for our English stage: but I should rather choose one that bordered upon Cato, than upon Shakspeare. One may imitate (if one can) Shakspeare's manner, his surprising strokes of true nature, his expressive force in painting characters, and all his other beauties; preserving at the same time our own language. Were Shakspeare alive now, he would write in a different style from what he did. These are my sentiments upon these matters: perhaps I am wrong, for I am neither a Tarpa, nor am

I quite an Aristarchus. You see I write freely both of you and Shakspeare; but it is as good as writing not freely, where you know it is acceptable.

I have been tormented within this week with a most violent cough; for when once it sets up its note it will go on, cough after cough, shaking and tearing me for half an hour together; and then it leaves me in a great sweat, as much fatigued as if I had been labouring at the plough. All this description of my cough in prose, is only to introduce another description of it in verse, perhaps not worth your perusal; but it is very short, and besides has this remarkable in it, that it was the production of four o'clock in the morning, while I lay in my bed tossing and coughing, and all unable to sleep.

> Ante omnes morbos importunissima tussis,
> Qua durare datur, traxitque sub ilia vires:
> Dura etenim versans imo sub pectore regna,
> Perpetuo exercet teneras luctamine costas,
> Oraque distorquet, vocemque inmutat anhelam:
> Nec cessare locus: sed saevo concita motu,
> Molle domat latus, & corpus labor omne fatigat;
> Unde molesta dies, noctemque insomnia turbant.
> Nec Tua, si mecum Comes hic jucundus adesses,
> Verba juvare queant, aut hunc lenire dolorem,
> Sufficiat tua vox dulcis, nec vultus amatus.[1]

Do not mistake me, I do not condemn Tacitus: I

---

[1] "Fav: April 4. Wrote in the Country, after his severe Illness, which left behind it continual Hectick, & Cough." (Gray's note in Pemb. Common Place Books.)

was then inclined to find him tedious: the German
sedition sufficiently made up for it; and the speech
of Germanicus, by which he reclaims his soldiers, is
quite masterly. Your New Dunciad I have no con-
ception of. I shall be too late for our dinner if I
write any more.

Yours.

Gray replies: "You are the first who ever made a
Muse of a Cough; to me it seems a much more easy task
to versify in one's sleep (that indeed you were of old
famous for)[1] than for want of it....These wicked remains
of your illness will sure give way to warm weather and
gentle exercise; which I hope you will not omit as the
season advances....I talked of the Dunciad as concluding
you had seen it; if you have not, do you choose I should
get and send it to you?"...He has been reading 'Joseph
Andrews' upon West's invitation. 'The incidents are ill-
laid and without invention' but 'the characters have a
great deal of nature. Parson Adams is perfectly well; so

---

[1] 'This is, I believe, founded in truth; for I remember
some who were of the same house mentioning that he often
composed in his dormant state, and that he wrote down in the
morning what he had conceived in the night. He was, like
his friend, quite faultless in respect to morals and behaviour,
and, like many great geniuses, often very eccentric and absent.
One of his friends, who partook of the same room, told me,
that West, when at night composing, would come in a thought-
ful mood to him at his table, and carefully snuff his candle,
and then return quite satisfied to his own dim taper, which he
left unrepaired.' *Bryant* (letter of reminiscences in Mitford's
2nd life of Gray).

is Mrs Slipslop' &c. 'These light things (I mean such as characterise and paint nature surely are as weighty and much more useful than your grave discourses upon the mind, the passions and what not.'... *His* 'paradisiacal pleasures' he says should be to read 'eternal new romances of Marivaux and Crebillon.' Then follows an answer to West's criticism on the style of Agrippina, parts of which have often been quoted, latterly by Mr Matthew Arnold – 'the language of the age is never the language of poetry : except among the French, whose verse, when the thought or image does not support it, differs nothing from prose.' &c. He ends by saying 'You need not fear unravelling my web....I believe my amusements are as little amusing as most folks...but...it is better than ἐν ἀμαθίᾳ καὶ ἀμουσίᾳ καταβιῶναι.'

37. WEST TO GRAY.

April [1742]

To begin with the conclusion of your letter, which is Greek, I desire that you will quarrel no more with your manner of passing your time. In my opinion it is irreproachable, especially as it produces such excellent fruit; and if I, like a saucy bird, must be pecking at it, you ought to consider that it is because I like it. No una litura I beg you, no unravelling of your web, dear sir! only pursue it a little further, and then one shall be able to judge of it a little better. You know the crisis of a play is in the first act; its damnation or salvation wholly rests there. But till that first act is over, every body suspends his

vote; so how do you think I can form, as yet, any
just idea of the speeches in regard to their length or
shortness? The connexion and symmetry of such
little parts with one another must naturally escape
me, as not having the plan of the whole in my head;
neither can I decide about the thoughts, whether
they are wrong or superfluous; they may have some
future tendency which I perceive not. The style
only was free to me, and there I find we are pretty
much of the same sentiment: for you say the affectation of imitating Shakspeare may doubtless be carried
too far: I say as much and no more. For old words
we know are old gold, provided they are well chosen.
Whatever Ennius was, I do not consider Shakspeare
as a dunghill in the least; on the contrary, he is a
mine of ancient ore, where all our great modern poets
have found their advantage. I do not know how it
is, but his old expressions have more energy in them
than ours, and are even more adapted to poetry;
certainly, where they are judiciously and sparingly
inserted, they add a certain grace to the composition;
in the same manner as Poussin gave a beauty to his
pictures by his knowledge in the ancient proportions:
but should he, or any other painter, carry the imitation too far, and neglect that best of models Nature,
I am afraid it would prove a very flat performance.
To finish this long criticism: I have this further
notion about old words revived, (is not this a pretty

G.   11

way of finishing?) I think them of excellent use in
tales; they add a certain drollery to the comic, and
a romantic gravity to the serious, which are both
charming in their kind; and this way of charming
Dryden understood very well. One need only read
Milton to acknowledge the dignity they give the epic.
But now comes my opinion that they ought to be
used in tragedy more sparingly than in most kinds of
poetry. Tragedy is designed for public representation,
and what is designed for that should certainly be most
intelligible. I believe half the audience that come
to Shakspeare's plays do not understand the half of
what they hear.—But finissons enfin.—Yet one word
more.—You think the ten or twelve first lines the
best, now I am for the fourteen last; add, that they
contain not one word of ancientry.

I rejoice you found amusement in Joseph Andrews.
But then I think your conceptions of Paradise a little
upon the Bergerac. Les Lettres du Seraphim B. à
Madame la Cherubinesse de Q. What a piece of
extravagance would there be!

And now you must know that my body continues
weak and enervate. And for my animal spirits they
are in perpetual fluctuation: some whole days I have
no relish, no attention for any thing; at other times I
revive, and am capable of writing a long letter, as
you see; and though I do not write speeches, yet I
translate them. When you understand what speech,

you will own that it is a bold and perhaps a dull attempt. In three words, it is prose, it is from Tacitus, it is of Germanicus. Peruse, perpend, pronounce.[1]

Gray answers from London, in the same month, that 'Agrippina is laid to sleep till next summer', and Mason adds that 'he never after awakened her'. He commends West's translation of Tacitus and sends him a version of Propertius (Works, ed. Gosse, Vol. I. p. 153).

38. * WEST TO ASHTON.

Dear Ashton,

Had I anything instructive or amusing to send you you should have it : but as I have neither you must excuse me both. but the end of this letter is a Petition. If you can find the burlesque imitation, I left with you of Pope's Verses on his Grotto, I sh^d be greatly obliged to you, to send it me. Vale mi   Reverendissime[2]

RV.

Tuesday April 15 [1742].

---

[1] This speech I omit to print, as I have generally avoided to publish mere translations either of Mr Gray or his friend. [Mason.]

[2] The reference to Pope's Verses, and this form of salutation, which shows that Ashton is now ordained, combine to fix the date of this letter to the time of West's *last* illness, rather than to that of 1737. It will be seen that on June 3, Ashton dates from Downing Street, and he was probably much in Walpole's company at this time.

My compliments to Walpole. I wish he would
write & comfort the Sick. 'tis a Christian duty. I
apply it to yrself, Doctour, likewise.

39. WEST TO GRAY.

Popes, May 5, 1742

Without any preface I come to your verses, which
I read over and over with excessive pleasure, and
which are at least as good as Propertius. I am only
sorry you follow the blunders of Broukhusius, all
whose insertions are nonsense. I have some objections to your antiquated words, and am also an enemy
to Alexandrines ; at least I do not like them in elegy.
But, after all, I admire your translation so extremely,
that I cannot help repeating I long to show you some
little errors you are fallen into by following Broukhusius. * * * * * Were I with you now, and Propertius
with your verses lay upon the table between us, I
could discuss this point in a moment ; but there is
nothing so tiresome as spinning out a criticism in a
letter; doubts arise, and explanations follow, till there
swells out at least a volume of undigested observations:
and all because you are not with him whom you want
to convince. Read only the letters between Pope
and Cromwell in proof of this; they dispute without
end. Are you aware now that I have an interest all
this while in banishing criticism from our correspondence? Indeed I have; for I am going to write down

a little ode (if it deserves the name) for your perusal,
which I am afraid will hardly stand that test. Nevertheless I leave you at your full liberty; so here it
follows.

> Dear Gray[1] that still within my Heart
> Possessest far the better part!
> What mean these sudden Blasts, that rise,
> And drive the Zephyrs from the Skies?
> The Winter yet is scarcely gone,
> And Summer comes but slowly on.
>
> Oh, fairest Month of all the year!
> In whom the Graces still appear
> Awake, & raise thy drowsy head
> From off the soft ambrosial Bed:
> Where, underneath your bower reclined
> You hear not the least breath of Wind.
>
> Awake in all your Glory dress'd
> Recall the Zephyrs from the West
> Restore the Sun, revive the Skies!
> Awake, sweet Month, arise, arise!
> Great Nature's self upbraids your Stay
> And misses her accustom'd May.
>
> See, all around demands your Aid,
> The Labours of Pomona fade;
> The Trees their daily Plaints renew,
> And dyeing Flowers exclaim on You.
> No more the Birds their ditties sing:
> With Storms alone our Forests ring.
>
> Come then, but haste thee, gentle May!
> No slumb'ring now, nor dull Delay.

---

[1] Modestly written 'Dear ——' by Gray in Pembroke ms.

Oh, come with that enchanting Face
That lively Look, that youthful Grace!
Come, & diffuse thy Spirit round,
Till Joy and Plenty do abound
That all Things may partake a Part,
And Heaven & Earth be glad at Heart.[1]

Gray replies (London, May 8, 1742): 'I rejoice to see you putting up your prayers to the May.' and then proceeds to some appreciative criticism.—With respect to his own translation of Propertius he says 'I never saw Broukhusius in my life....You see, by what I sent you that I converse with none but the dead; they are my old friends, and almost make me long to be with them'; an expression which anticipates Southey's 'My days among the dead are passed.' He sends West a quotation from Anacreon; and the lines

Sigilla in mento impressa Amoris digitulo
Vestigio demonstrant mollitudinem

challenging West to guess whence they come.

40. WEST TO GRAY.

Popes, May 11, 1742

Your fragment is in Aulus Gellius[2]; and both it and your Greek delicious. But why are you thus

---

[1] This poem, as printed by Mason, differs considerably from the text given above, which is copied from Gray's transcript in Pemb. mss.

[2] Mitford has a note to say that this is wrong, and that it is in Mori Marcellus, of course a simple misprint (caused probably by Mitford's minute writing) for Nonius Marcellus: Mitford adds that the passage is quoted by Marcellus s.v. 'Mollitudo'.

melancholy? I am so sorry for it, that you see I cannot forbear writing again the very first opportunity; though I have little to say, except to expostulate with you about it. I find you converse much with the dead, and I do not blame you for that; I converse with them too, though not indeed with the Greek. But I must condemn you for your longing to be with them. What, are there no joys among the living? I could almost cry out with Catullus[1] "Alphene immemor, atque unanimis false sodalibus!" But to turn an accusation thus upon another, is ungenerous; so I will take my leave of you for the present with a "Vale, et vive paullisper cum vivis."

*FROM CATULLUS.[2]

Lesbia, let us (while we may)
Live, and love the Time away,
And never mind what old Folks say.
Suns can set, & rise as bright:
No rise attends our little Light.
We set in everlasting Night.
  Count me a thousand kisses o'er,
Count me a thousand kisses more
Count me a thousand still, & then
We'll count them o'er & o'er again.
Why should I count? why should I know
How many kisses you bestow?
'Tis better let the Reckoning fall,
We'll kiss and never count at all,

---

[1] Cat. xxx. 1.   [2] Ib. v.

And thus we may avoid much Hate;
Since none can envy at our State;
When none shall know our total Bliss,
How often & how much we kiss.

Quæris quot mihi basiationes?[1] &c.

You ask how often you must kiss
To make me up my Sum of Bliss,
As many heaps of Lybian sand,
As lie upon Cyrene's Strand,
From Ammon's Shrine the whole Extent
On to old Battus' Monument;
Or as many Stars as spy
From their Watch-Tower in the Sky
The lawless Thefts of Soft Delight
That pass beneath the Silent Night:
So many Kisses you must kiss
To make me up my Sum of Bliss.
And when the Sum so great is grown,
That ne'er its number can be known:
The curious then their Tale will cease,
And Envy's tongue repose in Peace.

Fav: Wrote, May 11, 1742.
He died, the first of June following.[2]

Gray's last extant letter to West bears the date
London, May 27, 1742. West has taken him too seriously.
'Mine is a white Melancholy, or rather Leucocholy for the
most part...a good easy sort of state.'...'The May seems
to have come since your invitation' (let. 39) 'and I propose
to bask in her beams.' He reminds him of a contemporary
at Eton who is now a husband and father, and of states-
men whom they remember as 'dirty boys playing at

[1] Cat. VII.
[2] [Gray's note in Pembroke Common-place Books.]

cricket'; sends him a Greek inscription for a wood, and
with a long explanation) the Latin poem 'Sophonisba
Massinissae.' It is one of the brightest of Gray's letters,
with no shadow on it of the impending calamity. It was
the last of his that West ever saw, the next was from
Stoke with the ode on Spring; thus the first of Gray's
and the last of West's original efforts in English verse
were on the same theme. In the Pembroke Common
Place Book, Gray calls his poem ' Noon-tide, an ode'; to it
he has appended the note "at Stoke, the beginning of
June 1742 sent to Fav: not knowing he was then Dead."

41. *ASHTON TO WEST.

My dearest West,

The melancholy acct of your Health, is an
inexpressible concern to me, & I shall wait with an
impatient expectation of yr Recovery & rejoice sincerely in every little accession to your Strength.
But keep up your Spirits whatever you do. You
have Youth and the Season of the year on yr side.
I pray God to supply you with Strength, and bless
you with a perfect Vigour of body & Mind. Mr
Walpole sympathizes with you. As soon as you can
use your Hand let us hear from you. Nobody can
wish you better than we do.

                    Yrs
                         very sincerely
                              THOS. ASHTON.

Downing Street
    June 3. 1742.

When this was written West had already been dead two days. Gray's letter, written on the impulse of this sudden grief, and the verses by Ashton to which he there refers, may fitly close this strange and rather sad little history.

42. * GRAY TO ASHTON.

My dear Ashton,

This melancholy day is the first that I have had any notice of my Loss in poor West, and that only by so unexpected a Means as some verses published in a Newspaper (they are fine & true & I believe may be your own.) I had indeed some reason to suspect it some days since from recieving a letter of my own to him sent back unopen'd. The stupid People had put it no Cover, nor thought it worth while to write one Line to inform me of the reason, tho' by knowing how to direct, they must imagine I was his friend. I am a fool indeed to be surprizd at meeting with Brutishness or want of Thought among Mankind; what I would desire is, that you would have the goodness to tell me, what you know of his death, more particularly as soon as you have any Leisure;—my own Sorrow does not make me insensible to your new Happiness[1], which I heartily

---

[1] What this was, I do not know for certain, but it probably has to do with some piece of preferment, consequent on Ashton's ordination. It is stated in *Alumni Etonenses* that he was presented to the living of Aldingham in Lancashire,

congratulate you upon, as the means of Quiet, and Independence, & the Power of expressing yr benevolence to those you love. neither my Misfortune, nor my joy shall detain you longer at a time, when doubtless you are a good deal employd; only believe me sincerely yours

T. GRAY.

P.S. Pray do not forget my impatience, especially if you do not happen to be in London. I have no one to enquire of but yourself. 'tis now three weeks, that I have been in the Country, but shall return to Town in 2 days.

June 17 ——— Stoke, 1742.

> While surfeited with Life each hoary knave
> Grows here immortal, & eludes the Grave:
> Thy virtues prematurely met their Fate,
> Cramp'd in the Limits of too short a Date.
> Thy Mind not exercised so oft in vain
> In Health was gentle, & composed in Pain:
> Successive Tryal still refined thy Soul,
> And plastic Patience perfected the Whole.
> A friendly Aspect not inform'd by Art,
> An Eye that look'd the Meaning of thy Heart,
> A Tongue with simple Truth & Freedom fraught,
> The Faithful Index of thy honest Thought.

which he resigned in 1749; but the date of this presentation is not given. The 'happiness' was probably nothing matrimonial; an engagement, later, which promised him £12,000, was, according to Gray, broken off in 1746 (Works ed. Gosse, ii. 144), and he married Miss Amyand, on the 10th of December, 1760.

Thy pen disdain'd to seek the servile Ways
of partial Censure and more partial Praise.
Thro' every Tongue it flow'd in nervous Ease
With Sense to polish, & with Wit to please,
No lurking Venom from thy Pencil fell;
Thine was the kindest Satyr, liveing well:
The Vain, the Loose, the Base, might blush to see
In what Thou wert, what they themselves should be.
Let me not charge on Providence a Crime,
Who snatch'd thee blooming to a better clime
To raise those Virtues to a higher Sphere
Virtues which only could have starved thee here.

ASHTON [1].

[From Gray's MS. at Pembroke.]

[1] Mitford, Life of Gray, Aldine ed. vol. 1 p. xvi has the note "There is in the European Magazine for Jan. 1788 p. 15 a poem said to be written by West, called 'Damon to Philomel', and a copy of Verses on his death, supposed to be written by his uncle Judge Burnet." On turning out this reference, I find that the poem "Damon to Philomel" is by Mr West "who died Lord Chancellor of Ireland, Dec. 3, 1726"; i.e. by West's father, and the verses on the death of the younger West are no other than those above given, known to be by Ashton.

SECTION III.

GRAY TO JOHN CHUTE.

[LETTERS PUBLISHED FOR THE FIRST TIME IN
MR CHUTE'S HISTORY OF THE VYNE.]

SECTION III.

GRAY TO JOHN CHUTE.

THE following account of John Chute is compiled from Mr Chaloner Chute's *History of the Vyne*. He was born Dec. 30, 1701, and was thus nearly 15 years older than Gray. He was educated at Eton, when Dr Godolphin was Provost. From the death of his father (Edward Chute) in 1722, until that of his elder brother Anthony in 1754, he lived principally abroad, spending much of his time in Florence at Casa Ambrosio, the house of Horace Mann, the British Resident. It was here that he made the acquaintance of Gray and Walpole in 1740.

When Gray parted company with Walpole at Reggio, in the spring of 1741, he consoled himself with the companionship of John Chute and his young relative, Francis Thistlethwayte, of Southwick Park, Hampshire, who had recently taken the name of Whithed under his uncle's will. These three spent the festival of Ascensiontide 1741, in Venice together, after which Gray returned to England.

John Chute, who never married, died May 26, 1776, at the Vyne, and was buried in the Parish Church of Sherborne St John. (For an account of his correspondence with Walpole, see Mr Chute's *Hist. of the Vyne*, chap. v.) He built the Tomb Chamber adjacent to the Chapel of the Vyne and placed in it the beautiful recumbent figure of his ancestor Chaloner Chute (Speaker of the House of Commons under Richard Cromwell)—one of the best works of the sculptor Thomas Banks. He was a man of taste

and culture,—there is a quiet and graceful pleasantry in
his recorded *bons mots*. See further, Walpole, *Short
Notes*, &c., Letters I. p. lxvii (ed. Cunningham).

The following was obviously written just after Gray's
return from the Continent.

1. TO MR CHUTE.

[Sep. 7, 1741.]

My dear S^r

I complain no more. You have not forgot me.
Mrs Dick, to whom I resorted for a Dish of Coffee,
instead—thereof produced unto me from her Breast
your kind Letter, big with another no less kind from
our poor mangled Friend[1] to whom I now address
myself (you do'nt take it ill) & let him know, that as
soon as I got hither, I took wing for the Strand to
see a certain Acquaintance of his (for I then knew
not whether he were dead, or alive) & get some News
of him. I was so struck with the great resemblance
between them, that it made me cry out . he is a true
Eagle, but a little tamer, & a little fatter than the
Eagle Resident: I told him so, but he did not seem
to think it so great a Compliment as I did. his Wife
had miscarried but was quite well again ; his house
half pulled down, but riseing again more magnificent

---

[1] Gray soon after his arrival visited Galfridus, twin brother
of Horace Mann, in London. Mann was at this time much
tried by illness, which he bore most patiently. (Mr Chute,
Hist. of the Vyne, p. 86.)

from it's Ruins. he received me, as became a Bird
of his Race, & suffer'd himself to be caressed without giveing me one Peck, or Scratch. the only bad
thing I know of him, is, that he wears a Frock, &
a Bobb-Wigg. may I charge you, my dear Mr Chute
(I give you your great Name for want of a little tiny
one) with my Compliments to Dr Cocchi[1], Benevoli
(tho I hate him) and their Patient. particularly to
this last for recovering so soon, & so much to my
Satisfaction. I think one may call him dear Creature,
& be fond in Security under the Sanction of your
Cover. I carried his Mus^m Flor^m to Commissioner
Haddock, who is Liddel's uncle. that Gentleman had
left Paris, haveing been elected for some place in
this Parliament, & (tho' it is like to be controverted)
took the opportunity to return to England for a time,
but is now gone, I think to Spaw. Adieu! M^r M:

Nunc ad te totum me converto, suavissime Chuti!
whom I wrote to from Dover. if this be London, Lord
send me to Constantinople. either I, or it are extremely odd. the Boys laugh at the depth of my
Ruffles, the immensity of my Bagg, & and the length
of my Sword. I am as an Alien in my native land,
yea! I am as an owl among the small birds. it rains,

---

[1] Mann's Physician. Also an Author. Described in a
letter from the Earl of Cork to Mr Duncombe, Nov. 29, 1754,
as 'a man of most extensive learning; understands, reads and
speaks all the European languages.' [Wright.]

G.   12

everybody is discontented, and so am I. you can't
imagine how mortifieing it is to fall into the hands of
an English Barber. Lord! how you or Polleri would
storm in such a Case. do'nt think of comeing hither
without Lavaur, or something equivalent to him (not
an elephant)[1]. the Natives are alive, & flourishing.
the fashion is a grey frock with round Sleeves, Bob-
Wig, or a Spencer, plain Hat with enormous Brims, &
shallow Crown, cock'd as bluff, as possible, Muslin-
Neckcloth twisted round, rumpled, and tuck'd into
the breast ; all this with a certain Sā-faring Air, as
if they were just come back from Cartagena[2]. if my
pockets had any thing in them, I should be afraid of
every body I met. look in their face, they knock
you down ; speak to them, they bite off your Nose. I
am no longer ashamed in publick, but extremely
afraid. if ever they catch me among'em, I give them
leave to eat me. so much for Dress, as to Politicks,
every body is extremely angry with all that has been,

[1] Vide the anecdotes of Lord William Poulet (xxxv. of
'Walpoliana' vol. 1, p. 17). 'A gentleman writing to desire
a fine horse he had, offered him any *equivalent*. Lord William
replied that the horse was at his service, but he did not know
what to do with an *elephant*.'

[2] i.e. from the disastrous expedition to that place under
Vernon and Wentworth. The assault of Cartagena was aban-
doned on the 24th of April, 1741. The best account of this
sad affair is to be found in Smollett's *Roderick Random*.
Smollett was surgeon's mate on board one of Admiral Vernon's
ships.

or shall be done : even a Victory at this time would
be look'd upon as a wicked attempt to please the
Nation. the Theatres open not till to morrow, so
you will excuse my giveing no account of them to-
night. now I have been at home, & seen how things
go there, would I were with you again, that the
Remainder of my Dream might at least be agreeable.
as it is, my prospect can not well be more unpleasing;
but why do I trouble your Goodnature with such
considerations? be assured, that when I am happy (if
that can ever be) your Esteem will greatly add to
that happiness, & when most the contrary, will always
alleviate, what I suffer. many, many thanks for
your kindness ; for your travels, for your News, for
all the trouble I have given, & must give you. omit
nothing, when you write, for things that were quite
indifferent to me at Florence, at this distance become interesting. humble Service to Polleri; obliged
for his harmonious Salutation, I hope to see some
Scratches with his black Claw in your next. Adieu!
I am most sincerely, and ever Your's

TG:

London—Sept: 7: O: S:

P.S. Nobody is come from Paris yet.

A Mons?

Monsieur Chute, Gentilhomme Anglois chez
Mons? Ubaldini nel Corso de' Tintori à

Florence.

12—2

The foregoing is the earliest of Gray's letters to Chute; and for the convenience of those who would read this correspondence in its proper sequence, I will here give the dates of those letters which are already published in Mr Gosse's edition of Gray's Works, as they are determined by internal evidence, or by comparison with the letters of Walpole about the same time:

let. LIV	. .	May 24, 1742.
let. LII	. .	July, 1742.
let. LV	. .	Oct. 25, 1743.
let. LXXV	.	Oct. 1746 (early in the month).
let. LXXVI	.	Oct. 12, Sunday, 1746.

It is scarcely necessary to explain the steps by which this arrangement is arrived at; for if the letters are taken in this order, it will justify itself. The two letters of October 1746 are addressed to Chute upon his return with Mr Whithed to England; what follows (probably in the same, or early in the next month) expresses the same impatience on Gray's part to embrace his friends. To what has been said of Mr Whithed already we may add the following from Gray's first letter of Oct. '46, with Mr Chaloner Chute's note thereon.

'I readily set Mr Whithed free from all imputation; he is a fine young personage in a coat all over spangles, just come over from the tour of Europe to take possession and be married, and consequently ca'nt be supposed to think of anything or remember any body.'

['A portrait of Francis Whithed at the Vyne by Rosalba shows him much as this letter describes him, "a fine young personage in a coat all over spangles." The picture is matched by a portrait, also by Rosalba, of Margaret, daughter and heiress of John Nichol, of Southgate, Middlesex, the lady here alluded to, to whom he was engaged to be married. But

Whithed died at the Vyne in March 1751, and Margaret
Nichol eventually married James Brydges, Marquis of Carnarvon, afterwards 3rd Duke of Chandos.']

2. TO MR CHUTE.

Cambridge, Sunday [October? 1746].

Lustrissimo

It is doubtless highly reasonable that
two young foreigners come into so distant a country
to acquaint themselves with strange things, should
have some time allowed them to take a view of the
King (God bless him) and the ministry & the
theatres, and Westminster Abbey and the Lyons and
such other curiosities of the capital city. You civilly
call them dissipations, but to me they appear em-
ployments of a very serious nature, as they enlarge
the mind, give a just insight into the nature & genius
of a people, keep the Spirits in an agreeable agitation, and (like the true artificial spirit of lavender)
amazingly fortify and corroborate the whole nervous
system : but as all things sooner or later must pass
away, and there is a certain period when by the rules
of proportion one is to grow weary of everything, I
may hope at length a season will arrive when you will
be tired of forgetting me. 'Tis true you have a long
journey to make first, a vast series of sights to pass
through—let me see, you are at Lady Brown's

already; I have set a time when I may say 'Oh he is
now got to the waxwork in Fleet Street; there is
nothing more but Cupids Paradise and the Her-
maphrodite from Guinea & the original Basilisk
dragon & the buffalo from Babylon & the new
Chimpanzee & then I. have a care, you had best,
that I come in my Turn; you know in whose Hands
I have deposited my little Interests. I shall infallibly
appeal to my *best invisible* Friend in the country.

I am glad Castalio has justified himself & me to
You. he seem'd to me more made for Tenderness
than Horrour & (I have courage again to insist upon
it) might make a better Player than any now on the
Stage. I have not alone received (thank you) but
almost got thro' Louis Onze[1]. 'tis very well, me-

---

[1] The *Histoire de Louis Onze* of Duclos (Charles Duclos
Pinot, as M. Auger says we should spell his full name) had
been censured by an *arrêt du conseil*, of the 28th of March
1745 'comme contenant plusieurs endroits contraires, non
seulement aux droits de la couronne sur différentes provinces
du royaume, mais au respect avec lequel on doit parler de ce
qui regarde la religion ou les règles des mœurs, et la conduite
des principaux membres de l'église.' This decree prohibited
the reprinting of the work until the offensive passages had
been removed. Duclos' editor M. Auger (1820) affirms that the
order was disobeyed. Nevertheless it is perhaps significant
that an edition of the work in the British Museum, which
bears date 1745, 6, is printed at the Hague. However this
may be, in 1750 Duclos, on Voltaire's going to Prussia,
succeeded him as historiographer of France, on the strength of
having written the work thus censured five years before.

thinks, but nothing particular. what occasioned his
expurgation at Paris, I imagine, were certain Strokes
in Defence of the Gallican Church & its Liberties—a
little contempt cast upon the Popes, and something
here & there on the Conduct of great Princes. there
are a few Instances of Malice against our Nation,
that are very foolish.

My Companion, whom you salute is (much to
my sorrow) only so now and then. He lives 20 miles
off at Nurse, and is not so meagre as when you first
knew him, but of a reasonable Plumposity. He shall
not fail being here to do the Honours, when you
make your publick Entry. Heigh ho! when will that
be, chi sa? but mi lusinga il dolce sogno! I love
Mr Whithed and wish him all Happiness. Farewell,
my dear Sir

            I am, ever yours,

                        T. G.

Commend me kindly to Mr Walpole.

'Soon after writing these letters Gray joined his friends
in London, and in a letter to Wharton of Dec. 11, 1746
says, "I have been in town flaunting about at public
places with my two Italianized friends."' [Mr Chaloner
Chute, *Hist. of the Vyne*, p. 104.]

3. TO MR CHUTE.

[1762]

My Dear S^r

I was yesterday told, that Turner (the Professor
of Modern History here) was dead in London. if it be
true; I conclude it is now too late to begin asking
for it: but we had (if you remember) some conversation on that Head at Twickenham; & as you have
probably found some Opportunity to mention it to
M^r W: since, I would gladly know his Thoughts
about it. What he can do, he only can tell us: what
he will do, if he can, is with me no Question. if he
could find a proper channel; I certainly might ask it
with as much, or more Propriety, than any one in
this Place. if any thing more were done, it should
be as private as possible; for if the People, who have
any Sway here, could prevent it, I think they would
most zealously. I am not sorry for writing you a
little interested Letter: perhaps it is a Stratagem;
the only one I had left, to provoke an Answer from
you, & revive our—Correspondence, shall I call it?
there are many particulars relating to you, that have
long interested me more than twenty Matters of this
Sort, but you have had no Regard for my Curiosity;
& yet it is something, that deserves a better Name!

I don't so much as know your Direction, or that
of Mr Whithed[1].   Adieu! I am ever

Yours
T Gray.

To
    John Chute Esq.

The above letter concerns Gray's *unsuccessful* applica-
tion for the Professorship, which he obtained only in 1768.
The Professor appointed in 1762 was Mr Brockett of
Trinity.   See Mr Gosse's Life of Gray, pp. 157, 158 and
infr. Sect. IV. γ. n.   Also Gray to Wharton, Dec. 4, 1762
(Works ed. Gosse, III. p. 136), in a note to which Mason
states that Gray's name was suggested to Lord Bute by
Sir Henry Erskine.

[1] It is noteworthy, as indicating how completely this correspondence had been dropped, that Gray has no suspicion
that Whithed died more than eleven years ere this date.

SECTION IV.

GRAY TO PERCY AND BROCKETT.

.

SECTION IV.

GRAY TO PERCY AND BROCKETT.

THESE letters, &c. are in the Percy MSS. in the British Museum [Add. MSS. 32,329]. The note to Brockett is followed by a tantalizing fragment (? in the handwriting of Percy) "Short minutes of my Conversation with Mr Gray, the Poet.

[Though dated at the time, they were not written till a month after, when it was possible for some small particulars to have escaped my memory, and some trifling mistakes to have occurred to me.]"

And then, on the other side of the leaf is nothing but the well-known story of the reason 'assigned me by my Cambridge friends' for Gray's leaving Peterhouse—even this tale breaking off in the middle.

In Gray's observations on the Pseudo-Rhythmus [Works ed. Gosse, vol. I. p. 371], he mentions having read "'Death and Life in two fitts' and *Scottish Field* in a MS. Collection belonging to the Rev. Mr Thomas Piercy in 1761."

Perhaps to this year then belongs the note to Percy (a). That to Brockett is earlier than (a), and collected, it may be, by Percy on his visit to Cambridge, as a *relique*.

Brockett, it is to be noted, is not here Professor; he did not become so until 1762.

The first edition of Percy's *Reliques* was published in 1765.

(α) Mr Gray presents his compliments to Mr Piercy & is very sorry for the mistake he has made. concluded that he was lodged at Maudlin, & therefore sent the book this morning to Mr Blakeway's[1] Chambers, where he imagined Mr Piercy to be.

The Messenger is a little in liquor, therefore have a care of sending him to fetch it.   the letter* was in the book, wch Mr Gray thought was deliver'd to M^r P: own hands

　　* viz. Mr Evan Evan's Letter.

(β)　(On a separate piece of paper)

THE ABBOT OF _MEUX_.

Look in a Map of the East-riding of Yorkshire, & you will see, that at a few miles distance—north of _Lekenfield_ lies _Watton_ ; to the South lies _Bererley_ (the usual Burying-Place of the Percies); & to the S. East the Abbey of Meaux, of which there are still some remains visible; the name is pronounced _Meuss_. (Mr Mason dictates this note)

Mr Percy's note therefore is wrong.

(γ)　Mr Gray sends his compliments to Mr Brocket[2].　Shall be extremely obliged to him, if

[1] "To Mr Blakeway, late fellow of Magdalen College, the Editor owes all the assistance received from the Pepysian library."　Preface to _Reliques of Ancient English Poetry_, 1765.

[2] Of Trinity.　Tutor to Sir James Lowther ; Professor of History at Cambridge, 1762 ; supported the Earl of Sandwich

he would make inquiry (when he has occasion to
go into Trin: Library) after the following old
English Books

> Paradise of dainty devices 1578 4to & 1585
>
> England's Helicon   4to
>
> W. Webbe's Discourse of Eng: Poetrie 1585 4to
>
> Fr: Mere's Wit's Commonwealth : 1598 Lond:
> & 1634[1]
>
> Sam: Daniel's Musa, or Defence of Rhyme 1611[1]
> 8vo
>
> Stephen Hawes' Pastime of Pleasure 1555 4to
>
> Gawen Douglas' Palace of Honour 1533 London
> 1579 Edinb:
>
> Earl of Surrey's Ecclesiastes 1567 4to
>
> ——— —— 2^d & 4th Books of the Æneid
> 1557 12mo
>
> Gascoign's Works, 2 v: 4to 1577 & 1587.

If they should not be in the Library, Mr Gray
believes that Professor Torriano[2] could favour him
with a sight of some of them for a few days. he will
take all imaginable care of them.

in his candidature for the High Stewardship of Cambridge,
1764. 'On Sunday Brocket died of a fall from his horse,
drunk, I believe, as some say returning from Hinchinbroke'
[Lord Sandwich's place in Huntingdonshire]. Gray to Mason,
Aug. 1, 1768.

[1] The dates here are uncertain, being blotted or stained.

[2] C. Torriano was Regius Professor of Hebrew from 1753
to 1757.

SECTION V.

MISS SPEED TO GRAY.

G.   13

SECTION V.

MISS SPEED TO GRAY.

ALMOST all that we know of Miss Speed is to be found in the life and letters of Gray. The incident which led to the Long Story is well told by Mr Gosse in his Life of Gray, p. 100. In Cole's MS. note to Mason's Edition, p. 211 (Mitford, Works of Gray, Vol. I. Appendix D, p. cvii.) we find 'Such was the friendship between the late Lord Viscount Cobham & Colonel Speed, Miss Speed's father, that upon his decease, he esteemed her as his own child; brought her up in his family, and treated her with a paternal care and tenderness.' Gray relates with manifest pleasure that she used to say φωνᾶντα συνετοῖσι in so many words to those who could not understand his Odes. Let us add these notices[1] from Gray:

July 1760 (to Wharton): "I remain...still in town, though for these three weeks I have been going into Oxfordshire with Madam Speed; but her affairs, as she says, or her vagaries, as I say, have obliged her to alter her mind ten time's within that space: no wonder, for

[1] The earliest notice of her is by Pope to Martha Blount. Writing from Stowe the seat of Lord Cobham, July 4, 1739 he says "Lady Cobham and Mrs Speed who (except two days) have been the sole inhabitants, wish you were here." She was then 16 years old.

13—2

she has got at least £30,000 with a house in town, plate, jewels, china and old japan infinite [left her by Lady Cobham] so that indeed it would be ridiculous for her to know her own mind. I who know mine, do intend to go to Cambridge," &c.

Oct. 21, 1760 (to the same): "You astonish me in wondering, that my Lady C left me nothing. For my part, I wondered to find she had given me £20 for a ring; as much as she gave to several of her own nieces. The world said, before her death, that Mrs Speed and I had shut ourselves up with her in order to make her will, and that afterwards we were to be married."

Jan. 1761 (to the same) : "My old friend Miss Speed has done what the world calls a very foolish thing. She has married the Baron de la Peyriere, son to the Sardinian minister, the Comte de Viry. He is about 28 years old (ten years younger than herself) but looks nearer 40... The Castle of Viry is in Savoy a few miles from Geneva, commanding a fine view of the Lake .. Her religion she need not change, but she must never expect to be well received at that court till she does; and I do not think she will make quite a *Julie* in the country."

March 5, 1766 (to the same) : "Mad. de la Perrière is come over from the Hague to be Ministress at London... She is a prodigious fine lady, and a Catholick (though she did not expressly own it to me) not fatter than she was: she had a cage of foreign birds and a piping bullfinch at her elbow, two little dogs on a cushion in her lap, a cockatoo on her shoulder, and a strong suspicion of rouge on her cheeks. They were all exceeding glad to see me, & I them."

MISS SPEED TO GRAY.[1]

Sir,

I am as much at a loss to bestow the Commendation due to your performance as any of our modern Poets would be to imitate them; Everybody that has seen it, is charm'd and Lady Cobham[2] was the first, tho' not the last that regretted the loss of the 400 stanzas[3]; all that I can say is, that your obliging inclination[4] in sending it has fully answerd; as it not only gave us amusement the rest of the Evening, but always will, on reading it over. Lady Cobham and the rest of the Company hope to have your's tomorrow at dinner.

I am your oblig'd & obedient
HENRIETTA JANE SPEED.
Sunday.

The date of the above letter is probably August, 1750, in which month the *Long Story* was written.

[1] Mitford [Add. mss. 32,561 p. 208].

[2] Ann, widow of Field-Marshal Richard Temple, Viscount Cobham, who died in 1749, daughter of Edmund Halsey Esq. of Southwark : she lived at the *Old House* at Stoke Park. [Mitford.] Halsey was the predecessor of Thrale's father in the brewery. [Boswell's *Johnson*, B. Hill's ed. vol. i. p. 491 n.]

[3] 'Here 500 stanzas are missing.' *Long Story*. I think I have transcribed Mitford accurately.

[4] She probably means 'intention'.

MISS SPEED TO GRAY.

25 Aug 59.

My dear Sir,

I wonder whether you think me capable of all the gratitude I really feel for the late marks you have given me of your friendship. I will venture to say, if you knew my Heart you would be content with it. but knowing my exterior so well as you do, you can easily conceive me vain of the Partiality you shew me; in return for putting me in good humour with myself, I will give you pleasure by assuring you Lady Cobham is surprizingly well & most extremely obliged to you for the anxiety you expressed on her acct.—We now take the air every day, and are returnd to our old way of living, & hope we shall go on in the same way many years. We are both scandalizd at your being in Town¹ at this time of the year, not because (as you may think) that it is unfashionable, but because we think it very unwholsome from the heat of the Season. Now I know you are insensible to heat or cold, not but that your body suffers by either extreme, but you have not attention enough to yourself to seek a remedy. We beg now to point out one against the excessive heat of London, by desiring you wou'd come down to Stoke, where you will find everything cool but the reception, we shall

¹ *Sic* apparently in Mitford.

give you. There is always a Bed aired for you, &
one for your Serv[t] indeed I can make use of the
strongest argument to tempt you, which is that at
this time it will be a deed of Charity as we are absolutely alone. M[rs] Clavering and M[r] Crane the Apothecary left us yesterday. I don't know whether you
are acquainted with the latter, but I have such a
partiality from his attendance on Lady Cobham that
I almost wish for a slight fit of illness, that I may
have something to do with him—if you are at present
an invalide, let that prompt you to come, for from
the *affected Creature* you knew me, I am nothing
now but a comfortable nurse.

You sent me dreadful news in regard to the K. of
P.[1] I now begin to fear for him, it was vastly good
of you to give us a detail of what passes in the
World, for few people will be at that trouble, indeed
a Certain Countess with whom I correspond does not
spare Pains, but such news as she sends is not always
to be depended on.—I have kept her last letter for
your entertainment. I am an desespoire[2] about my
friend L. G. S.[3] and am sorry from difft. hands to

[1] Book xix. of Carlyle's *Frederick the Great* 1759—1760,
bears the significant heading 'Like to be overwhelmed.' The
disastrous battle of Kunersdorf had been fought on the 12th of
August.

[2] *sic.*

[3] Lord George Sackville, who being in command of the
cavalry at the battle of Minden (Aug. 1, 1759) declined to

hear that his narrative is about as much in his favour, as you seem to think his letter to Col: Fitzroy.—I hope to talk all these matters over with you, soon, therefore shall add no more at present, but that I am with great Truth

Dear Mr Greys'

faithfull Servt

HENRIETTA JANE SPEED.

Never make excuses about franks, for I shall never grudge the expense you put me to by your letters.

---

charge, and thus lost the opportunity of entirely routing the enemy.   He was tried by court-martial in the following year, and cashiered.   See Gray's letter to Brown (vol. III. let. iii. ed. Gosse).   In letter iv. *ib.* he gives him a fuller account of the battle ; while in letter v. Sept. 28 to Wharton he says ' The night we rejoiced for Boscawen [his victory in the Mediterranean over the French fleet] in the midst of squibs and bonfires arrived Lord G. Sackville.   He sees company ; and to-day has put out a short address to the Public, saying, he expects a Court-Martial (for no one abroad had authority to try him) and desires people to suspend their judgement. I fear it is a rueful case.'   He concludes ' I believe I shall go on Monday to Stoke for a time, where Lady Cobham has been dying,'—indicating a sudden change for the worse since Miss Speed's letter *supra.* (Gray's next letter is from Stoke Oct. 6.)

[1] *sic.*

SECTION VI.

GRAY'S NOTES OF TRAVEL.
FRANCE, ITALY, SCOTLAND.

(HITHERTO UNPUBLISHED.)

FROM THE COLLECTION OF MR JOHN MORRIS.

SECTION VI.

GRAY'S NOTES OF TRAVEL.

Mr Gosse (Gray's Works, vol. IV. p. 340) describes the following as 'rather dry and impersonal notes of the journey in France in 1739,' up to the point where the journal printed in vol. I. pp. 235--246) of his edition of Gray begins. It will be found, however, that they run considerably beyond that point. For instance, both sets of notes include Dijon, Chalons sur Saône, Tournus, Lyons, Geneva. I believe that Gray kept two records, meant to supplement each other. The general character, however, of the notes here given, as compared with the more or less parallel notes which Mr Gosse has printed, bears out his description of them. They are like an embryo catalogue or topographical history. It is significant that here he gives an account of Chalons-sur-Saône, through which, in the other journal he says he 'went without stopping.'

In the Italian notes, there is not the same parallelism. Those here given, headed ' Florence, April 1740[1],' are probably the earliest; next come those called by Mitford ' Criticisms on Architecture and Poetry during a tour in

---

[1] Mr Gosse [Gray's Works, II. p. 53] says that Gray's short remarks on the pictures which he saw at Florence and other places were published in 1843 by Mitford. I have not found any but the *Roman* notes, in the Aldine edition, vol. IV. 1836 ; [vol. V. bears date 1843].

Italy,' which will be found, however, on examination to belong entirely to Rome; and lastly—by far the most interesting—those under the heading ' Road to Naples June 12.' Even in Italy, however, it is probable that Gray kept two sets of papers. It has seemed best not to attempt to annotate this part of the work, which, if done at all, should be done by some one well acquainted with art and architecture. Accordingly only one or two references or explanations are here added.

Cathedral of Amiens[1],—Shrine of S[t] Firmin, of massy Gold—rich painted windows.

Abbey, and Cathedral of S[t] Dennis—Monuments of the Kings of France—Lewis 12 Francis 1st, Henry 2[d], Catharine of Medicis, particularly fine; some good Bas-reliefs, rich mosaic windows—the Treasury—inestimable antique Vase of oriental Onyx with admirable Sculptures representing the mysteries of Bacchus—Crown of Charlemagne; Rubies, Emeralds & Sapphires of vast bigness—Coronation robes & other Regalia.

PARIS.

1. The Palais Royal, built by Card: Richelieu, inhabited at present by the Duke of Orleans—a

---

[1] In a letter to Dorothy Gray April 1, 1739 [II. p. 16, ed. Gosse], he says ' the Cathedral is just what that of Canterbury must have been before the Reformation.' He is speaking of course only of the subordinate decorations ; in a letter to his mother architectural distinctions would have been out of place.

noble collection of near 500 Pictures of great masters
—the St John Baptist of Raphael—Naked Venus,
wringing her hair, by Guido—the Leda and Danae of
Corregio—a whole room of the finest Paul Veronese—
the 7 Sacraments of Poussin—small copies in Bronze
of the Toro, Lyon & Horse, &c:—the new Gallery,
design'd by Mansart, & richly adorn'd with sculpture,
gilding and furniture of fine embroidery; painted by
Coypel with stories from th' Eneid—The Walks
belonging to the Palace.

2. *The Palace Luxembourg*, built by Mary of
Medicis; at present the residence of the 2^d Queen
Dowager of Spain—the Gallery so well known, of
Rubens.

3. The Invalides—the Church, beautiful disposition of the Chapels, & Dome; Altar imitated from
St Peter's at Rome.

4. *The Val de Grace*—fine Chappel; beautiful
Statues of the Virgin & Joseph by Anguier.

5. The Hotel de Toulouse—the grand Gallery,
rich gilding, embroidery, and Glasses, on each side 5
Capital pictures—the Rape of Helen, by Guido, the
Sabine Wives separating the two armies by Guercino,
a Divorce, by P^{tro} di Cortona.—

6. *Cathedral of Notre Dame*—Statues of the
Virgin with the dead Christ, & those of Louis the
13th & 14th, by the 2 Coutoux, & Coysevox.

7. Church of the Carmelites—a fine Annuncia-

tion, of Guido—a Magdalen, of Le Brun. Statue of
Card! Berulle, by Sarazin.

8.   The English Benedictins.   Body of K. James
2ᵈ, deposed here.

9.   Abbey of *Sᵗ Genevieve*—fine Library—ancient
Church, Monument of Des Cartes.

10.   Abbey of *Sᵗ Germain de Prés.*—Library,
collection of antiquities—the Church sepulchres of
the Kings of yᵉ first race—great Altar, a handsome
piece of architecture. Monument of Casimir, K: of
Poland.

11.   Church of the Celestines—fine tomb of the
Const: Monmorency—Monument over yᵉ Heart of
Harry 2ᵈ—& of Charles 9ᵗʰ—another to the memory
of Francis 2ᵈ—Tomb of the D: of Orleans & his wife
—that of the D: of Longueville.

12.   Church of Sᵗ Eustache.   Tomb of Monsʳ
Colbert by Coysevox.

13.   Church of *Sᵗ Sulpice*, a vast, new building.
handsome enough.

14.   *The Sorbonne*, the admirable tomb of Card:
Richelieu, by Girardon.   3 figures.

15.   The College de quatre Nations—monument
& fine statue of C: Mazarin.

16.   The Grand Jesuits—Monument of Silver gilt
over the heart of Lewis 13:—Chapel & monument of
H: Prince of Condé with fine Bas-reliefs & Statues by
Sarrazin in Bronze.

17. Hotel de Mezieres, where the Cardinal Polignac resides—a collection of statues—4 figures representing the discovery of Achilles, the bodies and drapery Antique, arms & head modern. fine Sarcophagus with a Bacchanal in alto-relievo. Bust of Julius Cæsar young. several urns, some of Oriental Alabaster, Porphiry, Serpentine & Granate. Tables of Verde antico, and other precious marbles. Pictures. a St Sebastian's Head, very fine. an Endymion sleeping. an Adonis dead; by Guercino. a Woman & a child, Portraits; by Titian. a Virgin's Head, by Carlo Dolci View of St Peter's, by Paolo Pannini, &c:—

18. Hotel de Mylord Walgrave.—Susannah & the Elders, by Guido. Woman taken in Adultery by Luca Giordano. the Brazen Serpent, by Sebast: Bordone. fine Landscapes, of Claude Lorraine.

19. Hotel de Monsr Knight. death of Orpheus; & Bacchus with Ariadne, by Pietro di Cortona. Landscapes of Cl: Lorraine.

20. Hotel de Mr Hayes. David with the Head of Goliah, by Guido, exceeding fine. Lanscapes of Cl: Lorraine, very good.

21. *Place royale.* a handsome Square. fine equestrian Statue of Lewis 13, by Ricciarelli.

22. Place de Vendome. an Octagon of regular buildings. fine Statue of Lewis 14, on horseback by Girardon.

23. Place des Victoires. an oval, but small. huge gilt Statue of L: 14th with a Victory.

24. *The Chartreux.*—the Cloyster, with the life of St Bruno, by Le Sueur in 24 pictures, admirably fine ; figures about a foot high.—Cells of the religious, composed of a parlour, a bed-chamber, a library, a gallery, & a garden; very small, but excessively neat.

25. Hotel de Soubise—fine furniture, Tapestry, gilding, lustres of rock-Crystal, & embroider'd beds.

26. *Versailles.*

27. *Marli.*

28. Chantilly.

29. St Clou.

30. *St Germains.*

31. *Trianon.*

DIJON.

Founded by Aurelian, called Divio, usual residence of the Dukes of Burgundy : the Kings used to reside at Vienne, or Chalons. Hugues 3^d, D. of B: made it a City first, in 12th Century. bestowed upon a younger branch of the Ducal house, holding in fee of the Bishops of Langres. Robert, K: of France, haveing bought the Bishop's pretensions, bestows it on a younger Son of his own ; but the Dukes of B^{dy} find means to reunite to their other possessions, till at the death of Charles le Hardi Lewis 11th of France seizes upon it together with the whole Dutchy. Parliament held here. Monuments of the Dukes at the Carthusians.

CHALONS SUR SAONE.

Anciently Cabillonum, great causeway made by J. Cæsar between this & Bibracte (or Augustodunum) now Autun. Counts of Chalons independant of the D? of Burgundy. Kings of France passing thro' here are invested by the Bishop with the robes of a Canon, they bestow the robe on some Ecclesiastic, who from thence has a right to the next vacant stall in the Cathedral. Abelard died here in the monastery of St Marcel.

TOURNUS.

Trenurchium : an old & rich Abbey here, with two exceeding high spires, dedicated to St Philibert ; the Abbots were once sovereigns of the town. Margaret, Widow to Charles d'Anjou, K: of Sicily, built here a small palace, where she ended her days. it is now an Hospital.

MASCON.

Matisco.

DUTCHY OF BURGUNDY.

John, K: of France, seized upon it, & bestow'd it on Philip de Valois, his youngest Son, surnamed the Bold. this Philip married Margaret, Heiress of

G.   14

Flanders, & Widow of his Predecessour, Philip de Rouvré, who had died without Issue. Philip the Bold was regent of France during the Lunacy of Charles the 6ᵗʰ his nephew. Jean, Sans peur, succeeded Philip, his father. he had Lewis, D: of Orleans assassinated, & made himself Regent of France, for 12 years. he was murther'd at a conference with Charles 7ᵗʰ then but Dauphin, at the Bridge of Montereau in L'Isle de France. Philip le Bon, his Son, succeeded him, & enter'd into an alliance with England, after many years of War is reconciled to the K: of France. the Low-Countries are united in his Person, he founded the Order of the Golden-fleece.

Charles le Hardi succeeded him. he is defeated by the Swiss at Morat, & killed in Lorain at the battle of Nancy. Lewis 11ᵗʰ seizes upon Burgundy in prejudice to the rights of Mary, Daughter of D: Charles, and Wife to Maximilian, Son to the Emperour Frederick. Maximilian consents to a peace with Lewis, & gives his daughter Margaret to the Dauphin Charles with Burgundy, Artois, &c: for a Dowry.

LYONNOIS.

The way between Mâcon & Lyons runs thro' a fine Champain country, with Convents & Villages in view ; you pass thro' Villefranche, a small town, but the Capital of Beaujolois.

LYONS.

The distant survey from the streets exceeding narrow; the best point of view from the principal bridge over the Rhone, where once was a wooden one which broke down with an infinite number of people on it, as K: Philip Augustus & Richard 1st of England had just pass'd it in their way to the holy land.   this city was the Ancient Lugdunum, the first Roman colony was
in the time of Augustus
settled there by Munatius Plancus (whose monument is extant near Cajeta in Italy) it is situated in the Province of the Segusii.   Hannibal is supposed to have passed the Rhone hereabouts, & enterred (*sic*) Italy by the Country of the Insubri (the Milanese) by Chambery & the Vale of Aosta; here was then a small Island formed by the conflux of the Rhône & Saone, & a Canal, which is now filled up, & on which a part of the city is built, particularly the place des Terreaux. the Abbey of Aisnay stands, where was once the temple of Augustus; it was erected to his memory by 60 Nations of the Gauls.   Drusus is said to have consecrated it, the day his Son Claudius was born here.   the four pillars which support the mid Arch of the Abbey-Church, were made out of two, that stood at each Angle of the ancient altar; they appear of pure oriental Granite.   there are some bas-reliefs & inscriptions about the Abbey : it was consecrated in

14—2

the 12th century by Pope Paschal. the famous harangue of Claudius upon two brass plates is in the Hotel de Ville. it was made to introduce some great families of Gallia Lugdunensis into the Senate. in Nero's time, when the whole city was burnt, these tables were lost, but discover'd in the ruins of Mont St Sebastien in the year 1529. in the place de Ter- reaux, Cinq-Mars was executed in Card: Richelieu's Ministry. the Place de Bellecourt is magnificent. upon the bridge o'er the Rhone, the Emp: Gratian was murder'd by Andragatius, General to Maximus. the Castle de Pierre-Encise was once the Archbishop's palace, but is now a State-prison. on the side of a hill near St George's gate are still to be seen some remains of Agrippa's Causeway, it lies 12 foot deep & led from Lyons to Narbonne. the other 3 he made led, 1 to the Pyrenæans by Auvergne, the 2nd to the Rhine by Strasburg. the third to the Western Ocean near Mardyke. near the gate du Trion are the ruins of an Aqueduct built by M. Antony to carry water to the legions quarter'd on Mount Fourviere ; in this Mountain the Taurobolium was discover'd. some vestigia of the amphitheatre are visible at the Minims ; it was built by Claudius. the Jesuits have a cabinet of curiosities. at St Irenée are fragments of a Mosaic pavement ; at la Trinité abundance of Roman Epitaphs. a picture of St Thomas's unbelief by Salviati, at the Jacobins. the

Lyonnois belonged to the Constable, Charles of Bourbon, & on his defection was seized by Louisa of Savoy, Mother to Francis 1st who ceded it to the King, her son.

DAUPHINÉ.

VIENNE.

Vienna, Capital of the Allobroges; a Colony sent hither by the Senate in the year 693, another to Colonia Allobrogum (Geneva), and a third to Cularo (Grenoble, Gratianopolis). it was the Capital of the Burgundian Kings, and comeing to a younger branch of that house, they stiled themselves Counts Dauphins of the Viennois, Humbert, the last of them made it over to Charles, D: of Normandy, Son to King John of France on the well-known conditions. here is to be seen the old temple, or Praetorium.

GENEVA.

Anciently Geneva; Genoa in Italy is supposed by Livy to be a colony from this Geneva or Genua, or Gebennæ. it was the frontier town of the Allobroges towards Helvetia.

1. Gallos ab Aquitanis Garumna flumen, a Belgis Matrona & Sequana dividit.

Helvetii reliquos Gallos virtute praecedunt, quod fere quotidianis praeliis cum Germanis contendunt.

2. Helvetii continentur unà ex parte flumine Rheno latissimo atq altissimo, qui agrum Helvetium a

Germanis dividit: alterâ ex parte, monte Iura altissimo, quæ est inter Sequanos & Helvetios; tertiâ,
lacu Lemano, & flumine Rhodano, qui provinciam
nostram ab Helvetiis dividit.

3. Santonum fines non longé a Tolosatium finibus
absunt; quæ civitas est in provinciâ.

4. Ocelum, quod est citerioris provinciæ ex-
tremum.

5. Segusiani sunt extra provinciam trans Rhodanum primi.

6. Flumen est Arar, quod per fines Æduorum &
Sequanorum in Rhodanum influit incredibili lenitate,
ita ut oculis in utram partem fluit (*sic*) judicari non
possit.

7. Omnis civitas Helvetia in quatuor pagos
divisa est; Tigurinum[1], Verbigenum[1],

8. Bibracte, oppidum Æduorum longé maximum
ac copiosissimum.

9. Boios petentibus Æduis, quod egregiâ virtute
erant, ut in finibus suis collocarent[2], concessit;
quibus illi agros dederunt; quosq postea in parem
juris libertatisq conditionem,atq ipsi erant,receperunt.

10. Omnium rerum summa erat Helvetiorum
263,000, Tulingorum 36,000, Latobrigorum 14,000,

---

[1] Added by Gray to these words of Cæsar (De Bell. Gall.
I. 12). The *pagus Tigurinus* is mentioned 1. c; the *pagus*
Verbigenus I. 27. The other two Cæsar does not name.

[2] Gray writes 'collocassent'.

Ranracorum 22,000, Boiorum 32,000; ex his, qui arma ferre possent, ad 92,000. eorum. qui domum redierunt censu habito repertus est numerus 110,000.

11. Ager Sequanus, qui est optimus totius Galliæ.

1. Gallia propria, or the country of the Celtæ, was divided from the Belgæ by the R: Seine & Marne, from the Aquitani, by the Garonne. so that it contained of the modern France all Normandy W: of the Seine, Bretagne, the Orleanois, Poitou, Burgundy, Champagne, Dauphiné, Provence, & Languedoc with all the country contained between these ; & moreover Switzerland, the Franche-Comté, Alsace, & Lorraine, with most of Savoy. out of this, all comprehended between the Mediterranean on the South, the Alpes on the E:, a line drawn along the Rhone, under Auvergne as far as the Garonne about Toulouse, on the N, & that river & a part of the Pyrenees on the W: was the Roman Province of Gallia Ulterior.

2. Helvetii, the Swisses have still their ancient bounds; the Rhine divides 'em from Germany, Mount Jura from the Sequani, or Franche-Comté, & the Lake of Geneva, with the Rhône from Savoy &c: they still retain too their ancient valour.

3. Segusiani, supposed the inhabitants of La Foréz, & Beaujolois.

FLORENCE. April, 1740.

PALAZZO PITTI.

A vast Structure begun by a private Man, Messer
Luca Pitti. his Heirs finding themselves reduced by
the great Expence he had been at, & themselves
unable to finish it, sold it to Leonora of Toledo, the
Wife of Cosimo 1mo. it was begun on the designs of
the famous Ser Brunelleschi, who carried the building
as high as the 2^d Story of the Grand Front; afterwards Bart? Ammanati finish'd it on a Model of his
own. The Terreno has it's Windows placed at a great
distance from one another, the next order has 23
arched Windows in a manner close together with a
small & low Balustrade running alone before them of
neither Use nor Ornament. over this is a 3^d Story
smaller of only eleven Windows of the same fashion.
this whole front is charged all over with Rustick after
the Tuscan fashion in large Bozzi, & makes an appearance grand enough, opening upon a large Piazza
(tho' this Piazza is neither levell'd, nor paved. it has
one Gate, which brings you into a Cortile, square, &
surrounded on 3 Sides by a Loggia, over which run
the Apartments. this Portico is of the Tuscan order,
arched ; & both its Columns, & the face of its Arches
charged all over with Rustick in the Manner of th'
Hotel de Luxembourg at Paris. the 2^d Order is Ionic,
& its Pilasters have also a Rustick in square Bozzi,

but placed at some distance one from the other. the
highest Order is Corinthian, & this too has it's Bozzi
Round, like the lower one, but not close together.
the whole surmounted by a handsome & rich Intabla-
ture. the fourth side of the Cortile (which fronts
you, as you enter) rises no higher than the top of the
Loggia. in the midst of it is a kind of Grotta,
containing a large Bason of stagnated Water with
little leaden figures of Cupids, as it were swimming &
sporting in it. in a Nich opposite to you is a bad
Statue of Moses in Porphyry, & the Roof & Walls
adorned with Rock-work & paintings. in the Court
even with the front of this Grot are two large Niches
on each hand. in one a Soldier supporting the body
of a dead Youth, probably representing the same
Persons with that Statue near the old Bridge, but in
a manner much inferiour. in the other Hercules
lifting Antæus from the ground. both Antique, of
indifferent workmanship, & much damaged. over
this building, which joins the Ends of the Loggia ; &
even with the 2d Story, is a large fountain, & the
prospect lies open to the garden call'd Boboli. in the
Testate of the Portico are on one side a Statue of
Pluto naked with Cerberus by him; on the other a
Hercules Colossal in the attitude of the Farnese.
this is Antique & good; inscribed with the name of
Lysippus counterfeited. under it is the known Bas-
Relief of the Mule. You go up a Staircase by no

means answerable to the Greatness of the Palace, which brings you into the Sale des Gardes. on the left hand is the Apartment of the late Great-Prince Ferdinand. in the Salone are many Portraits of the house of Medici. a Square in the Cieling, but done in Oil—

Virtue presenting a Person to Jupiter &c—Luca Giordano

Some very large Battle-Pieces, much damaged—Borgognone

Nymphs surprized, & seized on by Satyrs, very bad indeed—Rubens.

Two very large Views of Bays with Gallys refitting. one is quite spoil'd by Damp; the other exquisitely fine, Sun-beams playing on the Water, an old Castle with Pine-trees, figures going into the Water, a Ship sailing at a distance & loseing itself in Air, & Sunshine. admirable! — — Salvator-Rosa.

In the other Rooms.

Christ standing on a kind of Pedestal. the Evangelists on each side, rather less than life. the Shades very black, & but disagreeable in the whole. — — Il Frate. — — — — —

A Madonna, with a figure by her like a Pallas, unfinish'd, his worst Drawing — Correggio.

Annunciation. there is a magnificent piece of Building with a View thro' into a Garden. it is a

sort of Loggia. on one side kneels the Virgin, the
Angel on the other, & two huge Columns between
them, so that it is impossible they should see each
other. — P: Veronese.

The Madonna sitting. on one hand St Peter
stands, one arm extended, a very noble figure, an air
of a head like Rafael, Profile. on the other St Sebastian, his hands tied behind him, & pierced with
arrows, naked, & finely painted. on the Ground sit
Mary Magdalen, & another Male-Saint in changeable
garments; they both squint extremely, as does the
principal figure who is a mere dowdy, & the Bambino
a Monster. St Bruno & other Saints standing by.
a peculiar Colouring like Andrea, but better. Large
— — — Il Rosso — — —

Madonna del Collo lungo. the fault which gives
name to the Picture immediately strikes the Eye.
She is sitting, & uncovers the Child who sleeps in her
Lap to several Angel-like figures, that crowd to see it.
there is a Groupe of 3 heads inexpressibly fine, one a
Youth's head in Profile (his whole figure appears, &
he bears a Vase in his hand) another a face as of a
Girl (seen full) with blew eyes & light hair dress'd as
fine as any antique statue, lovely beyond imagination.
the other is of a boy, who presses forward between
these two, his hair curled in Ringlets, & a most
Natural expression. the Virgin is not handsome, but
a most majestick Air, the head & dressing of the hair

in exquisite Taste. her Drapery in little folds, that shows the rising & turn of the breast to a wonder. it is cracked from top to bottom being on board otherwise well preserved. the Bambino is very bad, & lies sprawling in a strange manner. a building at a distance with a Man displaying a Scrowl. much finish'd & big as life — — — Parmeggiano — —

Madonna della Pescia. she sits on a high Throne under a Canopy, whose Curtains are supported by angels flying. on one side stand S: Peter & S:[1]

2 boy Angels on the foreground with Notes of Musick—extremely fine — Rafael — —

Disputation on the Trinity. St Austin is speaking, & addresses to S: Peter Martyr. St Laurence in his Sacerdotal habit, & S: Francis attending. Mary Magdalen, & S: Sebastian sit on the foreground. it is famous, particularly for the degrees of Conviction, that appear in the figures suitable to their several Characters. finely painted undoubtedly, & perhaps the principal work of this Master. from whence he got his great Reputation I know not, Grace & Beauty 'tis certain he was an utter Stranger to; Harmony in the Tout-Ensemble he was ignorant of; his Subjects are always ill-chosen, & if he colour'd a particular figure well, this is by no means sufficient to put him on a rank with the greatest Masters. tho' even in

----

[1] So left by Gray.

this he often fails, & there is a smeariness in his shades that makes all his figures appear dirty. it is so even here — — Andrea del Sarto — —

S: Mark, sitting in a Nich, a Colossal figure, with a book in his hand. a most noble Style, Drapery in marvellous folds, vastly great! — — Il Frate — —

Assumption of the Virgin : Apostles below looking into the Sepulchre. She looks like a dirty ordinary Girl, abundance of Boy Angels about her. much gaiety of Colours in the several draperies, no harmony — — — Andrea del Sarto — —

Another ; much the same, some few figures excepted — — Ditto — —

S. Andrea Corsini praying: the Virgin above with Saints & Angels. she is a most aweful beauty ; there is S. Peter almost lost in Glory, the head is exactly Guido. the whole finely colour'd with great Warmth and Harmony — — large as life — — Carlo Maratti — —

Ritratto of Card: Bentivoglio, easy and natural, yet perfectly great. the Colouring fine beyond all expression — — Vandike — —

Card: Hippolito of Medici, half length, in the habit of a Hungarian, very gentile — — Titian —

Seven more Portraits, half lengths—some very fine — — Ditto — —

Charles the 5th, whole length, standing—the air has somewhat low & disagreeable — — Ditto — —

Philip the 2ᵈ, same size, Young, pale & thin, a most unpromiseing countenance — — Ditto — —

A Lady, dress'd in Crimson Satin. Half-length; fat, red-hair'd, & the air of a Cook-Wench, but painted to the greatest perfection of Colouring — — Paris Bordone — —

Luther (as it is called, tho' undoubtedly not so) playing on the Harpsicord. his head turned over his Shoulder towards a Man, who stands behind with a Lute; on t'other side a Woman in a black Cap & feather. the two latter figures perfectly insignificant. but the head of the principal one has a most ex- quisite life & Spirit in the eyes, & is admirably painted. the Drapery is one great black Spot — — Giorgone — —

Secretary of Leo the 10ᵗʰ, head & hands. a sort of Man, that should not have set for his picture —- — something hard — — Rafael — —

The famous PORTRAIT *of Leo the* 10 *with the Cardinals Medici & Rossi*, as fine as a Portrait can possibly be, & excellently preserved! — — Ditto —-—

Pilgrims of Emaus, his dark, sooty
  Manner —
Apollo, fleaing Marsyas — same Style —
S. Sebastian, all blister'd & spoil'd —
          } Guercino

A fine Madonna, of Rubens — —

ROAD TO NAPLES. June 12.

You pass thro' the Porta Cœlimontana near S:
John Lateran, & continue along the road to Albano
with numberless little ruins of Sepulchres spread in
the fields all round you, particularly toward the
right hand, where at a little distance the Via Appia
runs along.   they have been all extremely injured by
time, & other means, so that there are but few, whose
external form remains.   some seem to have been
small Rotundas, raised on a square Base, & ending in
a Cupola ; others quadrangular buildings with a flat
roof, & adorn'd with Pilasters ; (unless perhaps these
last may have been little Sacella) they all are huge
Masses of Brickwork, whose walls are often many
Yards in thickness containing one or two appartments within ; & undoubtedly have been formerly
incrusted with marble, or Tiburtine Stone, for all
the ground is cover'd with fragments of it.   there
are every where remains of Aqueducts with 50 or 60
Arches standing entire and uninterrupted together
in many places, which add a vast deal to the prospect.
the Campagna of Rome is not alone ill-cultivated[1],
but naturally a barren & disagreeable plain, & has
need of these monuments of antiquity to add a

[1] To Dorothy Gray, Naples, June 17, 1740 (II. 81, ed.
Gosse) 'The minute one leaves his Holiness' dominions,
the face of things begins to change from wide uncultivated
plains to olive groves and well-tilled fields of corn,' &c.

beauty to it. one has always in view before one
the hills at about 14 miles distance or more with the
towns of Tivoli, Palestrina, & Frescati upon them, &
a mixture of other little cities, & villages. beyond
the Torre di Mezzavia one turns to the left out of the
Alban road towards S. Marino, a large town belonging to the Colonna family situated on the side of one
of those hills, that form a sort of natural bason,
or receptacle for the Alban Lake. in the principal
Church is a side Altar —

The Martyrdom of S: Bartholomew, a famous
picture, the 2 ruffians, who are employ'd about that
bloody work are greatly in character, & are figures of
much spirit. for the rest the Saint seems to feel
nothing of the matter, but all his thoughts are fix'd
on heaven. this is too tame, for if he suffer'd nothing he was no martyr, & he might have shew'd the
pains he endured, yet with dignity too : nor is his
figure very well drawn : there are other people
present; large as life; usual blackness in the Shades - -
— — Guercino — —

There is the Martyrdom of another Saint at the
upper end, seems also of him ; not good.

In the Church della Trinità behind the great
Altar is — — —

The Trinity, of a size more than half-life. the
Father with Sorrow in his countenance, & arms
spread, supporting on his knees the dead Christ.

some few Cherubs that form a Semicircle over them ;
no other angels. the same Giac: Freii has graved.
a fine picture. but much better treated by him
in the Ch: of the Trinità de' Pellegrini at Rome — —
Guido — —

Here way[1] ascends the hills, & continues by a
very pleasant & shady road along them—with the
Lake in the Vale below to the right, & C̣lọ̣ Gandolfo
appearing on the top of the mountains on t'other
side of it. on the left is the Mons albanus, & the
Dorsum running along it's side, on which Alba Longa
was once situated. you continue among the hills,
which are very green, & well cultivated to Velletri,
seated on the top of a little mountain with a pretty
Vale below it, anciently famous for nothing, as
Sil. Italicus says—Quos incelebri miserunt valle
Velitræ— upon descending these hills you have a
most extensive view of the plain to the right, &
the Marshes (Pomptina Palus) with the Sea beyond,
& the Circeïan Promontory, (that seems a huge
Mountain, all alone) stretching into it. here turning
something to the right one continues along the plain
to Cisterna, a small town, whose inhabitants are
Vassals of a Neapolitan Prince, of the Gaëtano
Family: he is also Lord of Sermoneta, & Caserta
with a pretty extensive Territory round about them.
a little farther we past thro' a large Park of his,

[1] Gray, 'was'.

G.   15

one part of which is a noble wild Scene all over-
run with huge old Oaks, & Cork-Trees. the Mountains now begin to thicken, & approach nearer to the
Sea, so as to leave but a narrow Tract of cultivated
land between themselves, & the Marshes. one soon
comes to the foot of a steep hill on whose top stands
Sermoneta (Sulmo Volscorum) just by it one crosses
a little stream of sulfureous Water, like the Albula.
'tis like that of a blewish white, & the Stench intolerable. they call it Aqua Puzza. we past by Sezza
(Setia) of ancient fame for its wines

—Ipsius mensis seposta Lyæi

Setia—   Sil: Ital: 8.

This is situated much as the last, & as all the
little cities are hereabouts, on a hill at the foot of
more lofty mountains, which shelter them on one
side from the North, & East Winds, while on the
other they lie open to the breezes from the Sea,
& are exalted above the noxious Vapours, that rise
from the marshes, which would infect, & render
uninhabitable Towns in a less elevated Situation, as
they do all the plains of the Campagna upon a level
with themselves. the ancients seem to have made
choice of an exalted Site, whenever they could with
convenience, & Virgil distinguishes the Cities of
Italy by this particular.

Adde tot egregias urbes, operumq laborem
Tot congesta manu præruptis oppida saxis,
Fluminaq antiquos subterlabentia muros. Georg: 2.

One has here the little river Ufens creeping along
on the right hand among the Fens, & slowly working
it's way into the sea.

Quâ Saturæ jacet atra palus, gelidusq per imas
Quærit iter valles, atq in mare conditur Ufens. Virg: 7.

———— pestiferâ Pontini uligine campi
Quâ Saturæ nebulosa palus restagnat, & atro
Liventes cæno per squalida turbidus arva
Cogit aquas Ufens, atq inficit æquora limo. Sil: Ital: 8.

Somewhat farther is Piperno (Privernum) also
seated on a high Hill. the Peasants here wear
a sort of Buskin, the sole of which is made of a raw
hide with the hair on, bound about the foot, & half
way up the Leg with Whipcord. Virgil distinguishes
the inhabitants when they came to war, by almost a
similar sort of Chaussure, only that they wore it on
one foot only—

vestigia nuda sinistri
Instituunt pedis, at crudus tegit altera pero. Virg: 7.

haveing past thro' a noble old wood of Ilex's,
Cork-trees, & Oaks one crosses the River Amaseno
over a bridge, & keeping obliquely to the right, for
so the course of the Mountains runs, which begin
now to grow exceeding lofty, one strikes into the
Via Appia (which has run strait along thro' the
middle of the Pomptina palus, & tho' in perfect
preservation, is useless by reason of the waters, that
cover it) at a place call'd Torre delle Mole, a few

miles on this side Terracina. 'tis I believe here as perfect as anywhere, not alone the midway for carriages remains, which is just of a breadth for 2 carriages to pass, but the raised causeway on each side for foot-passengers, the whole of a greyish coarse marble, the pieces of Irregular Shapes generally a foot or two, sometimes more in breadth, laid as they suit one another best. the side ways are raised better than a foot above the middle. Statius gives a good description of these immense labours in the 4th Book of his Sylvæ, 3.

> Hic primus labor inchoare sulco[1],
> Et rescindere limites, & alto
> Egestu penitus cavare terras:
> Mox haustas aliter replere fossas,
> Et summo gremium parare dorso,
> Ne nutent sola, ne maligna sedes,
> Et pressis dubium cubile saxis;
> Tunc umbonibus hinc et hinc coactis,
> Et crebris iter allegare[1] gomphis.
> O quantæ pariter manus laborant!
> Hi cædunt nemus, exuuntq montes;
> Hi ferro scopulos, trabesq cædunt;
> Illi saxa ligant, opusq texunt
> Cocto pulvere, sordidoq topho:
> Hi siccant bibulas manu lacunas,
> Et longé fluvios agunt minores.

There are frequent ruins on each hand of it, not only of Sepulchres, but the foundations of larger buildings, & arched vaults of brick disposed Particu-

[1] *Sic* ap. Gray.

latím. one continues along this way, which goes
up several mountains, & thro' deep vallies, still
running obliquely towards the Sea, till one comes
to Anxur, or *Terracina* seated on a fine hill with an
open view of the Sea—Æquoreis splendidus Anxur
aquis. Mart:———passing by which one goes on along
the shore between the Sea, & some exceeding lofty
rocky Cliffs; on the very top of one of 'em are large
remains of an ancient edifice. here are frequent
square towers along the Coast built to prevent sudden
descents of the Moorish Corsairs, but very inconsiderable, & ruinous. against the side of one of
these rocks are cut the 12 Numbers mention'd by
Addison in decimal proportion, decreaseing upwards:
a little further one enters the *kingdom of Naples*, the
bounds are marked by an Inscription on a large stone
monument erected in Philip 2$^{d's}$ time. one now sees
several tracts of land, & little Isthmus's stretching
into the Sea, which enters far in, & forms several
bays, & lakes (as it were)—which, with a mixture of
woods among them, form a view very agreeable to the
eye. now one turns again to the left leaving the
shore, & journeying thro' charming Vales to Fondi.
the hedges abound with the broad-leaved Myrtle,
Bay, Spanish-Broom, Laurustine & many flowering
Shrubs I never saw before. one comes round to the
Sea again very soon at Mola (Formiæ) most charmingly situated on the *Bay of Gaëta*, the Usual

Station of his Sicilian Majestie's Gallies. the air
here is all perfumed with the large plantations of
ancient Orange-trees about the town; they were at
this time all cover'd with flowers & ripe fruit at once,
& the first I had yet seen in Italy, that seem'd to
grow kindly in the natural earth, being of great bulk,
& beauty. The bay was full of Fishing-Vessels; on
the right hand lies the Town and Castle of Gaëta in
full view overlooked by a high hill on which is the
Monument of Munatius Plancus, like a round tower,
all alone. 'tis about half a dozen miles from Mola
cross (*sic*) the Bay to it. one still follows the Appian
way, which runs thro' this town, to the banks of the
River Garigliano: just on this side are pretty large
ruins of Minturnæ, a small aqueduct of brick entire
for a good way together, a Theatre, & something like
a Circus, with many other little remains of building
scatter'd about quite down to the Sea. one crosses
this River (the Liris) in a ferry. it retains it's
former calmness, and clearness, winding slowly thro' a
charming plain, & full to the very brink, not like the
generality of Italian rivers, shallow, and turbulent.
one now leaves the Appian, which goes off towards
the ruins of old Capua, that lay some miles more
inland, than the new City does. the road now grows
extremely spatious, like those in Lombardy, &, tho'
unpaved, is in extremely good condition, haveing been
repair'd, & in a manner new-made against the arrival

of the new Queen. one finds an extraordinary change
upon leaving the Pope's dominions, the roads grow
chearful, & frequented, the country cultivated, & the
towns populous. this part of Italy is indeed a
miracle of beauty, & fertility, these are the Massic,
the Calatine, & Falernian fields, & indeed nothing
can go beyond these. What must such a country be
in the times of liberty, when even under the execrable
government it has now long been subject to, it can
flourish in this manner? at Capua one crosses the
Vulturnus, which runs under it's walls, a shallow
muddy furious Stream at that time not near filling
it's Channel: the City is small, but full of people, an
Archbishoprick, & gives the Title of Prince to a Son
of the Royal family. the road passes thro' Aversa
(Atella) a city of the Saracen's foundation, very neat,
& airy. one enters Naples thro' a very handsome
Suburb, in which are several Palaces, Churches, &
publick buildings, large, & grand enough, but commonly of a very ill taste in Architecture, charged
with abundance of clumsy Ornaments. upon entering the grand Street (Strada di Toledo) the infinite
number of people, & coaches are somewhat amazeing,
it is with difficulty one passes, & it is one continued
market from one end to the other for Fruits, flowers,
& Provisions of all kinds, I believe near a mile in
length, reaching from the Porta della Spirito S^{to} to
the King's Palace; towards the further end it winds

something, otherwise quite strait, & paved admirably
well (as are the streets in general) with square Stones
laid corner-wise, so as to resemble the Opus reticu-
latum, flat, & of about a foot & ½ dimensions. the
houses are of the common people, but lofty (4 Stories
high) & equal throughout, & the breadth of the
street proportionable to it's length.

THE CERTOSA.

This Convent one of the richest in Italy enjoys a
most delicious Air, & Situation, being seated on a
very lofty hill just above the ancient Castle of S.
Elmo. from a Portico in it you have a noble prospect
of the *whole City* below you, & the Bay in it's whole
Extent with M: Vesuvius, Surrentum, & all the
country beyond it as far as the promontory of
Minerva on the left, & on t'other hand Pausilipo
stretching out into the Sea, & behind it a part of the
Bay of Baiæ, the view being bounded by M: Miseno.
before you is Capreæ (30 Miles distant) appearing as
a barren Mountain of a vast height divided into 2
Summits which lyes across the mouth of the Gulf,
& leaves a Passage on each side of it

　　　　　　　　　　　— Insula portum
　　Efficit objectu laterum, quibus omnis ab alto
　　Frangitur, inq sinus scindit sese unda reductos.

such a vast variety of buildings, mountains, woods &
water; and that composeing a scene every part of

which is mark'd out in ancient Story for some thing,
or other remarkable can hardly be any where else
parallel'd.   the fathers are 60 in number, the building
spatious, being begun by Charles of Anjou, D: of Cala-
bria, Son of Robert, King of Naples, & perfected, and
endowed by his Daughter, who succeeded her Grandfather by the name of Joan 1.ʰᵗ the great Cloyster
is light and airy.   it is a Portico supported by three-
score Columns of white marble, & in the midst, as
usual, is the common Burying Ground of the Convent
enclosed by a Balustrade also of marble with Skulls,
& such suitable decorations carved on it.   in the
Prior's Apartments are some Pictures, which they
esteem greatly, tho' I saw little considerable there.
a Crucifix, only a single figure, (of which the old
Story is told of the Porter) between 2 & 3 foot long.
Air like that of the Grand Duke, but not colour'd
like anything else I have seen of him - - - M: Angelo
Buonaruoti.

Martyrdom of S: Laurence, a Sketch in Oil for
that in the Escurial.   small figures......Titian.

THE SACRESTY.

The whole cieling painted with histories in squares,
small; & single figures between of a larger size.
better than ordinary for him; there are some fine
things — — Cav: Arpino — — — — —

Crucifixion, large as life, in Oil.   not good; no
nature at all — — Ditto — — — — —

Denyal of Christ; heads and hands. this on the
contrary is true nature indeed, and excellent in a low
way, but it is a perfectly Dutch Scene — — M: Ang^{lo}
Caravaggio.

Several others, but not good — — Luca Cangiari,
Giac^{mo} Puntormo &c.

THE TREASURIES.

a Pietà, large as life. only the Virgin, & S:
John; she has a fine expression of Sorrow, but without beauty, or grace; the other a very mean, &
ordinary figure: but the dead Christ, who is thrown
in a very uncommon attitude upon her knees, is a
most admirable figure both for drawing & colouring;
nothing can be more easy, & it perfectly comes
forward from the Canvass. the finest thing I ever
saw of him. it cost 4000 Ducats, but the Fathers
now esteem it at 10,000 — — Spagnuoletto — — —

Here are Ornaments for the Altar of amazing
richness. half-figures of several Saints bigger than
life, a Statue of the Virgin, great numbers of wrought
stands, & large vases, all of massy Silver, & a
Custodia adorn'd with Sapphires, Emeralds, Topazes,
& Rubies of a huge size.

THE CHURCH.

In the Choir behind the Great Altar is the Na-
tivity, fig: as large as life. the Joseph is the only
one quite compleat, for he left the picture unfinish'd.

it shews no decay of Genius at all, & the heads have all that Divine beauty one sees only in his works — — Guido — — — — — — —

The Crucifixion in the Arch over it in Fresco, very large — — Lanfranco — — — — — — —

The whole Vault of the Church in 3 vast Compartments, the Figures, that serve for Ornaments, & the 12 Apostles above the Cornice are all in general of the same Master, an immense Work, yet there are several others of him in Naples at least as considerable, as this. if you come to particular parts, there is no great grace, or expression, neither is the Drawing always correct; but in the whole a Greatness in the execution, a perfect Mastery in the management of his colours, & a great harmony, that strikes the eye all at once, a certain Furia in his Airs, & the Draperies always noble & simple. his works here are well preserved, & bright as if but just done — — — — —

THE ENVIRONS OF NAPLES. June 16, N: S: 1740.

M. *Pausilypo* lies on the right side of the city. it is a long Dorsum, or Promontory, that runs out a good way into the Sea; of a considerable height, cover'd with little woods, & Villa's with Vineyards intermix'd. the Chiaia runs along from Naples almost as far as the side of this Mountain, thro' the bowels of which is cut the famous *Grotta.* one passes

for some little space along a passage also pierced
through the solid rock, but this is carried quite thro'
to the top, & open to the Air, till one comes to the
mouth of the Cave, which is a tall Arch better than
50 (?)[1] Foot in height, & of a breadth sufficient
for 3 Carriages at least to enter abreast. these
latter dimensions are continued quite through it,
but the height greatly decreases, till a little beyond
the middle, where it appears not $\frac{1}{5}$ of what it was at
first; it then rises again till at[2] the mouth next
Puzzuoli, 'tis almost as great as before. the top is
form'd into an arch the whole way, & makes a solemn
appearance, like some long vaulted Isle of a Gothick
Church. upon entering it, as the light falls chiefly
upon the two ends, & one has in view the Outlet at
the opposite end, the eye is much deceived in it's
length, which seems not above 100 Yards, tho' in
reality near half a mile. there are 2 square passages
over each entrance at a great height, that run obliquely thro' the rock, & open into the vault contrived
to throw the light still a little further in, & admit
more air. in a fine day one sees very well, till
near the middle, where it grows somewhat dark, &
carriages that meet are obliged to warn one another
by crying out Alla marina, or Alla montagna. about

[1] The margin here renders the number doubtful.
[2] The margin here causes difficulty on both sides, but this
is doubtless the reading.

the midst of it in a small cave cut into the rock-side
is a small chappel of the Madonna with lamps burning
continually, tended by a Hermit. Alphonso the 1st
enlarged the Grotta, & in Charles 5s time D: Peter of
Toledo, the Viceroy paved it, & made an excellent
road, which still continues: as large Inscriptions near
it testify. when it was first made is uncertain; some
people name one Cocceius, as the author of it; but
these are of no authority. it is likely to have been
done in the earlier days of Rome, as it appears more
design'd for convenience than ostentation, for it seems
to have been but a disagreeable passage in Seneca's
time, & the aforemention'd king gave it it's present
loftiness. haveing passed the Grot one comes into
a most beautiful country, consisting of fertile hills
cover'd with Vines, & Figs; or else Corn with rows
of elms, & their Vines running up them, & hanging
in Festoons from one to the other. one turns a little
to the right of the Pozzuoli-Road, & ascending for
some time between the rocks one comes to the top of
a hill, from whence the Lake of Agnano discovers
itself with its charming borders surrounded with
mountains of a moderate height all cultivated &
planted to the top. Upon descending into the Vale
even at a distance the sulphureous Steams that rise
from the Lake & the Ground about it are easily perceived. at the time I saw it, the way thither for ¼ of
a Mile at least, & the whole country about the lake

was cover'd with an infinite swarm of very small frogs. there was no stepping without treading upon them. the Country people said it was common, & that they fell in the Rain; but it had not rain'd that day, nor for several before it. on the right side of the Lake under the rocks is the Grotta del Cane. they have closed up the mouth of it with a door, that locks; it is very small & low not above 5 foot & ½ high at the entrance, & does not extend above 3 yards into the rock growing still lower & lower. we made the usual experiment with a middle-sized Cur-Dog, that had frequently before undergone the same operation: the Man held his 4 legs, & laid him on the earth on his side with his head close to the ground. he struggled much, & began to pant in a few Moments. in 3 Minutes fell into Convulsions, his strength soon left him, & he lay without motion of his limbs, only fetching his breath shorter & shorter. we took him out, & laid him on the Grass, & in about 5 Minutes he was quite recover'd, whineing, & seeming to rejoice, that he was restored to life. several of the little frogs were put in, who hop'd about a little, but stretch'd themselves out, & died in less than half a minute. the torches went out immediately being dip'd in the Vapour, which is not visible, but the experiments proved it did not rise more than ½ a foot above the ground. one may enter the cave without hurt; there is a sensible

warmth in it, as in all the rocks hereabouts, & the
ground & sides are moist. the Lake is very agreeable
to the eye, almost round, & about a mile in compass;
it has much fish in it (Tench & Eels) but more frogs.
near the margin in some places it boils very strongly,
yet there is no perceptible heat in the water. a
little distance from the Cave is a building with
several little appartments call'd I Sudatorii di S:
Germano. in the innermost of them the Vapour that
rises is so violent as to put anybody into a strong
Sweat in some few Minutes. this is a visible smoke
issuing out continually, & the Smell of Sulphur is
extremely offensive. these places are used with
success in several distempers, particularly the Pox, &
the Itch, some say the Gout too. continuing along
the side of the Lake to the left one ascends again to
the top of a mountain, & thro' a narrow passage
comes into a large hollow, or plain of better than a
mile in compass surrounded with high Cliffs of a
naked dismal appearance, with a little thin herbage
scatter'd here & there the tallest of these towards one
end of the plain from several parts send forth a thick
white Smoke & that up to their very top. about the
roots of them, and in 3 or 4 places of the plain are
certain small cavities in the ground, from whence
rises the same Vapour, but more strongly; on throwing a large stone against the ground it returns a deaf
report, that shews all beneath is hollow. over several

of the smaller Vents they pile up broken Potsherds,
about which a Crust of Sal Armoniac[1] gathers in a
short time.　in this part of the Solfatara the heat is
very sensible to one's hand upon touching the earth;
the other end of it seems in comparison to have but
little of these warm springs & minerals; plants grow
there pretty thick: here they have built up Sheds
under which they make Alum.　the Rain-water that
falls hereabouts, naturally stagnates in the middle of
the plain, which is the lowest part of it, from whence
being impregnated with earth, they bring it hither, &
digest it in proper receivers, where the Alum forms
itself into a thin ice-like Crust on the surface, & sides
of the Vessels.　Petronius gives a good Description
of this wonderful Spot in his fragment of a Poem: it
was called Forum Vulcanium.　the Capucins have a
small convent a little above it; no very secure Situation.　*Pozzuoli* is about a mile distant from hence;
the country of extreme beauty and fertility with
openings every now & then among the hills, that
discover that part of the Bay between the little
promontory on which this town is situated, & M:
Pausilypo; with the little Isle of Nisida, that lies just
before the point of it; it is a high rock (but cultivated) & with a Castle on it's most elevated part,

---

[1] Gray might find a precedent in Chaucer for this spelling,
which probably rests on some false derivation.　See Skeat's
Etym. Dict., *s.v.* Ammonia.

which gives to a Neapolitan Cavalier the title of
Marquis of Nisida. it is about a Mile & ½ round,
anciently call'd Nesis, & remarkable for certain un-
wholesome exhalations; now no such thing is observed there: between this & the land is a low flat
rock with buildings on it, call'd the Lazaretto. from
Pozzuoli we took a large boat with 4 oars to go round
the *Bay of Baiæ* in, which presented a beautiful
calm Sea to the eye. from this town runs for a considerable way into the water the Mole of Antoninus
Pius. the large massy piles of Brick and Cement
appear not to have been all of equal width. we
went coasting the bay round, passing by Monte
Barbaro (the ancient Gaurus) eversince the strange
Eruption of M: Nuovo by it's side it has lain barren
& neglected, till within these few years past they
have begun to cultivate it anew, & to plant Vines in
some parts, which they find succeed very well[1]. a
little further on is the New Mountain itself, not so
high as the last mention'd, thinly cloath'd with a
burnt, and rusty herbage—Quæ scabie, & salsâ lædit
rubigine ferrum. it retains no other marks of it's
former horrours. every one knows how accompanied
with an earthquake, & vomiting out fire it rose out

[1] Cf. the last five lines of the Latin Hexameters on the
Monte Barbaro and the Monte Nuovo sent to West from
Florence Sep. 25, but written at Rome, July, 1740. (Works, I.
181, ed. Gosse.)

G.   16

of the earth in the space of one night about 200 years
ago, & destroy'd or overwhelm'd all the country about
it: it reaches from M: Gaurus to very near the lake
Avernus. between the foot of this Hill, & the Sea
lies the Lucrine Lake, whose present condition can
give but an imperfect Idea of its former beauty, since
the mountain has rose in it's place, & cover'd the
springs that used to supply it, so that nothing remains but a meer puddle, shallow & overgrown with
reeds, & dwarf-myrtle. the ground that at present
separates it from the Sea is not 10 Yards in breadth,
& one sees no traces of the Julian Port Virgil mentions. here we landed, & walked about ½ a mile up
among the Hills to the place, where the Avernus
discovers itself in a charming vally surrounded by
Vineyards & woods; now much frequented by Water-
fowl, & stock'd with fish. it is of a vast depth,
& near 2 Mile in compass. at one end of the margin
of it are the ruins of an Octagon temple of Brick,
round withinside with 7 large Niches, & as many
Windows over them: it is commonly named the
Temple of Apollo, & by others of Neptune, or of
Mercury. on another side of the Lake, after ascending some way up one of the mountains by a narrow
passage thro' the wood, one finds the mouth of the
Sibyl's Grotta; 'tis very small, & one bends almost
double to enter it; the straitness continues for a few
paces; & then the cave rises into a tall Arch: this

Vault continues strait on (being about 13 foot broad,
& 12 high) 95 Canes in length, where one sees the
Earth has fall'n in, & stop'd it up. not far from the
end by a very narrow winding passage one descends
into a little arched bathing room, where one can
hardly enter for the water that comes into it; the
cieling has been adorn'd with little Grotesque paintings, & Mosaic. there is also another little Cell near
it, where are the remains of a brick winding Staircase,
which is supposed to have led up to the top of the
mountain. it is very hard to imagine the Use of
these subterraneous ducts. in all likelihood they
were older than the Roman's time, & that their mere
age & oddness gave room to apply certain religious
Fables to them, that obtain'd among the Vulgar: some
of them they took for the mouth of Hell, others for
the habitation of a Sibyl, others for the Cave of the
Cimmerians, &c: the little rooms fitted up for bathing
seem to have been a Use they were afterwards put to
by people, near whose Villa's they happen'd to be.
this tho' call'd so, is undoubtedly not the Sibyl's
Grot of Virgil; that he says was

Excisum Euboicæ latus ingens rupis in antrum.

But the Euboic, or Cumæan coast was quite on
t'other side the promontory of Misenus, & near the
Remains of Cuma is still to be seen the mouth of a
Cave like this, running directly towards the Avernus,
but stop'd up within 50 paces of the entrance. from

hence returning back to the Sea we continued along
the bay, whose borders not here alone, but quite
from Pozzuoli are a most surprizeing Scene for the
Instances of Roman Magnificence, that shew themselves even from the Summits of those Mountains
that surround it down to their foot, & quite out into
the Sea for many Paces. vast vaults & arches of
Masons-work, that hang over, & seem to grow to the
sides of those Cliffs, still supporting themselves without the help of their foundations, which appear far
off below in ruins, being huge Masses of Brickwork,
that stretch themselves far into the bay.

> Marisq Baiis obstrepentis urges
>   Summovere littora,
> Parum locuples continente ripâ.   These were call'd
>   Cæmentis licet occupes   [Cæmenta.
> Tyrrhenum omne tuis—
>   Contracta pisces æquora sentiunt
> Jactis in altum molibus: huc frequens
> Cæmenta demittit redemptor
> Cum famulis—

A little farther we landed again at the *Sudatorii
di Tritoli*, supposed to have been the *Thermæ of
Nero ;* 'tis certain there are vast remains of building
up to the very summits of the mountain. the baths
are artificial caverns work'd far into the rock. one
enters by certain long & narrow passages, in one of
which the heat is almost insupportable, if you walk
upright; upon stooping pretty low you do not feel so
strongly the violence of it. this is 120 paces long,

& then one descends for 60 odd paces more, where a
spring of scalding water boils out of the rock: but
this is a little too far to be led by mere curiosity,
since two minutes at the entrance only of the Grott is
sufficient to sweat one violently. the steam is very
powerful & suffocating, & very visible at the mouth
withoutside, where it issues out continually. the
rich come hither in great numbers dureing the month
of June, & use it seven days running. it belongs to
the Annunziata, who send the patients of their hos-
pitals hither sometimes 1000 at once. from whence
we continued along an arch'd passage cut thro' the
rock, & by a narrow pav'd road work'd also between
the rocks, walk'd towards Baiæ: in the way we were
very sensible of the hot vapour proceeding from the
ground, & the mountain on our right: every now &
then for a Pace or too (*sic*) it was intolerable, then
one felt it no more, but only the common warmth of
the Sun reflected from the Rock. there were several
holes, in which one could scarce bear to thrust one's
hand for the heat. a little further where the hills retire
something from the shore, one sees a lofty Rotunda;
above half the Cupola is fall'n in, and a part of the
Inclosure. the Structure is of Brick (as are most
of the remains hereabout) neatly & strongly built.
it has 4 great Niches below, and 7 Windows over
them. there are so many ruins scatter'd about, &
joining to it, that it is imagined to have been an

appartment of the Baths of Piso, the famous head of
a Conspiracy against Nero : but however it goes by
the name of *Diana's temple*. a little further are
several large arch'd Vaults, which stand always
pretty deep in water, thro' which a Man carries you
under a little arch into another round Edifice adjoin-
ing, about 25 Paces in Diameter, with an opening
atop as usual, & 4 windows below it. here they make
you whisper, & it has the same effect, as in the Dome
of S. Pauls. this they name Truglio di Mercurio.
a little farther, & upon the Shore is an Octagonal
Edifice. the whole Recinto remains, but the top is
demolish'd. it has an arch'd opening atop for a
window in each side, & four great Niches. the shape
of the frontispiece remains, being a large Arch, &
two small ones on the sides; these make a strait line,
longer than the temple side they join to, & must
have had but a bad effect. this is call'd the Temple
of Venus. a little farther on the Shore is the Castle
of Baiæ, built by D: Pedro of Toledo, seemingly
pretty strong & in good repair. the body of it on
an eminence, but it's fortification's descend to the
Sea. something beyond it are some remains of Bauli,
where on the coast they shew you a sepulchre for
that of Agrippina Minor. it is almost cover'd with
earth ; they have made a hole, into which by a ladder
one descends. there is a vaulted passage runs round
between the double Walls, like that in the Mauso-

leum of Augustus, only in little : the roof has
some remains of Stucco with little figures in Compartiments & Borders of Grotesque, Sphinxes, &
foliage, but much damaged & blacked by the smoke
of Torches. a little distance from hence are the
Cento Camerelle. there is a large Vault, sustain'd
by about a dozen square pillars, & by a small staircase one descends under ground by narrow passages
into certain other appartments, whose use nobody
seems to conceive. there are many & various ruins
spread about the country here, to which they have
affix'd the names of various great Men, whose Villa's
are mention'd as situated somewhere hereabouts, but
upon trivial grounds. you now are not far from the
Bay of Miseno the Station of the Roman fleet upon
this Sea, & consequently almost at the end of the
promontory : one ascends up the charming hills
cover'd with Vineyards, & Plantations, that form the
Back of it, about 3.4 of a mile, & passes in the way by
rows of ruin'd sepulchres, in some of which is a little
Mosaic, & a few grotesque ornaments of painting.
this place they now call Mercato di Sabbato, & the
country about it Campi Elisii, it is indeed of miraculous fertility, & beauty. one has here a View of
the Mare Mortuum, a pleasant lake, or rather bay,
for it communicates with the Sea, & is only separated
from it by a little tongue of land, a few paces in
breadth, & M: Miseno beyond it which rises gra-

dually without precipices, & is cultivated up to the Very top, where it spreads into a plain, a fine situation for some Temple, or lofty building. there once was a Pharos upon it, but nothing now, it joins to the land by a narrow & low Isthmus. we tasted the wine of this country, which is of a full red, strong, & rough, like Bourdeaux Claret, & might with time come to be excellent. beyond Misenus are the Isles of Ischia & Procita (Arimæ or Inarime, & Prochyta) the former much the larger, very lofty, especially to the N: East; the more plain End of it has a large town, & several buildings, that make a great figure in the prospect, for it is much frequented on account of it's baths : Procita is much lower, less, & not so well inhabited. between the Mare Mortuum & Mercato di Sabbato is the huge antient Reservoir, call'd Piscina Mirabilis ; one descends into it by 40 Steps ; it is supported by 148 square Pilastroni. the whole work cover'd with a plaister as hard as stone itself. there are Spiracula in the roof for the passage of air & light. some attribute this work to Lucullus, others to Agrippa & say it was a Conservatory of fresh water for the Use of the Fleet, that lay at Misenus. the ruins of Cumæ lie but a little way on the other side of the Promontory however we return'd to Pozzuoli cross the bay, and made another day of it thither wholly by land, near the foot of M: Gaurus by which one passes we turn'd towards

the right to the place called Via Campana, where for
more than a mile are numberless ancient remains
without much distinguishable form or beauty indeed,
but huge, & massy; beside abundance of Sepulchres,
some of them open'd not many years since : one is
the most entire I have ever seen 'tis a square Colum-
barium with 4 or 5 rows of Niches; in the midst
of 3 of the sides are as many large Enfoncemens
with a Column on each side of them sustaining a
pediment, much like a modern Chimneypiece ; the
whole of brick cover'd with plaister, the roof & sides
between the niches adorned with little Grotesques of
painting, & Stucco in square Compartiments with
small figures in the middle prettily executed enough
& in tolerable preservation.   there are Centaurs,
Sphinxes, Loves, Harpies, &c : it seems to have
been the monument of some considerable family, but
all the inscriptions & Urns are taken away, & I
could get no information of what might have been
learnd from thence.   the road runs along the hills,
that form a circle about the Avernus.   less than a mile
on this side Cuma one passes under the Arco Felice.
it joins two Hills together, handsomely built of Brick,
& with vast Solidity, for the Mass is above 50 foot
in thickness.   the Arch is 20 foot wide, & 70 high,
& there are 2 or 3 little ones still atop of that, so
that it was even with the summit of the hills.   not
far from thence is the little temple call'd Del Gigante,

where is said to have been found the Colossal Statue of
Jupiter now before the Palace at Naples. it is square
with a vaulted roof in Compartiments, such as those
of the Pantheon. at the end is a large Nich, but not
near of a sufficient size to hold that statue. the remains of Cumæ are nothing in themselves very considerable, but (as every thing else hereabouts) vast,
& such as give one a great Idea of ancient art &
industry. the rock, on which the famous temple of
Apollo & Diana is supposed to have stood, is very
steep, & close to the shore; the Substructiones remain
on the sides of it, & are of hewn Stone, extremely
solid, & neat: this seems to have been the situation of
both Temple, & Citadel. below this hill, on one side,
where the rocks retire a little from the shore, is the
mouth of a Cave, perhaps the true Grotta della Sibylla.
this is very spacious, & only inconvenient by the number of loose stones that roll down into it, for it is a
gradual descent all the way. where the rock did not
seem capable of supporting itself, it has been propped
in several places of the sides by a wall of hewn stone
built up to it. some paces within it on the left hand
is a large & wide ascent of Stairs (I believe) more than
60 Steps. it goes strait at first, but winds a little
towards the top, where when you land, there seems
to have been another narrow flight of steps, leading
still higher, but this is quite stop'd up with earth, as is
the Cave itself not a great way further. this many

imagine to have been the other mouth of the Grot
near Avernus, but it is conjecture only. all this part
of the coast is exposed to an intense heat of the sun,
fruits are consequently in very early perfection here,
they used to have figs ripe at this Season, & Grapes
in great forwardness ; at the time we were there
indeed there was no appearance of it, the year being
remarkably backward I believe all over Europe ; however Barley was then ready to cut, & the Wheat had
chang'd colour. we made a *little journey* also on the
otherside of the *Bay of Naples to Portici*, where the
King has a Villa about 4 Miles out of town, the way
thither is thro' a number of small towns, & seats of
the nobility close by the Sea, for Mount Vesuvius
has not ever been able to deter people from inhabiting
this lovely coast, & as soon as ever an irruption is
well over, tho' perhaps it has damaged, or destroy'd
the whole country for leagues round it, in some
months every thing resumes its former face, and goes
on in the old channel. that mountain lies a little
distance from Portici towards the left, divided into 2
Summits, that farthest from the Sea is rather the
largest, & highest called Monte di Somma. this has
been hitherto very innocent; the lesser one, which is
properly *Vesuvio*, is that so terrible for it's fires; it
is better than 3 Miles to ascend & those extremely
laborious. 'twas extremely quiet at the time I saw
it: some days one could not perceive it smoke at all,

others one saw it riseing like a white Column from it,
but in no great quantity. about a mile beyond Portici we saw the Stream of combustible Matter, which
run from it in the last eruption; within $\frac{1}{8}$ of a mile,
or less from the Sea is a small church of Our Lady,
belonging to certain Zoccolanti, into this church it
enter'd thro' one of the side-doors without otherwise
damageing the fabrick, run cross it, & was stop'd,
I suppose, by the opposite Wall. the Fryars have
dugg away that part of it, & left it whole riseing in a
great rough mass at the door where it enter'd, as if
the miraculous power of our Lady had forbid it to
advance further : this is well-contrived, & carries some
appearance with it. that part of the Stream, which
comes along thro' the fields, at a distance resembles
plough'd Land, but rougher, & in huge Clods; they are
hard, & heavy, like the dross of some metals; the
people pile the pieces up, & make an enclosure to their
fields with them. this place is call'd Torre del Greco;
it is about 4 Years since the Eruption happen'd.
I imagine the river of fire, or Lava, as they call it,
may be 20 Yards, or more in breadth. it is not above
a Year since they discover'd under a part of the town
of Portici a little way from the Shore an ancient &
terrible example of what this mountain is capable of[1];

[1] See Walpole's letter to West of June 14, 1740 N. S. from
Naples (ed. Cunningham, I. p. 48). He gives, as obtained from
Gray, the quotation from Statius *infra*. Also Gray to his
mother, June 17, 1740 (ed. Gosse, II. 80 *sq.*).

as they were digging to lay the foundations of a house
for the Prince d'Elbœuf, they found a Statue or two
with some other ancient remains, which comeing to
the King's knowledge he order'd them to work on
at his expence, & continuing to do so they came to
what one may call a whole city under ground ; it is
supposed, & with great probability to be the Greek
settlement call'd Herculaneum, which in that furious
Eruption, that happen'd under Titus (the same in
which the elder Pliny perish'd) was utterly overwhelmed, & lost with several others on the same
coast. Statius, who wrote as it were on the spot,
& soon after the accident had happen'd, makes a
very poetical exclamation on the subject, which this
discovery sets in it's full light....

> Hæc ego Chalcidicis ad te, Marcelle, sonabam
> Littoribus, fractas ubi Vesbius egerit iras,
> Æmula Trinacriis volvens incendia flammis.
> Mira fides! credetne virum ventura propago
> [1]*Cum segetes iterum, cum jam hæc deserta virebunt,
> Infra urbes populosq premi, proavitaq toto
> Rura abiisse mari? nec dum lethale minari
> Cessat apex.   Silvæ: Epist: ad Vict: Marcellum L: 4.

The work is unhappily under the direction of
Spaniards, people of no taste or erudition, so that
the workmen dig, as chance directs them, wherever
they find the ground easiest to work without any

---

[1] This line is inserted, obviously afterwards, by Gray and
marked with an asterisk.

certain view. they have been fearful of the earths
falling in, & with reason, for it is but soft, &
crumbling, so that the passage they have made, is
but just sufficient for one person to walk upright in :
I believe, with all its windings it is now a good mile
in length & every day is increaseing. one descends
conveniently to the depth of about 30 foot by the
stone Steps of a Theatre, that they have found. one
walks a good way by the side of one of it's Galleries ; one see's buildings of brick with incrustations
of white marble, & here & there a solid column of
it, some upright, others fall'n, & lieing at length.
there is what appears the front of some edifice, an
arch with double pilasters on each side, these are
of brick cover'd with a coat of plaister, and painted
green with shades to imitate the trunk of a Palm-
tree. one passes by many walls cover'd with the
same plaister, painted in square compartiments either
green, or red, & sometimes a little figure, or piece
of grotesque in proper colours amongst it. most of
these buildings are still upright, it's plain ; other
parts seem overturn'd, & in ruins ; there is a mixture
of woodwork amongst the brick, all black, as a coal,
& tho' so firm as to show one even the Grain dis-
tinctly, yet upon being touch'd, moulders away into
dust. whether this be the effect of Fire, or merely
Age, I can not say: it is certain, there are no marks
of the first in any other instance ; what there may

be nearer the surface, I can't say. they have found an Olla with Rice, & Dates in it. the first I saw none of, but they say it retain'd it's hardness. the latter was as black as the wood ; & of a firmer consistence. there are inscriptions placed where the principal paintings, & Statues were found, which have been convey'd to the Palace, & there we went to see them. there are more than 40 pieces from half a foot square to 6 or 7 feet. as they are painted on Wall considering the difficulty of removeing, & conveying them one may call them well-preserved ; one may say the same of them, as to the colouring, with regard to their antiquity, it is not to be imagined very lively; it is sufficient if the Clair Obscur be distinguishable ; the colours are laid on in a bold manner with strong strokes of the pencil, & not much softned one into the other, but that is a delicacy time may easily have destroy'd. the Airs, particularly of heads, are commonly the best, in other parts there are frequent incorrectnesses of drawing: one of the most considerable is, I think The Chiron, & Achilles. fig^{res} a little less than life. the latter is a Boy, whom the Centaur is instructing to touch the Lyre, & a perfectly genteel figure ; he has a little drapery, about his middle, otherwise naked, & looks up in the other's face with a natural innocent air. the old Man's head is excellent for the air, & expression; the hair & beard

very great, & bold in a Style like Rafael; the naked
too of the human part is fine, but the Horse (his
hinder parts) is vastly too small, & out of proportion
to the rest: the Scene is the front of a temple with a
Portico. this is the best preserved among them.

Theseus after his victory over the Minotaur. that
Monster (a human figure with the head of a Bull,
but no horns) lies dead at his feet. the Youth are
flocking round him, & kissing his hands. they are
little figures with the proportions of full-grown people,
but not a quarter so big as life, tho' he himself is
rather larger. his head with the Sweep of the body
as far as the middle is very noble, & resembles the
famous Meleager: the legs & arms, particularly the
extremities vastly inferiour, & good for little. A Woman sitting on a rock, her head on her hand, looking
upwards, she is crown'd with flowers & (I think) has
a Cornucopiæ. before her a naked figure, like a Hercules, his back towards one, & face in Profile, &
beyond him a Victory half-appearing out of the
clouds. on the foreground a small Doe (Capreola)
giveing suck to an infant, & a little further an Eagle,
& Lion. the principal figures big as life. some good
things, but the extremities not good as in the
former......

There are other large pieces, but more damaged
than these. another old man (not a centaur) instructing a Youth ; this is almost vanish'd. somewhat like

a tryal, figures in Roman habits, & a Man seated, &
crown'd with Lawrel, who seems to judge them. A
Muse with two Flutes, &c: among the lesser are
2 Satyrs heads, one of them in a good taste ; a sort
of Landscape with buildings on each side a Lake,
where they lessen in proportion to their distance
according to the rules of perspective. A piece of
architecture, where thro' an opening is seen a Portico
with it's Columns showing, also according to art ; &
many others exceeding curious, as indeed the whole
discovery is one of the most considerable made for
these many ages. there are 6 Consular Statues of
white Marble in the Toga, & a Scroll in their hands,
as usual. the head of one of them, an elderly Man,
as fine as possible.

An Imperfect figure of a woman without head
or arms ; the Drapery perfectly good......

Part of a Horse, much bigger than life, Bronze ; &
many more fragments of brazen statues, several Ollæ ;
a Tripod of Marble with animals heads, & foliage ;
some Inscriptions, one very large to the honour of
Vespasian, another to Domitian's Wife, before he
was Emperour (he is call'd Cæsar in it) several Medals,
particularly of Claudius Cæs: many small Gold and
silver instruments; but these were in the King's own
hands, & we could not see them. the view of Naples,
& it's Bay in returning from hence is as beautiful,
as possible. it forms a huge Semicircle, & the moun-

G. 17

tains, that rise behind are (not like the barren ones
of Genoa, but) as deliciously fertile as one can imagine, all cover'd with Verdure, & woods intermix'd
with Villas, so is the whole Chain of Côteaux, that
run along to the S:E. of the City in a line parallel
to it. Naples has not the stately buildings of Genoa,
the materials are not so rich, nor the tast so
good, but in recompense it is larger, and it's bay
with the country about it infinitely more beautiful.
the streets are spacious, & well paved, the houses
high, & of equal goodness for a great way together;
they reckon it 9 mile in circumference without the
Suburbs, of which it has 7, & large ones. it is peopled
to a redundancy; they reckon 500,000 Souls, & it
seems not hard to believe : there are a greater number of children than ever I saw anywhere; they walk
at 6 months old, and go stark naked for 4 or 5 Years
which the Climate will easily bear. the people are
lively to a degree, and seem less inclined to Laziness
than the rest of Italy. every body is busy, till the
evening : then they give themselves up to diversion ;
the Men take their Colascione (a great sort of Lute)
or their Guitarre, & walk on the Shore to enjoy the
Fresco, sometimes singing in their Dialect in concert
with their instrument. the women sit at their doors
playing on the Cymbal, to the sound of which the
children dance with Castanets. this one sees all
along *the Chiaia*, which runs out from the City near

a mile in length towards Pausilypo, on one side are houses, chiefly of the common people intermix'd with some great ones, the other open to the Sea with Trees, & here and there a fountain. hither the Coaches resort in the evening, & drive slowly in 2 ranks backward & forward for an hour or two. a little beyond the end of this, & halfway up the side of Pausilipo is the little Church founded and endowed by Sanazarius in honour of the Partus Virginis ; at the end of it, where you enter, opposite to the high-Altar is his Monument, of the finest white Marble. on a spatious Basis are situated the figures of Apollo and Minerva sitting, & between them is a square bas-relief of Satyrs with Neptune & other figures, that shew he was the inventor of Piscatory Eclogues. above rises a Sarcofagus of a handsome figure with his bust upon it, an elderly man in long lank hair. the whole is a fine performance of Girolamo Santa Croce, a Neapolitan artist, compleated by Frà Gio: da Montorsoli, the Florentine. over the Mouth of the Grotta almost is *the Tomb call'd of Virgil;* 'tis of difficult access, & all cover'd with Shrubs, that grow over it, a square sepulchre with a vaulted roof, & 10 little Niches like the Columbaria : it belonged to be sure to some family. The Grand Street (di Toledo aforemention'd) winding a little toward the further end opens into an irregular Piazza, one side of which (to the left) is form'd by the Palace,

a fine piece of Cav: Fontana's Architecture; it is
of 23 Windows in front, & 3 Orders, Doric, Ionic,
& Corinthian, the first of them is a Loggia, the
other 2 the Apartments. the Great Gate consists of
4 Doric Columns of Granite, that support a Ringhiera
of 50 Palms in length; the whole front is of 520
Palms, the 2 ends of 360 ; the height 130 Palms:
these buildings enclose a Cortile, where the same
Orders are observed.

JOURNEY INTO SCOTLAND, FROM ROSE-CASTLE
IN CUMBERLAND. Aug: 1764. Bᵖ of Carlisle.

To Netherby. Rev: Mʳ Graham's, who has built hot-
houses there, & made a fine Kitchen-Garden, &
great plantations. here was probably the Æsica
of Anton: Itiner:
Cross the Sark (3 miles N: W:) & enter Scotland ∧ good road. ugly country.
          Annandale in Dumfries-Shire
To Annam, at dinner. bad inn. excellent Mutton.
Claret 3 S: a bottle. wretched appearance, &
dwellings of the common People. huts of mud,
& no chimneys.
To Dumfreis, at night. a large & handsome Town.
excellent Inn. fine views from the walks, particularly that on the Galloway-side of the R: Nid
a little above the Bridge, & another on yᵉ other
side of the Town along the River. 5 hours thro'
a fertile vale (Nithesdale)

To Drumlanrig, chief seat of the Duke of Queensbury, in a dreary wild country. Castle very large & strong, erected about 80 years ago. many portraits in the Gallery. 36 miles thro' Dresdear (where the Queensberry Family lie buried) to Car-
michael-House _{in Lanark-Shire} (Earl of Hyndford's) & only one Inn in the way. the House is now building. many pictures here. great plantations here. country naked & mountainous. 6 miles to

Corr-house-Lynn. where the *R: Clyde* falls by three different cataracts about 200 feet high, in a landscape of woods & rocks worthy the hand of Poussin. walk from hence a mile along the River to

Bonnington-Lynn, where it falls again in a single sheet. above the fall is a beautiful quiet pastoral scene. a cut thro' the wood in returning discovers *Lanerke,* a large Town not far distant on an eminence.

Lanerke. thro' bad roads to

Hamilton _{also on the Clyde} pretty large Town with one tolerable Inn. Hamilton-Palace stands in a spacious Park at the end of ye Town. a great ill-contrived edifice. grand Front built within these 50 years: Back-Front about James the 6^th^s time. Gallery full of fine pictures: much of Gibbons's carving here. bad turnpike road to

Glasgow _{still on the Clyde} an elegant City. Roman inscriptions at

the College. M.ʳ Foulis' Picture-Gallery. the
Kirk was the ancient Cathedral, a noble Gothick
Building, miserably spoil'd with Galleries & out
of repair: 12 miles to the banks of

Loch-Lomond _{in Dumbarton-Shire} row'd to Inys-Mary _{Inch-Mirin} an island with a
Park of yᵉ Duke of Montrose's, whose House at
Buchanan stands on the edge of yᵉ Lake. exquisite Landscape round the Lake. view of Ben-
Lomond, the second mountain in Scotland for
height Ben-Evis _{read Ben-Nevish in Inverness-shire} being the first. return to Glasgow, by

Dunbarton. Castle on a lofty rock garrison'd. immense view from thence. set out for (in one day)

Stirling. by Kilsyth thro' an ugly country cross
Graham's Dyke, (the wall of Antonine). fine
View from the Castle.

Thro' *Falkirk;* dine at Borrowstonness _{in Linlithgowshire} good roads,
& fine corn-countrey. it is a Sea-Port for Coal.
fine rich prospect over the Firth. along the
coast to

Abercorn (now *Hopton-House*). fine situation on a
bold ascent from the Firth. the House built early
in the present century, irregular & ugly. small
appartments. well-furnish'd & good pictures.
two hours to

Edinborough _{in Mid-Lothian} miserable Inns. noble views from the
Castle. Holy-rood House, some of it 200 years

old at least, but mostly built by Sr Wm Bruce 100 years later. here in the Earl of Braidalbin, & Duke Hamilton's lodgeings are a number of pictures. room where Rizzio was murther'd shewn here. Nave of ye Abbey Church standing, but ready to fall ∧ went out of Town to
_{now repair'd} placed above between "fall" and "went"

Dalkeith (Duke of Buccleuch's). fine tapestry & rich old furniture. many pictures. an hour's drive to

Rosslen. in a lovely Valley. ruins of a Castle. the famous chappel built in 1440. not far off is Hawthornden remarkable for its caverns, & romantic situation. return to Edinburgh. go by dinner time to

Duddiston (E: of Abercorn's). thence to

Newbattle (the Marq: of Lothian's) once an Abbey, seated in a Park ill-kept, but full of pictures. go to dine at

Drum (Ld Somerville's). a new House with some good Portraits. from Duddiston by Dallhousie ∧ thro' a naked countrey by good roads to *Bank-End*, where is a good Inn. thence by the evening to
in Berwickshire

Melross (or Meurs) a small Town ∧ with a great linnen manufacture on the R: Tweed. noble ruins of the Abbey-Church built about our Edw: 2^{ds} time, & exquisitely adorn'd. Colony of Masons still dwelling here. difficult road to
in Roxborough-Shire

Kelso. by Dryburgh, a ruin'd Abbey, & Fleurs (the
D: of Roxburgh's seat). Kelso is a poor dirty
Town, but with noble ruins of an Abbey in the
Saxon style. dine at Cornhill[1] in England, oppo-
site to *Coldstream* in Scotland. here is a neat
Inn. in the afternoon to

Tweedmouth. separated only by a fine Bridge from
Berwick passing (some miles out of the road) by

Norham-Castle on a high rock, of w^(ch) only one vast
Tower is standing. at Tweedmouth is an excel-
lent Inn. two hours driving at Low-Water from
Berwick to

Holy-Island. the Saxon Church there. return thence
to

Belford. about 6 miles ˄ to
　　　　　　　　or more (intricate road)

Bamburgh-Castle. very large. the Keep has been
repair'd for the Minister's habitation.

JOURNEY INTO SCOTLAND FROM DURHAM;
Aug: 19, 1765.

To Newcastle, 15 Miles. cross the Tyne.

To Morpeth (in Northumberland) a neat and well-
built Town standing in a pretty, but narrow,
valley, on the R: Wanspeck. Gateway of the old
Castle (now a Gaol) remaining on a hill, that
overlooks the Town, West of the Bridge. the

---

[1] Substituted over 'Coleshill' erased.

Countrey hitherto cultivated, but naked & un-
pleasant. 14 miles.

To Alnewick, 19 miles, a very good Town on the R:
Alne, in a narrow valley, but inferior in beauty to
the former. the Castle is built on an eminence,
tho' far lower than the neighbouring hills, that
border the valley on either hand.

(N.B. The corrections and interlineations in the account of the first Journey to Scotland were made at a
later time, as appears from internal evidence, and by the
less faded character of the ink. Perhaps on this 2nd
Journey, a year later?)

SECTION VII.

THOUGHTS AND VERSE FRAGMENTS.
GRAY.

SECTION VII.

THOUGHTS AND VERSE FRAGMENTS.

(a) EXTRACTS MADE FROM MR GRAY'S POCKET-BOOK.

[IN PEMBROKE Mss.]

P.B. of 1754

Contrast between the Winter Past and coming Spring. Joy owing to that Vicissitude. many that never feel that delight Sloth envy Ambition. how much happier the rustic that feels it tho he knows not how.

Then follow a few lines of the ode Now the golden Morn etc. so that the note above appears to be a kind of argument to that fragment. Four lines also as follow are among the others

> Rise my soul on wings of fire
> Rise the raptrous choir among
> Hark tis nature strikes the Lyre
> And leads the general Song.

On another page

Gratitude:

> The Joy that trembles in her eye
> She bows her meek and humble head
>   in silent praise
>   beyond the power of Sound.

(Mr Pope dead)

> and smart beneath the visionary scourge
> — 'tis Ridicule and not reproach that wounds
> Their vanity and not their conscience feels.

On another page

> a few shall
> The cadence of my song repeat
> and hail thee in my words.

Pocket Book of 1755

The Province of Eloquence is to reign over minds of slow perception & little imagination to set things in lights they never saw them in—to engage their attention by details or circumstances gradually unfolded, to adorn & heighten them with images & colours unknown to them, to raise & engage their rude passions &c.[1]

P.B. of 1760

The Grub that breeds in & perishes with the Common Mass of Putrefaction without being regarded, if a few Drops of Amber fall on it is embalmed for ages, and becomes a rarity[2].

---

[1] [In a note to a letter from Gray to Norton Nicholls (Mitford's Gray, Ald. ed., vol. IV. p. 196), Mason has quoted the above, but in a characteristic fashion. He has either invented or foisted in from another letter a passage upon which to engraft the quotation, and then, as Mitford points out, added to Gray's incomplete sentence words of his own.]

[2] Pope, *Prologue to the Satires* (1732—3).

> Pretty! in amber to observe the forms
> Of hairs, or straws, or dirt, or grubs, or worms!
> The things we know are neither rich nor rare,
> But wonder how the devil they got there.

The *Goût de Comparaison* (as Bruyère stiles it) is the only taste of ordinary minds. They do not know that Tibullus spoke the language of nature & love. that Horace saw the vanities and follys of mankind with the most penetrating eye and touched them to the quick, that Virgil * * * But they know that Virgil is a better poet than Horace, and that Horace's Epistles do not run so well as Tibullus' elegies, they * * .

(β) " Dumay the agreeable counsellor at Paris, after he was blind, sent Menage these two lines, having previously been told that his friend was laid up with the gout ;

> Qui mala nostra tulit praestanti dote valebat ;
> Ede viri nomen, dos tibi talis erit.

To which Menage instantly replied by the servant who waited

> Œdipodem tecum facio. Tumet aeger uterque
> Pes mihi. Caligat lumen utrumque tibi.

The answer is prettiest

> In Œdipus alone I read
>   Our miseries united ;
> My lameness was to him decreed,
>   His eyes like yours benighted.

I could do nothing with the RIDDLE itself—Mr Gray did me the honour to turn it thus

> He who our ills united bare,
>   The art of divination knew;
> If you the prophet's name declare,
>   I'll hail you prophet too.

And while the world owes him solid obligations, let him neither be angry nor ashamed that it sees he can trifle to oblige or divert a friend."

Piozzi, British Synonymy, vol. ii. p. 223.

Mitford quotes the above passage in his note books iii. p. 237 [Add. mss. 32,562] under the heading 'Verses by Gray,' with no suggestion of any difficulty; yet I know of no edition of Piozzi's *Synonymy* earlier than 1794, and Mrs Piozzi seems to speak of Gray as still living. The explanation perhaps is that some of the materials for her book were put together long before this.

(γ) "I asked Mr Bryant, who was next boy to him at Eton, what sort of a scholar Gray was; he said a very good one; and added that he thought he could remember part of an exercise of his on the subject of the freezing and thawing of words, taken from the Spectator, the fragment is as follows:

> ......'pluviaeque loquaces
> Descendere jugis, et garrulus ingruit imber.'"

Norton Nicholls. Reminiscences of Gray.

Bryant himself writes that Gray made these verses 'when he was rather low in the fifth form.' The theme however was not from the Spectator, but from the 254th Tatler.

SECTION VIII.

COLLECTANEA AND CONJECTURES.
GRAY.

[MITFORD'S EXCERPTS.   ADD. MSS. BRIT. MUS.
32,561 ; 32,562.]

G.   18

SECTION VIII.

COLLECTANEA AND CONJECTURES.

GWEDDI'R HWSMON[1].

By the Vicar of Llandyfry in Q. Elizabeth's reign.

(Lluniwr daiar, Helpwr dynion.)

Literal Translation.

Thou former of the earth, Helper of Men
Author of the Seeds of the Earth fruitfull
Giver of rain, increaser of corn
Hear the prayer of an Husbandman earnest

I am going to till the ground
And to sow in this my provision of Corn
Without seeing again of it
If thou dost not give a blessing on it.

Lord, vain it is to plant
To sow with an even hand & harrow,
Except thou make it to sprout forth,
And give a blessing & increase to it.

There will not come a grain thro' the earth
Of all that I have of provision
If thou wilt not make it sprout
Grow out and increase
I do therefore beg earnestly,

[1] (i.e. The Husbandman's Prayer.)

18—2

Oh! God! thy blessing upon my corn
That I may have from it
Means, like a Christian, me to maintain.
Open to me the Windows of Heaven
Rain down a blessing upon my Lands,
Feed the seed with the fat of the earth,
And give prosperity to my Crop.
Let not the Heavens turn to brass
Nor the earth to iron by too much heat
Let not the fields large fail
For our backwardness in serving thee.
Give by measure the former rain
In it's season & the latter rain
A temperate Season, heat moderate,
Blessing & prosperity upon thy People
Forbid the locust, forbid the Lindis,
Forbid the Mildew, that freckles the barley,
Forbid the Scorch & Wind & Lightning
Wh^{ch} occasions to the Corn hurt.

Crown the year with thy goodness
Pour ye fatness of thy blessing on it
Cloath the meads all with Sheep,
And our Mountains with beasts.

Give food to the Children of Men
Give fodder to the beasts dumb
Give Wine and Oil in plenty
To satisfy thine inheritance
Give us a harvest fruitful
A blessing from the fields and ye Cornstocks
Seed from the garden and fruit from the orchard
Honey from ye rock and milk from the fold
And bless the Work of our Hands
Lord gracious now & ever
So we will bless thee too
Upon our knees, night & morn.

(From Mrs Newcome, the B^p of Landaff's lady.)

GRAY MSS.[1] (IN MASON'S COLLECTION).

(Mitford's Excerpts, Add. MSS. Brit. Mus. 32,562, vol. IV. p. 1 *sq.*)

Sir R: Walpole raisd himself by the H. of Commons in defiance of the Chiefs of his own Party. Mr Pelham never speaks well but when provokd. Sir R: W did not understand foreign affairs; had no friendship but with persons much below him. jealous of his Power, drove all considerable Men from Court. Ps authority not depending on the Ks favor, he cares less who obtains it. Timid, scrupulous, proud, incommunicative. K. lost his eldest son, but glad of it. did not love his children when young, now does as well as most fathers. Q. of Denmark died of a rupture conceald[2] (like her mother) who said to her Louisa remember I die by being giddy and obstinate in maks a Secret of my disorder. K. of Denmark, tho' very fond of her, kept a Mistress, & gave her great uneasiness. (She) told her family at parting, if she was unhappy, they shd never know it. moving letter, when dying.

[1] The authorities for Gray's anecdotes are Mason (Mn or M) from Warburton (W—n); Horace Walpole (Mr W); and Dr Heberden. Who T. is, I do not know, but he seems to have been a friend of the Mrs Bonfoy who 'taught' Gray 'to pray'. (Works, ed. Gosse, iii. 152, ii. 378 n.) Some of these stories are already familiar to us through Horace Walpole.

[2] Cf. Walpole's Reminiscences (*Letters*, vol. 1. p. cxxxi *sq.* Cunningham.)

D. of Newcastle raisd a Troop in the Preston Reb:
and in which M^r P: behavd with bravery—betray'd
Lord Sunderland his first Patron to Ld Townshend
who was therefore much agst Sir R W making him
Secretary. betrays Townshend to Walpole when they
began to disagree. The first insists on his dismission
in order to a Reconciliation. King consents to take
Methuen, Queen and Sir R Walpole save the Duke.
on the Fall of Sir R. W. he deals with the opposition
to compass his ruin. D. of Argyle (disappointed) bid
Ld Ila tell R. W. that the Duke N: & Chancellor had
long leagued with himself and Granville agst him.
N: betrays Granv: to Chesterfield. Lord Gr. swore
he would be a Page of the Backstairs, rather than
quit the Court again. same to Willes "What is it
to me who are judges and Bishops? I make Kings
and Emperors." Early attempts to unite with R: W.
by Lord Hervey's means, but he refusd, being persuaded he had connections with Pretender. Ld Orf^d
applied to by the P^s comes to Town, writes to K: who
dismisses his ministers. Gr. & Bath keep up connection with K: by Yarmouth and persuade not make
Pit (*sic*) Secret: at War. Resignation. Wilmington
mediates. Ld Granv: had offerd the great Seal to
Willes and the Seals to Ld Cholmondely. Privy Seal
to L: Carlyle. D. of Grafton went into the Closet
laughing & said, 'Sir, I am come to direct your
Majesty, who shall be yr Minister.' Scheme to govern

by P[s] Emily. —— to Queen "Gad Madam I wish I could have been that man you could love." if the 3 days Ministry[1] had lasted, Lord Harlington (*sic*) was to impeach L[d] Granv—

...Sir R W. astonishd to hear the K: sh[d] behave well at the Battle of Dett[n]. Sir James Lowther left the Court & went to the Prince on the act for reducing interest to 4 per c. K: sunk his Father's will[2]. Pr: s[d] to Ld Donerayl 'My Lord, whoever are my Ministers, I shall be King' — on the Friday of the Rebels' march was for going to Portsmouth with his Wife & family. Supper on the Princ: lyeing in, during the Siege of Carlisle at which my Lord Stair was present Desert was the Citadel of Carlisle, w[ch] was pelted & taken with Sugar-plums[3]. L[d] Chesterfield never coughs & says, nobody need.

Window tax in Scotland returnd not a Shilling. Davidson Min[r] of Naver, Braes of Angus and...... Parishes prosecuted for wilful Fire-raising havg made bonfires on Dukes birthday. Coach tax first year £1000. 2[d] year, nothing. Lord Ila betrayd the burrows (*sic*) trusted to him to his brother, in 1741...

---

[1] 1746, when Lords Bath and Granville tried in vain to displace the Duke of Newcastle.

[2] Walp. *Rem.* chap. vi. (*Letters*, i. p. cxx *sq.*, ed. Cunningham.)

[3] Walpole to Mann. (*Letters*, i. p. 407, ed. Cunningham.)

before Sir R. Walpole's fall[1]. ...Murray and Cresset disciples of Bolingbroke and his bequest to late Prince. Income of the Pret[r] before Rebellion 23000£ a year. Ld B. advisd he sh[d] resign to his Son. Bp of Norwich finds the Pretender reading P. d'Orleans[2]. Murray and Bp of Norwich. L[d] H a cypher. L[d] W. too young to govern, & too old to be governd.......

...M[r] E: W[s] German footman, because he could not find one M[r] Abbot, that his master wanted, fetchd another M[r] Abbot that he thought would do as well— M[rs] Le Neves maid desird her Mistress picture and s[d] the Man (she knew) had bought the best of Colors, & anybody could lay them on. G: Townshend put under arrest for 5 hours.

Pope was extremely desirous that M[r] Allen sh[d] invite P[ty] Blount to his House near Bath, w[ch] he accordingly did ;—some time after the Men went out together on some Party or other, and at their return,

[1] 'But how will Walpole justify his fate?
He trusted Islay till it was too late.
　　　　　Sir C. Hanbury Williams on 1741.

Horace Walpole notes 'Archibald Campbell, Earl of Islay, brother of John Duke of Argyll, in conjunction with whom (though then openly at variance) he was supposed to have betrayed Sir R. W. and to have let the Opposition succeed in the Scotch elections, which were trusted to his management. It must be observed that Sir Robert Walpole would never allow that he believed himself betrayed by Lord Islay.' [See Cunningham's ed. of *Letters of Walpole*, I. p. 135.]

[2] Voltaire's *Pucelle*.

found Mrs Blount had quarrelld violently with M^r
Allen & was determind to leave the House. at parting she took a little bawble, that hung to her Watch,
and gave to Miss Tucker[1] (then a Child whom Warburton afterwards married) for (she said) she was the
only Person in the House, that had been civil to her.
She went away directly, and Pope with her[2], & from
that time there was a coldness between him & Allen.
Mrs Warburton remembers that she lay at that time
in the next room to Pope, & that every Mor^g between
6 & 7 o'clock, Mrs Blount usd to come into his
Chamber, when she heard them talk earnestly together
for a long time. & that when they came down to
breakfast, M^rs B: usd alys to ask him how he had
rested that night.

That after this, M^r A: & his family came a time
to Mr Popes at Twick'nam, & that he wrote a letter[3]

---

[1] Niece of the Allens. "In 1745 Warburton married
Allen's favourite niece, Gertrude Tucker; he owed to Allen's
interest several steps in his ecclesiastical advancement; and
eventually, after the owner's death, he became the possessor
of Prior Park." ⌐Courthope, *Life of Pope*, p. 338.]

[2] Not so: Pope left her with the Allens at Bath, as appears
by a letter from her to him, 1743 (*Pope's Works*, Courthope, ix.
332)....In reply to this Pope writes 'I think it best still to
enclose to Mr Edwyn. *I should not wonder if listeners at doors
should open letters.*' (Ib. p. 335.)

[3] Probably that dated 25 March 1744 (Ib. p. 336). It was
only Allen who came, in Pope's account of the matter. Pope
died about two months after (May 30).

to Mrs Blount excusing it, in which he spoke slight-
ingly of them. This letter she show^d about & it was
told M^r Aⁿ which much increasd the Quarrell.

That she obligd Mr Pope to insert in his Will that
article of the 300£[1] returnd to M^r A: and threatend
she wd not accept of what he had left her, unless he
did so (M: from M^r & M^{rs} W—n)

W—n has a long & extremely fine character of
the D of Marlboro' wrote by P. on the margin of his
Characters of Men[2], but severe beyond measure. M.
could remember only these two lines

'In vain a Nation's wish, a Senate's cares;
God said—Let lust & madness be his heirs.

　　*　　*　　*　　*　　*　　*　　*

[1] £150. "Allen accepted the legacy, which he gave to the
Hospital at Bath, observing that Pope was always a bad
accountant, and that, if to 150*l.* he had put a cipher more, he
had come nearer the truth." (Johnson.) Johnson repeats the
Warburtonian legend about Martha Blount's conduct in this
matter, but it is contradicted by her own statement to Spence,
that she tried to persuade Pope to omit this mention of Allen.
(Courthope, *Life of Pope*, p. 341.)

[2] Gray was mistaken on this point. It was in the margin
of the 4th Epistle of the Essay on Man. A facsimile of the
page is given in Courthope's *Pope*, vol. III. (ad in.). The
design of the change was to make the well-known reference
to Marlborough in the passage beginning

'Mark by what wretched steps their glory grows,
　　From dirt and sea-weed as proud Venice rose'—
more direct and pointed. The lines, says Mr Courthope, were
evidently well known in Pope's own circle, since Warton says

When he [Bolingbroke] came to die, he appeared
to expect nothing but annihilation (M:)

The D^c of Marlboro' seriously own^d & lamented
to Sir J: Vanbrugh, that he c^d not part with half-a-
crown, without Pain (T: from Mrs Bonfoy)

He has been often seen during a Campain, &
receiv^d Officers in his Tent, mending his old gloves
himself (Mr W.)

Bp Atterbury, while in France, lost much of the
friendship he had once had for Pope, and has been
heard to say, of him, that he was as crooked in mind
as in body. He own^d that he could bear to read no
other Historian of modern times, than Burnet; and
s^d there were many things in him, that were commonly
look^d upon as Fictions, which to his own knowledge
were very true. (T: from Mr Morris[1])

that Pope in some verses which he suppressed made Marlborough lament the loss of his son

'In accents of a whining ghost.'

This is a reminiscence of the words

'Hear him, in accents of a pining ghost
   Sigh, with his captive, for his offspring lost'—

as the lines quoted by Gray are of the words

'In vain a nation's zeal, a senate's cares.
  "Madness and Lust" (said God) "be you his heirs;
  O'er his vast heaps, in drunkenness of pride,
  Go wallow, Harpies, and your prey divide."'

(See Courthope's *Pope*, vol. III. p. 87 *sq*.).

[1] Perhaps the Mr Morrice spoken of by Walpole (*Short
Notes of my Life, Letters*, Cunningham, I. p. lxx) as the

Atterbury, about the time of Q: Anne's death, offerd himself to the Ministry to go in his Episcopal ornaments to Charing-cross, & solemnly proclaim the Pretender there (M^r W: from Sir R W). The late Pr. of Wales had among his Papers, one given him by Ld Bolingbroke containing a Scheme to govern without Parliament by getting the revenues settled on him for 5 years. He had a very great influence over the P^{re} for some time before he died. (Mr W. from the E of E—t, who had the Paper a good while in his own hands)

Ld Egmont was never seen to laugh but once, & that was at Chess (the same).

The late Ld Hervey asked the D. of Cleveland (an idiot) how his Ebony-dutchess did? He answered him that an Ebony Lady was as good as an Ivory Lord.

*   *   *   *   *   *   *

Tom Earle & others passing by H. Walpole's[1] house at Whitehall, saw a great Smoke come out of the Laundry below. "What the Devil" (says one of

Bishop's grandson. Walpole said of Burnet ' It is observable, that none of his facts has been controverted, except his relation of the birth of the Pretender, in which he was certainly mistaken—but his very credulity is a proof of his honesty.' (*Walpoliana*, I. p. 22.) Perhaps he does but speak after Atterbury.

[1] The brother of Sir Robert—and afterwards Lord Walpole of Woolterton.

them) "does Horace's Wife ever wash her Linnen?" 'No, no' says Earle, 'but she takes in other People's.'

* * * * * * *

Sʳ R W gave his brother Horace a little Horse for his Son to ride upon. but the boy not being big enough, or not caring to ride, the horse continued in Richmond Park a year or two, & when the present Ld Orford was grown up, of an age fit for it, Sir Rᵗ let him ride it. as soon as Mʳˢ Walpole heard of it, she sent directly to demand the price of the Horse[1].

[1] Here is the story as Hor. Walpole told it to Sir Horace Mann, [the date is noticeable, Oct. 8, 1742, when Walpole and Gray were estranged]: 'We expect some company next week from Newmarket: here is at present only Mrs Keene and *Pigwiggin*—you never saw *so agreeable a creature*,—oh yes! you have seen his parents! I must tell you a new story of them: Sir Robert had given them a little horse for Pigwiggin, and somebody had given them another; both which, to save the charge of keeping, they sent to grass in Newpark [Richmond]. After three years that they had not used them, my Lord Walpole let his own son ride them, while he was at the Park, in the holidays. Do you know that the woman Horace sent to Sir Robert and made him give her five guineas for the two horses, because George had ridden them? I give you my word this is fact.'

'Pigwiggin', says Walpole, is the 'eldest son of old Horace Walpole.' 'He was afterwards the second Lord Walpole of Woolterton, and in 1806, at the age of eighty-three, created Earl of Orford. He died in 1809.' (Wright.)

The miserable and malicious gossip of Walpole is only worth quoting, as showing how religiously Gray echoed him in social scandal. This is certainly the weak side of the poet's character.

Sir R: W: us'd to say, that no Man ought to be first Minister, least he sh^d conceive too bad an opinion of Mankind.

Mrs Russell (by no means famd for her Wit) a Grand-daughter of Oliver Cromwell was dressing the Princess Amelia one 30th of January, when late Pr: of W: came in to her apartment & said, this is a day that every body ought to be at Church, & especially you, Mrs Russell, sh^d be mortifying & doing penance S^r (says she) do you think it is not mortification enough for a descendant of Ol. Cromwell's to be here pinning up your Sister's tail.   (the same[1])

If Voltaire had stay'd longer in England, he would have been *hangd* for forging bank notes   (Mⁿ from Warburton)[2]

*   *   *   *   *   *   *

In the D. of Bedfords gallery at Woburn is a Portrait of that Earl of Courteney, whom Q. Mary would have married, & who was supposed to have been in Love with Q. Elizabeth. He is a pale Man with a wild look, & red hair & beard. he was long

---

[1] i.e. Horace Walpole.

[2] This is followed by an anecdote which it is quite impossible to repeat, of Voltaire's conversation at Pope's table. The authorities for it are 'T: from Ld Bathurst & Mⁿ from Warburton'.   It confirms the statement of Johnson, who probably heard the same story, that Voltaire 'talked with so much grossness that Mrs Pope was driven from the room.'

in the Tower, & died at Padua, as was thought of
Poison.

The D of Bedford has a volume of the Lady Rus-
sells orig: letters. there are several to a Dr Fitzwil-
liams soon after her Husbands death with his answers,
wherein he tells her by way of Consolation that she
ought to be thankful that Providence has separated
her from a Man, who had dipped his hands in rebellion
agst his Sovereign;—a letter from her at the Revolu-
tion to the same Clergyman, persuading him to take
the oaths, tho' to no Purpose, for he gave up his Pre-
ferments—a very elegant one to Tillotson, intreating
him to accept the Archb. of Canterbury (this will be
publishd in his Life wrote by Birch) one of Q. Mary
to L^dy Russell just before the battle of the Boyne
expressing great desire to have the matter soon de-
cided &c.

In the same gallery at Woburn are Portraits of
two young Men. behind one of them is seen a
Woman in a Labyrinth, behind the other a Man gnawd
by Serpents & Monsters. In the family they are
calld by the names of Polydore & Castalio, & said to
have been Twin Sons of the 2d Earl of Bedford, they
add that the youngest was married. (M^r W: from
the D: & D^ss of Bedford)

When Pope was senseless & dying, Ld Bolingbroke stood by him, & broke into violent Exclama-
tions & blasphemies agst Heaven, for suffering its

noblest, divinest Work to be reduced to such a wretched Condition. (M^r W from Mr Spence[1])

After his death, & the discovery made of the Patriot Prince, printed & hid in a Cupboard, Ld B: made it his business to abuse & expose him. Among other things he said, that the story of stealing & printing Popes letters, was all a juggle, and that he had seen them long ago wrote out fair in a book, and ready for the Press[2]. (Dr Heb^n & M^n from W—n)

[1] Spence appears to have toned down this anecdote at another time. "Spence says that Bolingbroke was greatly affected when Pope spoke of the suffering he experienced at not being able to think, and wept over him, exclaiming several times, interrupted by sobs, "O great God, what is man?" (Courthope, *Life of Pope*, p. 344, referring to Spence's Anecdotes p. 320.)

[2] 'Bolingbroke had instructed Pope, in 1738, to have printed for him a few copies of "Letters on the Spirit of Patriotism, On the Idea of a Patriot King, and On the State of Parties." After Pope's death, Wright, a printer, brought and gave over to Bolingbroke an impression of fifteen hundred copies which the poet had ordered him to retain secretly. Pope had, according to Bolingbroke's account, "taken upon him further to divide the subject, and to alter or omit passages according to his own fancy."' (*Life of Pope*, pp. 346, 347.) How Curll was tricked by Pope into publishing his correspondence is told by Mr Courthope at length in the *Life of Pope*, pp. 283—290.

CONJECTURAL READINGS ON SHAKESPEARE,
Theobald, ed. 1740.

The following readings are annotated with the help of the Cambridge Shakespeare, because it seems probable that Warburton derived some of the conjectures he put forward as his own, from Gray. Warburton said of Hanmer, 'Having a number of my Conjectures before him, he took as many as he saw fit to work upon, and by changing them to something he thought synonimous or similar, he made them his own.' He had himself, I believe, already dealt with Gray in the same fashion, and perhaps accused Hanmer of stealing that from him, which he had himself stolen from another. The slight differences between Gray's suggestions and Warburton's prevent our supposing that Gray was simply transcribing *his* annotations; to say nothing of the fact that he had no high opinion of the man whom in a letter to John Chute (the proper date of which is July 1742) he calls 'a very impudent fellow.' Again, one of these conjectures, that on Merry Wives v. 5. 49, is certainly Gray's; at least it finds no place in the Cambridge Shakespeare, and may be supposed to be quite new to the world. These notes perhaps belong to 1742. The Oxford edition of Shakespeare (Hanmer's) was first published in 1744; that of Warburton (Pope and Warburton) in 1747.

P. 12. In Ant: Pegafetta's voyage round the World with Magellan, he says the Giants of Patagonia call the chief of the Demons Setabos (*sic*) and the inferior one Cheleule. see Ramusio 1. 353.

[See Dr Aldis Wright's note, Tempest, 1. 2. 350 (Clar. Press Series.]

G.   19

P. 31. This ancient *morsel*, this Sir Prudence....
l. moral.

[Act ii. 1. 277. Warburton also conj. *Moral.*]

P. 54. Harmonious charmingly........l. charming
lays.

[iv. 118, 119

Fer. 'This is a most majestic vision, and
Harmonious charmingly.

charming lay Hanmer. *charming lays* Warburton.]

P. 72. Your words I'll catch......l. yours would
[I catch].

[M. N. D. i. 1. 185, 186

Sickness is catching: O, were favour so
Your words I catch fair Hermia, ere I go

So QQ and F_1. *Ide* $F_2F_3F_4$. *Yours would I* Hanmer.]

P. 86. The middle summer spring......l. that.
[M. N. D. ii. 1. 82

And never, since the middle summer's spring
Met we on hill, in dale, forest or mead &c.

that Hanmer (Warburton).]

P. 87. The human mortals want their Winter
here......l. harried i.e. celebrated.

[M. N. D. ii. 1. 101.

Winters heryed. Warburton.]

P. 114. Opening on Neptune with fair blessed
beams......l. far-blessing.

[M. N. D. iii. 2. 392.

far-blessing Hanmer (Warburton).]

P. 128. That is hot ice, *and* wondrous strange snow. l. a......shew.

[M. N. D. v. 1. 59.

a wondrous strange shew. Warburton.]

P. 238. This Punk is one......l. Pink.

[Merry Wives II. 2. 123

This Punk is one of Cupid's carriers.

pink Warburton.]

P. 245. Try'd game......l. cry'd aim!

[Wives II. Sc. 3. 79, 80

I will bring thee where Mistress Anne Page is, at a farm-house a feasting; and thou shalt woo her. *Cried game* (Q₁ Q₂) said I well?

Cried-Game Ff.Q₃. *Try'd game* Theobald. *Cry aim.* Warburton. *Cried I aim!* Dyce (Douce conj.) and modern editors generally.]

P. 281. Raise up the organs......l. rein.

[Wives v. 5. 47 sq.

......Go you, and where you find a maid
That, ere she sleep, has thrice her prayers said,
Raise up the organs of her fantasy;
Sleep she as sound as careless infancy.]

P. 299. Leavend choice......l. levelld.

[Measure for Measure I. 1. 52

We have with a leaven'd and prepared choice
Proceeded to you.

prepar'd and level'd Warburton.]

SECTION IX.

LATIN POEMS. GRAY.

SECTION IX.

LATIN POEMS.

1. FROM THE GREEK.

Fertur Aristophanis fatorum arcaua rogatum
    tempore sementis, rusticus isse domum ;
(Sideris au felix tempestas, messis an esset
    magna, vel agricolam falleret ustus ager)
Ille supercilio adducto multâ anxius arte
    disposuit sortes, consuluitque Deos :
Tum responsa dedit: vernus suffecerit imber
    Si modo, nec fruges læserit herba nocens;
Si mala robigo, si grando pepercerit arvis,
    attulerit subitum pigra nec aura gelu;
Caprea si nulla, aut culmos attriverit hædus :
    nec fuerit cælum, nec tibi terra gravis :
Largas polliceor segetes, atque horrea plena.
    tu tamen, ut[1] veniat sera locusta, cave.

                      [Pembroke Common Place Bks.]

2. [Imitated from the Greek] of Bassus.

Non ego, cum malus urit amor, Iovis induor arma
    nil mihi cum plumis, nil mihi cum corio :
Non ego per tegulas mittor liquefactus in aurum
    promo duos obolos: sponte venit Danaë.

                              Ib.

---

[1] *Sic.*

3.   Oh ubi colles, úbi Fæsularum
     Palladis curæ, plaga, Formiæq
     Prodigæ florum, Genuæque amantes
             Littora soles?
     Abstulit campos oculis amœnos
     Montium quantus, nemorumque tractus!
     Quot natant eheu medii profundo
             Marmore fluctus!

          Pemb. Common Place Bks. I. 381.
          Not dated, but obviously written after his
          return from the continent in 1741[1].

4.   On p. 83 vol. III. of Mitford's MSS. is a MS. Poem which has no other description or designation, but which seems, from the place in which it is found, to be Gray's. Compare the English Poem of West on p. 109. The Latin may also be West's; it is obviously in the rough.

     Gratia magna tuæ fraudi quod Pectore, Nice,
       Non gerit hoc ultra regna superba Venus:
     Respirare licet tandem misero mihi, tandem
       Appensa in sacro pariete vincla vides
     Numquam ...... uror; liber sum: crede doloso
       Suppositus Cineri non latet ullus amor.
     Præsto non ira est, cujus se celet amictu;
       Sera, sed et rediit vix mihi nota quies.
     Nec nomen si forte tuum pervenit ad aures
       Pallor et alternus surgit in ore rubor,
     Corda nec incerto trepidant salientia pulsu
       Irrigat aut furtim lacryma fusa genas.
     Non tua per somnos crebra obversatur imago
       Non animo ante omnes tu mihi mane redis.
     Te loquor; at tener ille silet sub pectore sensus
       Nec quod ades lætor; nec quod abes doleo.

[1] It is an echo of the stanza beginning 'Horridos tractus &c.' prefixed to letter to West from Genoa Nov. 21, 1739.

Rivalem tacitus patior; securus eburnea
    Quin ego colla simul laudo, manusque tuas.
Longa nec indignans refero perjuria: prodis
    Obvia, mens certâ sede colorque manet.
Quin faciles risus, vultusque assume superbos;
    Spernentem sperno, nec cupio facilem.
Nescit ocellorum, ut quondam penetrabile fulgur
    Ah! nimium molles pectoris ire vias;
Nec tam dulce rubent illi, mea cura, labelli[1]
    juris ut immemores imperiique sui.
Lætari possum, possum et mærere; sed a te
    gaudia nec veniunt, nec veniunt lacrymæ.
Tecum etiam nimii Soles, & frigora lædunt;
    Vere suo sine te prata nemusque placent.
Pulchra quidem facies, sed non tua sola videtur
    (forsitan offendam rusticitate mea)
Sed quiddam invenies culpandum, qua mihi nuper
    parte est præcipuè visus inesse lepor.
Cum primùm evulsi fatale ex vulnere telum
    Credebam, ut fatear, viscera et ipsa trahi;
Luctanti rupere (pudor) suspiria pectus,
    tinxit et invitas plurima gutta genas.
Aspera difficilem vicit Medicina furorem;
    ille dolor sævus, sed magis asper Amor
Aucupis insidiis, et arundine capta tenaci
    sic multo nisu vincula rupit avis;
Plumarum laceros reparat breve tempus honores
    nec cadit in similes cautior inde dolos.
Tu tamen usque illam tibi fingis vivere flammam
    Et male me veteres dissimulare faces.
Quod libertatem ostento, fractamq: Catenam,
    tantus et insolitæ pacis in ore sonus,
Præteritos meminisse jubet natura dolores;
    quæ quisque est passus, dulce pericla loqui.
Enumerat miles sua vulnera; navita ventos
    Narrat & incautæ saxa inimica rati;

[1] *Sic.*

Sic ego servitium durum, & tua regna. laborant
  Nice nullam a te quærere dicta fidem:
Nil nimium hæc mandata student tibi velle placere,
  Nec rogito quali perlegis ore notas.

5. After some Latin Alcaics signed 'Antrobus' comes in the 3rd volume of Mitford's Excerpts a Latin translation of Philips's 'Splendid Shilling,' to which he does not assign the authorship.

Oh! nimium felix! cura et discordibus armis
Cui procul exiguâ non deficiente Crumenâ
Splendet adhuc Solidus. non illum torquet egentem
Ostriferi Cantus, non allae[1] dira Cupido.
Ille inter Socios gelido sub vespere notum
Tendit iter, genialis ubi se Curia pandit
Juniperive Lares[2]: hic Nympham, si qua protervo
Lumine pertentat Sensus, uritque videndo
(Sive Chloe, seu Phillis amanti gratior audit)
Alternis recolit cyathis, tibi, virgo, salutem
Lætitiamque optans, et amoris mutua vincla
Nec minus interea fumique jocique benignus
Non lateri parcit, si quando argutior alter
Fabellam orditur lepidam, vel Scommata spargit
Ambiguosve Sales, festiva Crepundia vocum.

*   *   *   *

6. "The following Poem is written with Ink by Mason over Gray's Pencil, which was very faint, in order apparently to preserve it. N.B. Gray's writing perceptible below the Ink-letters." (Mitford.)

---

[1] Explained by a reference to the original

               ...'he nor hears with pain
  New oysters cried, nor sighs for cheerful *ale*.'

[2] 'To Juniper's Magpie or Town-hall repairs.' Two ale-houses at Oxford.

Vah, tenero quodcunque potest obsistere amori
    Exulet ex animo & Delia cara meo
Ne timor infelix, mala ne fastidia sancti
    Gaudia distineant, Delia cara, tori
Quid si nulla olim regalia munera nostras
    Ornarunt titulis divitiisque domos?
At nobis proprioque et honesto lumine claris
    Ex meritis ortum nobile nomen erit.
Dum tanto colimus virtutem ardore volabit
    Gloria dulce sonans nostra per ora virum.
Interea nostram mirata Superbia famam
    Talis splendoris tantum habuisse gemet
Quid si Diva potens nummorum divitis auri
    Haud largo nostras proluit imbre Lares?
At nobis erit ex humili bona copia sensu
    Vitaque non luxu splendida, læta tamen
Sic horas per quisque suas revolubilis annus
    Nostra quod explerit vota precesque dabit
Nam duce natura peragemus, Delia, vitam
    Vita ea vitalis dicier una potest.
Et juvenes et amore senes florebimus æquo
    Et vitæ una alacres conficiemus iter
Nostros interea ornabit pax alma Penates
    Iucundum Pueri pignora cara torum
Oh quanta aspicerem lepidam dulcedine gentem
    Luderet ad patrium dum pia turba genu
Maternos vultu ridenti effingere vultus
    Balbo maternos ore referre sonos
Iamque senescentes cum nos insederit ætas
    Nostraque se credat surripuisse bona
In vestris tu rursus amabere pulchra puellis
    Rursus ego in pueris Delia amabo meis.

"N.B. The above is a free translation of Gilbert Cowper's Ode, 'Away let nought to Love displeasing.' See Essay on Taste p. 97." (Mitford.)

We may conjecture that it is an early effort. Nothing
but immaturity can account for some peculiarities in it;
'vestris' for example in the last line but one.

7.   EARLY ALCAICS OF GRAY.

O Tecta, Mentis dulcis amor meæ
Oh! summa Sancti Relligio loci
   Quæ me laborantem perurit
      Sacra fames, et amicus ardor?
Præceps volentem quo rapit impetus!
Ad limen altum tendo avidas manus
   Dum lingua frustratur precantem
      Cor tacitum mihi clamat intus
Illic loquacem composuit domum
Laresque parvos Numinis in fidem
   Præsentioris credit ales
      Veris amans, vetus Hospes aræ:
Beatus ales! sed magis incola
Quem vidit ædes ante [focos Dei [1]]
   Cultu ministrantem perenni
      Quique sacrâ requievit umbrâ
Bis terque felix qui melius Deo
Templum sub imo Pectore consecrat
   Huic vivida affulget voluptas
      Et liquidi sine nube Soles,
Integriori fonte fluentia
Mentem piorum gaudia recreant
   Quod si datur lugere, quiddam
      Dulce ferens venit ipse luctus
Virtute virtus pulchrior evenit
Nascente semper, semper amabili
   Æterna crescit, seque in horas
      Subjiciet per aperta cæli.

[1] [An erasure here, he seems certainly to have written
'focos'.]

Me, dedicatum qui Genus, et tuæ
Iudææ habenas tempero, Regio
    Madens olivo, dexter audi
        Nec libeat repulisse[1] Regem
Lux una Sanctis quæ foribus dedit
Hærere, amatæ limine Ianuæ
    Lux inter extremas Columnas
        Candidius mihi ridet una'
Quam Seculorum Secula Barbaros
Inter Penates sub trabe gemmea
    Fastus tyrannorum brevesque
        Delicias et amœna Regni ;
Feliciori flumine Copiam
Pronâque dextrâ Cælicolum Pater
    Elargietur, porrigetque
        Divitias diuturniores.

The above is the 84th Psalm. (Mitford.)

[N.B. The above ode is written in Mr Gray's Hand ; but evidently when young, the hand being unformd and like a schoolboys, tho' very plain & careful. The Leaf on which it is written, apparently torn from a Copy-book...... Some of the expressions resemble those in the Gr. Chartreuse Ode. (Mitford.)]

----

[1] *Sic.*

INDEX.

www.ingramcontent.com/pod-product-compliance
Lightning Source LLC
Chambersburg PA
CBHW060515030726

47498CB00004B/953